Animan 11

By

Michael K Chapman

Harry was a man once.

Now a skilled Tigris warrior, Harry, and his Ursidae companion Secuutus, find themselves in the middle of a species war. A battle for supremacy between the Lupus and the Ursidae Casts over the right to rule the neutral town of Indutiae.

A war in which Harry has no choice but to choose a side.

Animan

ISBN: 978-0-9927317-5-5

Cover Image by Tamsin Chapman.

Other titles by this Author.

Humour
A Fly on the Ward
A Fly on the Garden Wall
A Nautical Novice (A Fly on the Boat)

Children's
Billy the Hero
Sally to the Rescue

Non fiction
Humanology

Fantasy Sci-Fi
Animan

Table of Contents

Chapter One: A New Land.

I awoke flat on my back. Before I opened my eyes I knew from the breeze on my body I was alive. That along with the fact I was conscious and breathing of course. I didn't move, I merely stared up at a crystal clear blue sky while my hands brushed through the grass on which I lay. The cry of an eagle in the distance caught my attention and I sat up to stare curiously in that direction. From the silhouette of the eagle soaring high in the sky, I switched my gaze to the world around me.

I was sitting in a large clearing amidst a huge forest, with trees stretching away as far as I could see. The air smelt clean and the only other sound to reach my ears was that of bird song. With resignation I knew I was not back in Manchester, no vehicle fumes in the air and no thumping music could be heard. I had not returned home at all but yet again had awoken in a strange world. I peered down at my body to see it remained covered in a pale golden brown fur with thin lines of black running through it, my limbs were still strong and lithe.

I was dressed in homespun trousers and shirt, both of which had tears in the fabric and stained with blood. Lying next to me on the grass was my heavy wooden and metal banded staff, its secret blade hidden from view. Secured in my belt was large evil looking knife, one that I had acquired long ago and to which I owed my life on many occasions. I patted my body all over, making sure I was not injured in any way. I had collected several minor cuts and bruises though not enough to cause concern. One pleasant discovery was finding my purse still loaded with coin, a fact I was grateful for. So I had arrived here, wherever here was, armed and with coin. A good start so far I concluded.

Looking around at the countryside it was obvious I was no longer in the Kingdom of Janiz and the riders. I had no idea where that small green jade box had sent me this time, but here I was and there was little I could do to change that. I suspected I was still on Totus-Terra but exactly where I had no idea. I sighed, here we go again. My Manchester flat had never felt so far away as it did that at moment. I stared at the land around me, wondering which direction to travel. To be honest, I didn't care, the disappointment of not waking in my own kitchen weighed heavy on my soul. I lay back on the grass in despair, fighting back tears, not sure if I would ever get home again.

Just then, I heard a groan very close behind me. I jumped up and swung round ready to fight, or run. To my total surprise and shock, I saw a huge body lying on the grass only a few feet away from me. I grabbed my staff and held it ready, always expecting the worst. Cautiously I approached the prone figure and prodded it none too gently with the butt of my staff. It stirred, groaned again before it slowly and ponderously raised its head, farted and stared back at me.

'Hello Secuutus.' I said.

With a start, the large figure leapt to his feet, his eyes darting frantically about him. 'Where are we?' he cried, 'What happened to Janiz and the palace? What just happened?'

'Take it easy mate,' I said as I took a pace towards him and laid my hand on his huge shoulders.

'Mate? I'm not your mate!' he growled, shrugging off my contact.

'Sorry Secuutus, I didn't mean that type of mate, where I come from it's another word for friend,' I apologised with a grin.

'Well don't call me that, other animan will think we're laying down together. Anyway, where are we?' he asked again, a slight tremor entered the voice of the Ursidae.

I could not answer my friend, my fellow rider and comrade, because I simply didn't know. The last thing I remember was standing in the king's chambers after defeating the fake sorcerer, and deliberately opening the green jade box. I had wrongly assumed that as the box initially transported me to the world of Totus-Terra, it would return me home to Manchester when I opened it again. I was wrong. Now I stood on the edge of a forest and faced an uncertain future. A sense of déjà vu filled my mind as I remembered the first time I opened that box and awoke to find myself in this strange land.

I had met the short-legged, stocky and huge shouldered figure of Secuutus while riding with the outlawed Prince Janiz. Secuutus was a member of the Ursidae Cast and had the slight characteristics of a bear in clothing. Like me, his body was covered in a faint layer of fur, his fur was brown in colour. He had deep brown eyes and his nose and mouth protruded slightly, giving the impression of a muzzle. Secuutus was dressed similarly to me, no high street fashions but the rough garb of a warrior. Neither of us looked like the animals we had evolved from, we simply retained a few subtle indicators. Our species had advanced. In a world where humans had never evolved, the four main predators had taken their place. Here lions, tigers, bears and wolves had evolved through the ages into upright biped creatures with humanoid abilities and it was they that ruled the land.

Secuutus rubbed at his eyes and peered around at the unknown landscape as the same bewilderment filled his head as it had mine. I gave him space to think as I remembered my recent past. I had awoken in a normal biped body that walked upright, except my body was now very tall and powerful, had speech and intelligence equal to that of a human, but had retained many characteristics of a tiger.

I was of the Tigris Cast. The Tigris are the biggest and most ferocious of the four Casts, often following a military or mercenary path. The lions or Leo Cast, ruled much the same as they do on the plains of Africa back home. Only moments ago, Secuutus and I had fought alongside a Leo, Prince Janiz, in his successful attempt to invade the royal palace and destroy a sorcerer. The sorcerer who had control over the prince's father, King Fastus. It was at the successful conclusion of Janiz's quest when I foolishly opened that damn box again. Poor Secuutus must have been standing too close and, he also became embroiled in its effects. Hence our presence in this new land, the terrain of grass plains and sparsely wooded hills replaced by the biggest forest I had ever seen.

'I'm sorry Secuutus, it seems you were caught up in the magic of that jade box, the one the sorcerer wanted, remember?' I said, breaking into the thoughts of my companion.

'I remember,' he growled.

'You were standing close to me when I opened it and, somehow, it transported you along with me. It was how I came to your world in the first place. You, Janiz and all the riders considered me strange, well I have a confession to make. I appear strange because I'm not of your world.' I finally admitted the truth.

Secuutus's eyes went wide as he stared at me, the concept of another world and the implications it implied had never been considered by an animan before. Poor Secuutus was not the sharpest of animan, I could see a twinkling of understanding flicker in his eyes before it died again. He peered at me for a moment or two longer, then a shrug of those huge shoulders testified he didn't understand or care. I watched as he inspected himself for injuries, checked his sword, all as I had done, and looked around our wider location.

'I knew you were different, with your strange magic, we all did. So I'm not surprised to hear you admit it,' he finally replied. 'But that's the past, we are here now, all we need to discover is where *here* is. We also need to survive. I want to get back to my home.'

I didn't have a chance to reply for at that very moment a figure burst from the treeline of the forest and ran straight at us. I could see it was from the Lupus Cast and obviously very frightened, the slight figure ran as if his life depended on speed, he ran as if a monster chased him. Moments later I saw that a monster was indeed pursuing the terrified figure, when it leapt out from the forest's gloomy edge, bounding after its intended prey.

Both Secuutus and I immediately readied our weapons, Secuutus drew his sword as I pushed the tiny hidden button on my staff which triggered a long narrow blade to emerge from the head of it, turning it into an effective spear. Secuutus moved to his left, I leapt to my right, both crouching as the Lupus approached, screaming in fear. Without pausing, the figure ran straight between Secuutus and me as the creature hurtled closer. A memory stirred in the recesses of my mind, I had seen such a creature before. It was a cat of some kind, though this was the size of a full grown male lion. The absurdity of the moment suddenly struck me, here I was, a tiger standing side by side with a bear to save a wolf from a huge cat. However, I didn't laugh, it was all too real.

The cat was approaching fast but at the sight of a Tigris and an Ursidae standing firm in front of it, it began to slow its charge. Finally, it appeared to recognise the threat and the huge cat came to a cautious stop. Golden eyes stared back at us while the Lupus cringed behind us, whimpering in fear. I stared at the cat, identification fighting to the surface of my brain. I saw a cat with upright, almost triangular ears, each with a tuft of fur rising from the apex. A wild and carnivorous feline face, strangely bearded by white fur under its chin. Its coat was a reddish brown with dark, almost black spots covering its body, not as closely spaced as a leopard but clearly visible. The tail appeared short and stubby in comparison to the moggies that led a lazy life as domestic pets at home. At last, I remembered, I realised what the animal was as it lowered itself to the ground in the age-old posture of hunting. It was a huge, and I mean a huge lynx, and we were its next meal.

Secuutus and I watched the animal and tensed, I recognised the signs and knew it would attack, as did Secuutus. Surprising as it may seem, I had never actually faced one until now I had only seen a lynx on the telly. I knew a lynx was a cat, though I knew some that though it a deodorant. Here it was real, and I was on the menu. I glanced over to Secuutus and saw him nod back at me, then to my complete surprise, the huge Ursidae let out a mighty roar and charged straight at the crouching lynx. I was a second behind as I realised his intentions. Together we ran at the beast, sword and spear ready to cut it down. I suspected the lynx had never experienced its prey suddenly turning the attack, for it leapt high and turned in mid-air as only a cat can, before landing with all limbs running, disappearing at full speed back into the forest.

Secuutus and I slowed to a halt, both relieved it had not come down to a fight. I remembered Sophos the Sage warning me about the animals that had, in turn, stepped up to fill the evolutionary gap left by the four main predators. I turned and looked back at the still cowering Lupus. Secuutus remained holding his sword as I retracted the blade into my staff. We both turned back to investigate who the terrified Lupus was and what was he doing in the forest by himself. As we approached, the whimpering finally stopped and two yellow eyes looked up at us. With a start, we both realised the cringing figure was a female, a Lupus femina.

'Okay, I didn't expect that.' I muttered to my equally surprised companion.

I had assumed the figure was male, for what reason I don't know but I had. Smaller than Secuutus and me by more than a head, the Lupus had faint pale grey fur covering what I could see of her body, again with a slightly protruding mouth and nose. Her figure was slight but wiry, the characteristics of a wolf shining through. Now faced with a terrified female Lupus, both Secuutus and I stood in a moment of surprise. I made to step towards the figure but it shuffled further from me, his . . . , her wide eyes staring in fear at Secuutus.

'It's okay, we wish you no harm,' I spoke gently. 'There's no reason to fear now.'

The Lupus femina clearly didn't believe me as she remained crouched on the ground, her eyes locked on the mystified face of my Ursidae companion. Realising he still held his sword, Secuutus slowly returned it to its sheath and then raised both hands to show he was no threat. Still the female animan cowered.

'Why are you still afraid? I asked. 'The lynx has returned to the forest. It won't hurt you now.'

The terrified creature finally raised its eyes to peer at me, though her frightened gaze constantly flickered back to Secuutus. Moments passed then with a sob, the Lupus whimpered a reply, 'The lynx may not hurt me, but he will kill me!'

Both Secuutus and I recoiled in shock at this statement, Secuutus's face turned from shock to horror then bewilderment. It was clear he had no understanding of what the Lupus was implying as he turned to me in puzzlement. I knew both of us were strangers in this land, neither of us knew where this land was. So how could this female fear my companion, a gentle giant whom she had never met?

'I'm sorry, we don't understand. We are strangers here and have no reason to kill you. Why would you say such a thing?' I asked.

The Lupus stared at me for several minutes, indecision showing on her frightened face. Again she turned to study Secuutus who remained with his hands raised and open, a questioning frown upon his face.

'You are strangers you say? From whence do you come then?'

I decided truth or the most recent truth may be best in this situation. 'We come from the land of Regnum, ruled once by King Fastus, now by King Janiz. We don't know of this land for we have travelled far.' Perhaps not all the truth I thought.

'I know not of that land or its king. It must be far from here else I would have heard of it. You have travelled far indeed. So you have no knowledge of this land and its troubles? No knowledge of the war?' answered the Lupus in surprise.

'No, none at all. As I said, we are strangers here. I am Harry and my friend is Secuutus. I repeat, we mean you no harm.'

'I am called Pabulor. I gather food from the forest for my kin. This is the land known as Silva Homines and there are no rulers, yet. That is why the war rages, two sides battle to become the rulers of our land.'

'But with whom do you war? And why are you so frightened of Secuutus?' I asked gently.

Pabulor stared at me as if I had lost my mind for a moment before her eyes turned to stare at Secuutus again. After a moment's hesitation she replied, 'We Lupus are at war with the Ursidae!'

As soon as the words left her mouth, the Lupus shot to her feet and sped away back to the forest at a run, catching both Secuutus and myself by surprise. She had moved so fast, neither of us stood any chance of catching her.

Now we were alone again, in a land that was at war. The whole concept appeared familiar to me, I had been through similar before. I looked over at Secuutus and knew his thoughts were the same. It seemed like only moments ago we were battling palace guards and a fake sorcerer alongside Prince Janiz. A prince who was now King. Had we gone from the frying pan into the fire I wondered? Plus there was the odd detail of the Lupus femina's words, Lupus fighting Ursidae. Two species of animan warring to decide who would rule this land. Were there no Leo? It was custom here for a member of the Leo Cast to rule,

Lupus traded and schemed while the Ursidae tended to be farmers or blacksmiths, labourers.

My own Tigris Cast are the warriors, of course, this is not a set rule, Lupus fight and also farm, Ursidae can turn their hand to most things, including fighting. Nonetheless, a war between the Lupus and the Ursidae over the right to rule a land was unusual, to say the least. Being a Tigris, I hoped it would not involve me, however, my companion was of the Ursidae Cast, it could most certainly involve him.

I worried for my friend but the situation was lost on Secuutus. He didn't share my concerns, and in truth, I believed he had almost certainly not made the connection between himself and the animan war that raged in this land.

His next words verified my assumption. 'Right she's gone, whoever she was, but I'm hungry, let's find some food. Which way?'

I looked about me once more and concluded whichever way we travelled, it would involve making our way through the forest. Bearing in mind the direction taken by the Lupus, I turned away and decided upon a different route. No sense in walking into an area that contained Lupus, so avoidance seemed the best plan, at least until we had more information about the land we found ourselves in. Judging from the position of the sun, the Lupus had entered the forest in a westerly path, I set off towards the south, with Secuutus quietly plodding along beside me. I noted that since my arrival on this world, I appeared constantly to be travelling south.

However, at that point it made little difference because we had no idea where we were going anyway. Secuutus made no reference to the news that members of his Cast were at war with the Lupus. I wondered why at first, until I remembered he had very recently been ripped from the land he knew, from all that was familiar, including his fellow riders. He had fought alongside animan he had known for many years. He had been loyal to his prince and commander, a Leo. Less than an hour ago, he had been stood in the palace and witnessed the defeat of the sorcerer and the rise of a new king. Now here he was, in the blink of an eye, so to speak, he had been transported from his land, his friends and his prince. No wonder he didn't react to the news of a war between the Ursidae and the Lupus. He was still in shock.

I had been through this before when I opened that damn box in Manchester and awoke in this world. I had been allowed time to learn, lessons that on occasion, were the difference between life and death. My leg remained sore from my battle with the Hyaenidae, a species of hyena that had evolved into a creature the size of a grizzly but twice as nasty. I still recalled the shock of seeing my changed appearance for the first time, from a lowly human into a magnificent Tigris warrior, an evolution of a Bengal tiger. A tiger that walked on two legs, used hands and speech as a human, socialised and lived like a human, but was not human. My tiger features were only faint but could still be recognised, as with the other Casts, any resemblance to their animal origins were slight. I didn't have the roaring head of a tiger, simply a resemblance. Humans don't look like apes, but there is a resemblance, a slight one I agree, but it's there. It took me some time to come to terms with my changed features and this new world and though Secuutus's features had remained the same, he had still been ripped from the life he knew. So, I empathised with Secuutus and remained quiet at his side, allowing him to come to terms with the recent events.

A boreal forest screened the horizon all around us as we left the clearing and entered the woods. Trees I recognised shared the sunlight with other species I had not seen before. I concluded most were coniferous trees, such as pine, spruce and larch, but I could not say for sure, I couldn't see the wood for the trees. Sounds began to register on my hearing, sounds of birds I expected, but these sounds indicated the presence of a variety of species. I had no idea of where I was in this world but as a single landmass, animals, birds and insects had no barrier to confine them to a continent.

Sophos the sage had explained that on this world, the Earth's plate tectonics had not divided into continents, here on Totus-Terra the landmass remained joined, as it did when called Pangea. Free travel right across every country in the world was available to every species, insect, reptile, mammal or bird. Not that any sensible creature would want to journey across this massive landmass.

Personally, I thought flying would be a better option than walking, especially considering the distances involved. I just needed someone to invent the aeroplane.

My thoughts wandered and I continued to ponder on the Dodo, as I had ever since I arrived on this one huge landmass, did the Dodo still exist? With no barrier in the form of oceans or seas creating borders between continents, did the kangaroo or the koala exist? Was Bigfoot a reality here? Yeah I know, I wandered off track there for a moment, but the fact remains, what differences are there in this world? I knew humans did not exist, they had not evolved from apes here, and other species had stepped up to rule the land. But what else had changed, I had fought an overgrown hyena, just recently encountered a lynx the size of a lion, horses had grown larger to cope with the bulk of the animan, but what other creatures had evolved? Did I really want to know? I wasn't so sure.

I made my decision for the route we would take and so our new journey began. Secuutus and I exited the clearing and disappeared into the trees.

Chapter Two: A Bear Hunt

Our feet trod a ground that was soft and quiet, the earth almost totally covered in pine needles with no crunching deciduous leaves to give us away to any hidden threat. I noticed the temperature had a definite chill about it, we were certainly no longer in the warm climes of Regnum. As if to reinforce my thoughts, Secuutus gave a slight shiver.

'Why is the air cold here? It was never this cold at home,' he grumbled.

'I think we've found ourselves in a northern land my friend, it can get very cold up here, even snow.' I replied with hidden amusement.

'What's snow?'

Ah I thought, my huge companion had never before experienced weather other than that of his homeland. There, apart from the infrequent but extremely powerful hurricane like winds and the odd rainstorm, the climate was warm and dry. Secuutus had no experience and was ill-prepared for colder climates. Although all animan have a light covering of fur on their bodies, it's very faint and would be little use in maintaining body temperature. I decided we needed more suitable clothing, but where to get it? I had no idea, I was sure the likelihood of stumbling across a Burtons or Asda would be zero. I then attempted to explain snow to my non-scholarly companion. I think I may have given him the basics, however, the concept of frozen flakes of water falling from the sky was simply too alien for him to grasp. I gave up. If my assumption of where we are is correct, he'll find out soon enough.

We travelled on walking at a cautious pace, knowledge of where we were and what our future held still a mystery. There was also the threat of wandering into a war zone to be considered, being an Ursidae, Secuutus was most at risk. If we encountered a band of armed Lupus, it could be the death of him. As for myself, I was a Tigris warrior, known to be a mercenary Cast, fighting for coin. I would be assumed to have taken the side of the Ursidae as a soldier of fortune and I too would be at risk.

I was also aware that Secuutus shambled along with his head down, not caring where we were or the consequences of being caught, I needed to snap him out of his despondency, because our lives may depend on him being alert and aware. I stopped walking and turned to face my sad companion.

'Secuutus,' I began. 'I realise you are hurt and confused, I know all this is very strange to you and you miss Janiz and the camaraderie of the riders. I felt the same when I awoke on your world. Nonetheless, you must accept it, we're here and only the jade box can send us home. In order to get home, we must first stay alive. We'll search for the jade box in due course but first, we have to survive. So be alert, be ready and accept what has happened, for now at least.'

Secuutus turned and looked at me with his large brown eyes, the sorrow and confusion were plain to see and my heart dropped.

'If we find this box of yours, can we use it to return to Janiz and the riders? Are you sure?' he pleaded quietly.

I prayed for forgiveness as I looked straight back at him and lied. 'I'm sure. If we can find that box or another here, we can use it to get home. I promise. But first, we have to discover more about this land to ensure we stay alive. The jade box will not help us if we are dead!'

I knew the jade box would send us somewhere if we could find it of course. I also suspected it would be unlikely to return us to Regnum. After all, it had not sent me home to Manchester when I had foolishly opened it for a second time. It could send us anywhere, even a different dimension. I had convinced myself that's what happened to me, I don't believe in magic so some form of science must be behind that small inconspicuous jade box. But Secuutus needed the lie so I provided it. It appeared to work for after a few moments of contemplation, the Ursidae warrior straightened his huge shoulders, hitched his sword belt higher and finally began to take notice of his surroundings.

'If we can get home then all well and good,' he replied. 'I don't like this place, there are too many trees and it's too cold. If we have to fight, then fight we will, until we find a way home. Then we shall see.'

Secuutus slowly returned to his old self, his gaze studying everything, his whole manner corrected itself into readiness, aware of the sounds and sights of the forest and watchful for any danger. My lie had served its purpose, and I again felt comforted by the presence of a very capable killer at my side. Now we were two, two ex-riders who were familiar with battle, familiar with killing, we would find our way together.

The forest through which we travelled was heavily populated with conifers that reached high into the sky, creating spectacular splashes of light and shade. It was by these occasional glimpses of the sky that enabled us to continue travelling south, or at least in that general direction. As the sun dropped, we plodded onwards in what we hoped was a southerly course, but in truth, it didn't matter. We had nothing and nowhere to use as a destination so we simply kept moving. On the forest floor, one could only see a matter of fifty yards in some places, less than thirty in others due to the thick growth. Where the trees were dense, little vegetation filled the forest floor, in contrast, ferns, brambles and other foliage I didn't recognise made travel difficult in areas where the trees thinned and let the light through.

Birds sang around us, patches of blue and gold above the canopy lit our way and allowed us glimpses of mule deer and even a moose. The wildlife was plentiful as there were no hunters with high powered rifles, telescopic lenses or other assorted modern weapons. Nor did the large game appear overly frightened unless our path took us too close. A good bowman may make a kill but without guns, the animal's chances of survival were more evenly balanced. The animan did not kill for fun as humans do, food and survival was their only reason for killing an animal. Rabbits, squirrels and other small furry things paused to watch us before scampering away. One particular nosey rabbit failed to move fast enough and Secuutus's blade provided us with the evening's meal. Meagre pickings but at least it would help keep hunger at bay for the night.

After walking for some time, drinking from streams and rivers in which otters played and fish jumped, but as the day faded, we sought a location in which to spend the night. We chose a small stony beach beside what I took to be a sizable lake. Gathering wood for a fire was no problem, we were in a forest after all. We set the fire on the shore of the lake to avoid any risk of igniting the trees. With no bedding or extra clothing, it was going to be a cold night so boughs of fir were cut, collected and placed on the stony ground as makeshift beds. Some of the branches with thicker foliage were put aside as cover against the cold. They offered little in warmth but would help keep us dry and give a pretence of blankets. Secuutus needed to be convinced that although the sky was clear now, rain or snow could fall at any time. I wondered how he would cope in my homeland of Britain, where rain, cold, snow, sleet and fog were the norm.

We set our camp mid-distance from the forest edge and the water, I assumed the lake was not tidal but considered it wise anyway. While Secuutus built up the fire, I wandered down to stand and stare at the lake, its water's just reaching the tips of my boots. Why people everywhere inevitably stare out over an expanse of water and lose themselves in thought was one of my ponderings as I too did that very same thing. My staff was in my hand as I gazed across the water and memories flooded my mind as the water splashed at my feet.

What? I was broken from my reverie as realisation dragged me back to the here and now. Splashed I thought? Lake water doesn't splash. Shifting my gaze to the water directly in front of me, I could see fish darting to and fro, small grey fish oblivious to my presence. It was the easiest fishing I have ever experienced, which says little in truth, I had only caught one fish in my entire life, and that was by accident. Here though, I released the hidden blade in my staff and simply stabbed it down into the water. I had caught two lovely lake trout before the fish realised the danger and swam out of my reach. Now our evening meal offered more than just a few mouthfuls of rabbit.

Darkness fell and with full bellies, we settled down to sleep beside the flickering light of the fire. It was a clear night and the velvet black sky was dotted with more stars than I had ever seen, due to the modern light pollution of my world, such a display of heavenly bodies overwhelmed my spirit with its beauty. The sound of the forest changed from the clamour of bird song to the rustling of the night creatures. I felt it unlikely we would be attacked by Hyaenidae here by the shore of a lake surrounded by boreal forest. Nonetheless, caution remained high on our survival list, our weapons shared our beds, grasped tightly in our hands.

I remembered my old friend and fellow countryman, Sophos the Sage who like me had arrived here after opening a green jade box. He had warned me that many of the animals I knew at home had evolved here, most had become even more deadly. The only animal of threat here that I could think of, would be the Gulo gulo. This beastie had evolved from the already vicious and nasty wolverine into something even worse. Sophos had advised me to stay well clear of this creature, and I intended to do just that.

Though, it wasn't a snarling Gulo gulo that woke us in the silence of the night. It was something far more dangerous. Sounds not of the forest registered on my sleeping ears, causing my eyes to snap open and my breath to still. The night was clear and stars pierced the black blue blanket of the sky. The air was cold and I gave an involuntary shiver before the reason for my awakening became apparent. There were animan in the forest and heading our way. I glanced at our fire and was relieved to see it had died down as we slept, its feeble glow would not give us away unless someone came too close. I sensed that Secuutus was also conscious, remaining absolutely still beneath his blanket of fir. I tensed but did not move as the voices grew nearer. From the snippets of conversation I could hear, I realised the oncoming animan had no idea we were there, so our best plan was to remain quiet and still and hope they passed us by.

On the beach in the darkness Secuutus and I lay, our bodies motionless. Barely daring to breathe as the voices approached. Suddenly a footfall crunched the stony shoreline, evidence of their proximity, swiftly followed by sounds of more feet moving over the stony ground towards the water's edge. From where I lay, I could make out the shapes that now crouched at the lake and filled water bottles or cupped their hands and drank. The nearest figure was only four long strides from our prone bodies, lying invisible under a covering of conifer boughs. I could see enough to identify them, I knew the animan to be a group of Lupus, and from catching bits of their conversation, I discovered with shock that they were a hunting party. The Lupus were on a bear hunt, bear in the form of Ursidae, an Ursidae like Secuutus. Now I knew if we were discovered, our lives would end that night.

Fear now froze our bodies and adrenaline flowed through our veins. There were too many Lupus for Secuutus and me to overcome, we had one option and one alone, to pray we were not detected. At the water's edge, the Lupus appeared to be in no hurry to move on so I listened to as much as I could. Unwittingly it seems, we had wandered into an area controlled by the Lupus, and this was a military patrol. The constant clink of weapons as the Lupus refreshed themselves signified they were heavily armed, we would not stand a chance.

As my thoughts niggled at possible plans of escape, one of the Lupus stood up and moved away from the water. He walked back up to the tree line and began to urinate on the ground only feet from where I lay. Others soon followed his actions and within moments Secuutus and I were lying prone beside a stream of urine. In midstream, one of the Lupus suddenly looked up and appeared to sniff the air.

'Be still!' he rasped, 'I smell something.'

I nearly lost my bowels there and then. Lying on a rocky shore, covered in conifer boughs in the middle of the night with a stream of urine running past my prone head. We were on the verge of being discovered. I held my breath, willing my body deeper under the branches, wishing I was home, in my own bed. The whole line of urinating Lupus paused in their banter, some even managing to halt their flow as each responded to the command.

After what seemed a lifetime, one of the Lupus laughed, 'I smell nothing but your piss! There is nothing here, stop worrying. The likelihood of an Ursidae hiding in the bushes, ready to pounce on us is nonsense. Finish up and we'll get moving, the sooner this patrol is over, the happier I'll be. I've had enough of these boring night patrols and I want my bed.'

With that, the other Lupus joined in with comments and ridicule at the instigators unwarranted fears. If only they knew. At last, all were relieved and collecting their water bottles, the group of

Lupus could be heard climbing the shore and entering the forest once more.

Secuutus and I were alone again, and still alive. We waited long moments before moving even a finger, making sure the Lupus were well away from our camp on the shore. Finally, I slowly raised my head and peered into the darkness, my ears straining for any sounds of the Lupus returning. There was nothing, the night was quiet again and it appeared we were safe, for the moment at least.

I pondered on the intelligence of the patrol and its leader, not wondering why there should be two piles of conifer branches placed side by side on the stony shore. Surely two mounds of branches, one noticeably higher than the other, should be cause for investigation. I am pretty certain one does not encounter piles of fresh cut fir branches on the shore of a lake every night. Randomly placed branches may be considered the work of beavers, or wood gathers, but not two uniform piles on stony ground in the middle of nowhere. I thanked the Lupus group for their useless attention to detail, else Secuutus and possibly I would be dead seconds after our discovery.

'What just happened?' whispered Secuutus as he too raised his head and looked over at me. 'Did I just dream those Lupus standing and almost pissing on top of us?'

'No, you're not dreaming Secuutus, we just had a very lucky escape, thanks to the stupidity of the group and their leader. How they didn't see us I'll never know. Just be thankful they didn't.'

'Oh I'm thankful, that's for sure. I've not been so certain of death for . . . Well for a while anyway,' he finished as memories flooded back of his past life, lost in the briefest of moments.

'Yeah, I know what you mean, but it doesn't make it any easier. Perhaps we should move on and find better cover to wait out the rest of the night,' I suggested as I wriggled out from under my conifer blanket.

The new day found us walking through the forest, making our way south as usual. Neither of us knew where we were heading or what to expect when we got there. All we knew was we had to keep moving and hope we find a friendly face in this strange land of trees. The weather had a definite chill this morning and Secuutus grumbling incessantly about how cold this place was compared to his home. As for myself, I was much more acclimatised to cold and rain than my friend. The dawn had risen grey and overcast, moisture glistening on the trees and undergrowth. All I needed to see was an empty beer can and a potato crisp wrapper and the scene would be complete.

Wildlife here was abundant, rabbits, deer, elk and moose were frequently spied flitting through the trees. I realised that as yet, I had seen no sign of predators, and perhaps the presence of two killers in the area was enough? All the animals could see, hear and certainly smell Secuutus and me and would instinctively know what we were. They knew that if they kept just a safe distance from us, they had nothing to fear. I was hungry, I wished I had a gun.

The day moved on and we grew increasingly cold and hungry but so far we had not seen or heard any signs of civilisation on our travels. I feared we would spend another night under branches, shivering in the darkness. We both agreed it would not be safe to light a fire, following our lucky escape the previous night and the knowledge that the area was patrolled by Lupus soldiers. However, we did agree that any resting place should be deep in the undergrowth and well away from paths or tracks that occasionally crisscrossed the forest floor.

We had found no shelter nor saw another animan all day and that night we followed our plan. We searched out a patch of overgrown ground deep in the woods, and well away from any open spaces or paths. Once again we used boughs from the trees to lay on and to pile over ourselves in an attempt to hold the worst of the cold at bay. Thus we spent another cold night and this time, a night with no fire or food to warm us.

At first light we resumed our journey, both of us feeling very cold, hungry and despondent. Sleeping when cold can be difficult and a bed of boughs is no fun either. We had cold camped at the foot of what I took to be a hill, the morning light showed my assumption to be out in its measurements, the hill now appeared to be a huge great mountain. Not Himalayas I will admit, but in my hungry and weakened state, it would dominate Everest. We had little choice, either turn back the way we came, which we knew led to nothing or start climbing, so up we went.

As we climbed I soon discovered that whenever there was a gap in the tree, I could see for miles across the land. To my delight I saw in the distance, thin trails of smoke lifting into the grey southern morning sky, signs of habitation at last. Luckily, what I took to be a hill, turned out to be just that, a hill. It was my weary mind that exaggerated the size, for it was certainly no mountain. By early afternoon we were climbing and scrambling down the opposite side, heading towards those enticing wisps of smoke I had seen earlier.

By now we were both exhausted, little sleep and no food was weighing on our bodies and minds. We found a path and followed it, too fatigued to worry about encounters with whatever enemy lay in wait for us in this new land. The hill over which we climbed was but one of a range of hills that stretched towards the horizon, but now ahead of us, the land flattened before the next hills in the distance.

We had entered a valley of sorts, still thick forest but at least it would be less tiring than journeying over countless wooded hills. While at the elevated position, we saw not only smoke trails but water, rivers and streams glinting in the daylight. Perhaps here we could find food and possibly risk a fire, we had travelled a good distance from where we had encountered the Lupus, and there was now a hill between us. We mutually agreed we would risk a fire that night. On we travelled, down off the hill and into the valley.

Reaching the foot of the hill, we almost stumbled right past a dishevelled shack. Hidden amongst the trees with weeds and climbing plants creeping over it, as nature attempted to reclaim the space. At first glance, it appeared not only uninhabited but years since anyone had stepped foot in the place. Secuutus looked at me and I nodded in agreement, this would be our home for the night. Uninhabited it may look but we both approached cautiously, weapons ready and senses alert. No indication of animan in residence did not mean it was empty, there were many animals, reptiles and assorted nasties that may abide within its crumbling interior.

As we drew closer, I gestured for Secuutus to check around the shack from the left while I did the same from the right. Carefully stepping over thistles and other such stinging or prickly plants, we each made our way around the shack but found no obvious sign that anyone had been here for many years. Returning to the front of the shack, Secuutus impatiently grasped the doorknob and pushed. Nothing happened at first so he rolled his huge shoulders and pushed again, harder. This time the door opened and Secuutus's momentum carried him inside amidst a cloud of disturbed dust and cobwebs. I followed immediately, my staff held ready to defend against, against what I had no idea, but I was ready.

When the dust settled we could see that the shack had been vacated a long time ago and set about searching through the building, which didn't take long as it only had one room. A homemade bed sat against the back wall, a table stood beside an old sink beneath the only window, and shelves held numerous brick-a-brac and mouse nibbled books. A small fireplace, the built-in stone stood against the one remaining wall, rickety looking wooden chairs standing guard beside the hearth. A few scattered boxes completed the scene about us. Secuutus appeared delighted while I remained sceptical. Secuutus had lived much of his life in barracks or in the saddle, I on the other hand had lived in a small but comfortable and modern flat in Manchester. My own standard of living expectation was several levels above what pleased my companion.

I was volunteered by Secuutus to give the shack a bit of a clean, a bit being the operative words, and gather wood for the fire. Meanwhile, Secuutus disappeared in search of food. Neither of us were true expert hunters, but it has to be said, as a city lad I was still learning my skills. Sometime later Secuutus returned, cautiously calling out a greeting before entering the shack, it wasn't that he didn't trust me but he had no wish to be perforated by my bladed staff.

I was delighted to see him, or rather I was delighted to see the two haunches of meat held tightly in his huge hands. It appeared he had managed to bring down a Mule deer in a brief period of luck. Catching the animal with its head down, drinking from a stream, he had lobbed the biggest stone he could at the animals head, and actually hit it! A swift follow up with his sword and we had food for a couple of days, more if we decided to hang around as Secuutus had wisely stashed the remaining carcass for future use. That night we sat under a roof by a roaring fire and feasted upon flesh once again and to hell with the consequences.

The next morning found us rested and fed, and the world began to look brighter, for the moment at least. Rummaging through the boxes, under the unused bed, we had slept on the floor close to the hearth, we found an assortment of clothing. Most we discarded as being too small or beyond use, but I did find a couple of suitable thick coats, one for myself alone with a pair of trousers that didn't quite reach my ankles. The other coat we had to *adjust* as best we could to make it fit the massive frame of my companion. It still didn't fit well so I chose the least flea-ridden blanket from the bed and using my knife, I made Secuutus a rough poncho by cutting a slit in its centre. We dressed over our own thin clothes, least we would be warmer now.

Better prepared against the cold and with meat in our bellies, we made ready to move on. In the still of the morning, I looked out across the landscape and pondered our next move. A brief discussion with Secuutus proved to be fruitless, he had no plans or ideas either, this land was as strange to him as it was to me. Finally, we settled on a day of exploration, using the shack as a base to return to at night.

Feeling slightly more comfortable in the assortment of garments we now wore, we set off in the approximate direction of those smoke trails. An hour or so later we came across a small clearing in the wood and in its centre stood a cabin, a log cabin of course. A few chickens and pigs scratched or muzzled the ground in search of food, and hand tools for woodworking lay against one wall. We could see from our position under the cover of the trees that this place was indeed inhabited, but by whom we had to discover. Friend or foe.

We waited, lying flat in the undergrowth and watched the cabin, fearing to approach the unknown abode. We didn't have to wait long. Suddenly the door of the cabin open and a tall robed figure stood silhouetted in the doorway. The figure glanced cautiously around before throwing table scraps out for the scrabbling animals. The figure had a cowl covering its face in shadow, making it impossible to identify the wearer. However, the long sword hanging from the figure's waist gave warning that this individual could be dangerous.

'What do you think?' I whispered to Secuutus, 'should we approach?'

Following a brief pause, Secuutus replied also in a whisper, 'No, not yet. I have doubts about this animan, I feel we must be cautious. Let's just watch a while.'

The figure disappeared back into the cabin, only to reappear moments later with a wooden bowl grasped in one hand. As we watched, the animan investigated under small bushes, around the cabin and in every possible nesting place. When satisfied with the results, the cowled animan returned to the cabin, the bowl now containing several chicken eggs. As the figure turned to close the door it paused and its head suddenly lifted, as if scenting the air and cast another wary glance around the clearing before retreating inside.

I was curious, who would live in such an isolated location deep in the forest? Did they have something to hide or were they hiding from someone? The figure certainly didn't appear to be a lonely hermit or sage like Sophos. For all I knew the figure may be hideously disfigured, hence the hooded robe. It could be a religious figure, a thought instantly dismissed, the animan had no religion, they believed in what they could see about them. Apart from the odd demon, I knew they feared demons.

Secuutus and I lay hidden long enough for him to begin dozing, a sign perhaps that we had waited long enough. I prodded him awake and gestured it was time to move. We stayed right where we were, for at that very moment the door opened again and the figure again stepped out into the daylight. We watched as the figure scanned the area, nudging a chicken away from its feet while its eyes peered into the shadow of the trees. Finally satisfied, the figure appeared to relax then surprised both Secuutus and me by reaching up and removing its hood.

I had no idea what to expect. A grizzly old animan perhaps? Living a solitary life by choice or necessity? A hideously scarred figure shunning the world and hiding from the gaze of others?

My expectations fell false, I found myself staring at the last thing I would ever have expected. There in front of me stood an animan of a Cast I instantly recognised, I was staring a Tigris warrior. A female Tigris and her eyes were boring into mine.

Chapter Three: An Ally

At first, I was certain she stared purely by chance at where Secuutus and I lay, but the stare continued to a point where I grew anxious. Eventually, curiosity overcame me and I rose from the undergrowth and stared back at the female Tigris. Immediate her hand shot towards her sword and grasping the pommel, she moved to turn side on to us in a clear indication she was an experienced fighter, posed and ready.

I did nothing, I simply stared at the figure, not moving. I had one hand on my staff, the other hanging by my side. I saw her eyes search my body, looking for the blade she expected to find. Of course, there was none, there was just me and the banded wooden staff. Surely no threat to a Tigris armed with a deadly blade? Least that's the message I hope my stance portrayed, though a tall powerful male Tigris appearing from the bushes could be considered daunting to anyone. I had no wish to fight her or frighten her away. She was the first female of my Cast I had ever seen.

'We offer no threat to you,' I said softly. My companion and I are strangers in this land and simply wish to find our way home.'

Well, it wasn't a lie, we were strangers here and we both wished to return to our respective homes. However, I doubt that in her wildest dreams she could imagine what I meant by the phrase; return home. A short pause followed as we continued to stare at each other, the pause suddenly broken by Secuutus slowly rising to his feet. The imposing sight of a huge armed Ursidae ascending from the forest floor should have gained some form of reaction, but it didn't. The Tigris female remained in her stance, a flicker of her eyes being the sole change in her features. Still she did not speak, and I was pleased to see she had not drawn her sword either, so I waited. The silence grew, the female Tigris stared and Secuutus soon became impatient.

'Well? What are you waiting for?' he demanded of the figure. 'Speak Tigris, we mean you no harm. Either fight or allow us to your er . . . home? We would welcome knowledge of where we are and what this land is.'

The Tigris femina remained silent for another moment or two, then she turned towards the cabin and gestured for us to follow. Wearily we entered the clearing or whatever it was, a farm, a smallholding or just a home with some chickens and pigs? I didn't know nor care. Once at the door, the femina turned and held up a hand to stop us from entering. Secuutus began to growl but I placed a hand on his shoulder and he quietened. The femina looked us both over then pointed at the sword hanging from Secuutus's belt, and then pointed at the outside of the door. Her meaning was obvious and with a glance at me, Secuutus did as bid. Then the Tigris looked at me and to my shock, she pointed at the place where my evil knife was hidden in my clothing, then at the same spot where Secuutus had rested his blade. With a slight smile to indicate I recognised her skill, I laid the knife beside the sword. I remained mute about the blade hidden in my staff and she appeared not to consider a wooden staff as a weapon, I was allowed to keep it with me. Wisely, a rare occurrence in my Ursidae friend, he too kept his mouth shut about the blade. The Tigris femina stepped aside and pushed open the door and with a short gesture, she invited us into her cabin.

The inside of her cabin was much the same as our shack in the woods, though it had to be said, the cabin was much cleaner and well maintained. Personal items and clothing lay tidily about the place, supplies of grain were stored on a shelf and a hunk of meat hung from the ceiling in one corner of the room. The roughhewn furniture consisted of a table and two chairs, one bed and a small cupboard. A half-barrel served as a sink and over the one window draped a leather curtain. A narrow stone chimney rose from a small fireplace with cooking tools laying close by. It was a small but functional home.

Another gesture indicated Secuutus and I should take the only two chairs at the table. Once seated, our host provided two crude clay cups and placed a jug of some substance in front of us. Still she said nothing. Secuutus eagerly helped himself to a drink but I was more cautious, not because I feared betrayal, but rather that I had no idea what the beverage was. I had been caught out once by Sophos and I did not intend repeating that brain explosive moment. I poured just a little into my cup and took a sip. To my delight, I found it was a form of fruit juice, not the battery acid I expected.

We both offered thanks to our host and I gave a brief and very simple explanation of our situation, hoping to place her at ease. I informed her we had been separated from a travelling merchant's caravan. We had been the hired guards but when chasing off some bandits, we had become lost. We knew we were far from our home, the Kingdom of Regnum, but did not know how far or which direction to travel to return. Secuutus gravely nodded to reinforce my words, even though they were only half truths.

We could not admit to being transported here by a dimension shifting green jade box. Our host listened quietly, offering no interruptions or questions, she just sat and listened. When I finished my tale, she moved over to the cupboard and picked up a piece of pale wood, a small square of pine I thought. Next, she grasped a small stick of charcoal from beside the fire before returning to stand by the table.

As we watched with interest, the Tigris scratched on the wood with the charcoal, and then laid it on the table between Secuutus and me. On it she had written in a shaky script, "Can you read?" I stared at it for a moment as realisation struck home, Secuutus stared in confusion. Looking up at our host, I held out my hand for the charcoal. I then wrote one word on the piece of wood. "Yes."

I wondered why all this writing and Secuutus was now totally baffled. 'What's that, are they words? What is she drawing?' he asked while his gaze flashed between me and the Tigris. 'She is a Tigris femina. That much I can see, but what's this stuff with words?'

Without a word, the female picked up the charcoal and continued to write. When she finished, she once again placed the wood on the table. This time she had crossed out her first question and my reply, and underneath was now written, "I am Silĕre. I do not speak."

At last, I understood her silence, she was mute. As politely as I could, I passed this information onto Secuutus. For a moment he remained quiet, then to my surprise, he rose to his feet, looked straight in the eyes of Silēre and wiped one finger across his mouth. The Tigris femina hung her head again and nodded in reply and Secuutus gave a grunt of understanding before sitting down once again.

'No tongue,' he said in way of an insufficient explanation. I frowned at him to expand. 'She, like you, is a warrior. Both male and female Tigris can be hired as mercenaries, assassins or guards, anything that requires a skilled sword. Unfortunately, it is the practice of those who hire such animan, to remove the tongue if that animan fails in their given task. She has failed.'

I stared in amazement as my brain digested this news, it was a purely barbaric practice and shocked my city boy mind. Nevertheless, as an animan in a world were health and safety didn't exist, one killed or was killed, the act of losing one's tongue for failure is definitely preferable to losing one's life. The Samurai in Japan would fall on their own swords if they failed, I think perhaps, the animan way is more acceptable.

'So why does she live here, in the middle of nowhere? Surely she could continue as a mercenary, albeit a quiet one? I queried.

'She is shamed,' replied Secuutus as Silēre stared at the floor. 'She can't hide her mutilation, everyone will know she has failed. Most will never hire her and her own Cast may shun her. Living alone, hidden from the world is better than the ridicule and rejection she would receive from the humblest to the highest animan.'

Though my mind recoiled at this stigmatisation, as a human I was well accustomed to the vilification of others, from the sick and the poor to different race and even different religion. As for myself, I lived by the rule where I accepted everyone unless they pissed me off. Be right by me and I'll be right by you was my philosophy. All I saw was a female Tigris, an attractive and lithe animan of my species, my Cast.

'It matters not to me,' I said. 'I'm grateful for the invite into your home and for my drink. Thank you.' I directed these word to Silēre as I turned to face her. I was rewarded with a slight smile and that made my day.

'Ok, back to what we do and where we go from here,' I said, the previous conversation forgotten as far as I was concerned. 'Silĕre, can you tell us where we please?'

Silĕre nodded in affirmation and reached for her piece of wood again. Taking care, she began to draw a rough map of the area. Peering over her shoulder, I could see we were indeed in a huge forest, scattered with villages, towns and even a city, all concealed within the forest. Next to my surprise, Silĕre drew a line down through the middle of the map and then pointed at Secuutus before placing her finger on the west side of the map.

'Ursidae,' said Secuutus with a nod of understanding.

Silĕre moved her finger to the opposite east side of the line and looked up at both of us in turn. I quickly realised her meaning and said simply, 'Lupus.'

Again Silĕre nodded, indicating I was correct. Our Tigris femina host then explained in a series of hand movements and gestures that the two sides were at war. Following a question from me, Silĕre pointed at a spot on the map, showing our present position. We were in the Lupus controlled half of the forest, close to the border. A fact both Secuutus and I understood immediately, we were in the wrong place.

'I don't see my home, Regnum, is it far from here?' asked Secuutus in a soft voice.

Silĕre appeared to think for a moment before gesturing off the map in a southerly direction. Then she wrote one word at the bottom of the map, she wrote, "Far."

Have you ever seen a bear cry? Well, I came very close to seeing an evolved humanoid bear cry that day when I spoke Silĕre's word. A look of such sadness lined the face of Secuutus that I almost felt compelled to give him a hug. Nonetheless, I wisely declined the compulsion. Man hugs and even male contact was not as freely used here as at home, and I didn't want my friend to get the wrong idea. Instead, in a show of empathy, Silĕre herself moved close to Secuutus and gently laid a hand on his shoulder.

There we all were, Secuutus, Silĕre and me, troubled by our thoughts and regrets. Secuutus was homesick, Silĕre was shamed and I, well I didn't really know what I wanted. I had felt I would stay in this land, but when the time came, I chose to open the jade box, hoping it would send me home to Manchester, but it didn't. Now though, I knew for certain if the opportunity arose again, I would still seek to return to my small flat in the city. Here, with no Sophos to share my thoughts of home with, I was truly alone. I could not speak of my own race of humans, they didn't exist here. The ape had never evolved into man.

A sound broke our reverie, voices could be heard faintly in the forest and sounded as if they were heading our way. Quickly Silĕre gestured for us to hide, she pointed at the door and mimed us running and hiding the undergrowth behind her cabin. At a questioning frown from me, Silĕre again pointed at the door and us before placing a hand on her breast and then sweeping both hands around at the cabin. I understood, she lived here and was probably known by the locals and the Lupus. She would not be in any danger, but we would. I followed Secuutus from the cabin, picking up our weapons as we went and as quietly as only an animan can be, we crept some fifty yards across the bare ground and back into the cover of the trees. There we lay amongst the undergrowth and watched the cabin, both of us tense and ready to fight.

The voices grew nearer until into the clearing around the cabin strolled a small group of Lupus. Now in daylight, we could make out a uniform of sorts, they were soldiers. The group numbered six that I could see, little problem for two Tigris warriors and an Ursidae fighter if the need arose. However, neither Secuutus nor I wanted to get involved in a local war. We had ridden as outlaws and fought soldiers, mercenaries, wild beasts and a fake sorcerer only days ago, in another land. We had no wish to resume that lifestyle just yet. Sadly, it appeared the decision was not ours to make.

Secuutus and I watched as the soldiers approached the cabin, calling for Silĕre to open the door. Acting the part of being surprised, Silĕre took just a moment or two before obeying the order and we could hear the sound of a latch being withdraw and then the door opened. I gave Secuutus a nudge, I wanted to see what was happening at the front of the cabin. Stealthily we half crawled, half slithered our way over the forest floor until we gained a clear view of the group standing at Silĕre's cabin door. There, framed in the doorway stood the figure of Silĕre, her head was slightly bowed and she purposely avoided direct eye contact with the Lupus. I remembered she was considered shamed and any sign of pride or defiance could lead to instant rebuttal, most likely in physical form. I felt ashamed to see such a magnificent figure brought so low, but this was the nature of things in this land, it was I who had to adapt.

The lead soldier began shouting at Silĕre, he was obviously demanding something but I could not quite catch his words. It was evident that Silĕre was not responding how he wished and I watched his anger grow. The lead soldier stepped back as the other soldiers moved close and grabbed Silĕre, dragged her from the doorway and forced her out onto the ground. Once pinned down, the lead Lupus swung a vicious kick at her face.

This was too much for a once feared Tigris and in a flash she leapt to her feet and grabbed the soldier by the throat, lifting him clear off the ground.

Immediately his comrades rallied to his defence, raining blows on Silĕre and driving her back to the ground. I tensed, ready to attack but Secuutus placed a warning hand on my shoulder while placing a finger against his lips, telling me to be still and stay quiet. Deferring to his greater knowledge of the animan, I quietened, though every muscle in my body screamed for action.

To my horror, I realised what the Lupus intended to do next. Silĕre was pinned to the ground by four of the soldiers while the one who appeared to be in charge began loosening his trousers. They intended to gang rape Silĕre!

This time, Secuutus did not hold me back and both of us leapt to our feet, erupted from our hiding place and changed at the startled soldiers. I released the hidden blade in my staff and held it out in front of me like a spear, Secuutus had his sword gripped tightly out in front of him. The soldiers could do little as shock froze their muscles, fear on their faces as two huge animan bore down on them. Their fear was heightened as neither Secuutus nor I made a single sound as we appeared like apparitions from the dark forest.

Abruptly the soldier's training took over and they too drew their weapons. Their second mistake of the day, by reaching for their swords, they had to let go of Silĕre and in a flash she was on her feet and ripped a weapon from one of the soldiers, before immediately giving it back to him, through his stomach. Now five soldiers faced two Tigris and an Ursidae, the tables had turned.

As I reached my first opponent, he swung his sword up in a slashing movement intended to gut me there and then. I dodged aside and whacked my staff butt down on his head. The soldier was fast, and with a slight shake to clear his head, he leapt right at me, his sword aiming for my stomach. I was faster, still using the butt of my staff I knocked his weapon aside before reversing the staff and whipped up my blade. In one slicing movement, I swept it down across his body. The blow began at his shoulder and sliced down to his gut, opening a long wound. As my blade reached his soft vulnerable belly, I pushed, forcing the blade deep inside him.

Dragging out my blade I turned to see Silĕre facing two soldiers, until I rammed my blade into the exposed back of one, leaving her to finish the other. Wrenching the blade free I spun to fend off another attack by a Lupus soldier, bringing up my staff ready to defend, just as a sword tip suddenly appeared where his belly button should have been. I barely had time to acknowledge Silĕre before I was set upon by the last remaining soldier. I was surprised he hadn't run, his chance of survival against the three of us was not a bet I would put money on. With me at his front and Silĕre at his back, the soldier was cut down in moments, my blade in his throat, Silĕre's sword slashing through his back and severing his spinal cord.

All five soldiers lay on the ground, their life's blood staining the dark earth even darker and the two of us stood wild eyed and posed for more bloodshed. I say two of us because Secuutus, having dispatched his opponent, the lead soldier, rapidly with one mighty blow of his sword, had simply sat on the ground with his back leaning against the cabin wall and watched Silĕre and I finish the job. Seeing him there grinning brought forth a few choice words from me, while Secuutus grinned even wider.

'What the heck are you doing sat there, grinning like an idiot?' I demanded.

'Well I had nothing to do, you two had the situation under control. I had time on my hands so thought I'd rest up a bit. What more could I do?' Secuutus grinned back at me.

A tap on my shoulder turned me to face Silĕre, who stood staring into the trees, her attitude suggesting caution so Secuutus and I quit our banter and moved beside her, staring in the same direction. I listened, at first I could neither see nor hear anything other than the sounds of the forest. Then in a moment of awareness, I realised that from the direction that held our attention, there were more sounds in the forest, marching feet. I knew that could only mean one thing, more soldiers were coming our way. The other two realised this as well and with a nod of her head, Silĕre indicated we should move. Silĕre dashed back into her cabin to grab a few things, then as quickly and quietly as possible, we slipped into the trees and away.

We crept, we slithered, we crouched our way silently through the woods, casting frequent glances to our rear, we moved like the animals from which we had evolved. We moved like ghosts for several hundred yards before building speed, behind us voices now clear in the air, and coming from the direction of the cabin.

Thinking we needed information, I raised a hand and signalled my two companions to a halt, and following my lead, we sank to the ground with our ears searching to catch any indication of our uninvited guests. Though we were too far away to hear all that was said, raised voices soon came to our assistance. Shouting grew from the muted voices of before. It became evident that the dead soldiers had been discovered, and unfortunately for us, it was by a larger patrol of soldiers. I knew we would be hunted. I gestured for Silĕre that we needed to move and that she should lead the way. Secuutus and I had no idea which way to run, so our best chance of survival would be to follow Silĕre.

Nodding her understanding, Silĕre rose to a low stoop and led us off and away from the voices at the cabin. The shouts we heard had turned into commands as a search was organised. We had no way of knowing how many soldiers now sought our blood, but I knew their number was greater than ours from the diversity of voices we heard. We needed to run, to get away as quickly as we could. Secuutus and I followed Silĕre, trusting her local knowledge to keep us safe.

We continued to move as quietly as possible under the coniferous canopy, however, stepping on the occasional twig or branch was impossible to avoid. I prayed the sound would not be picked up by our pursuers. My prayers were answered as the voices behind us began to fade, it appeared we had made good our escape, until another patrol of soldiers loomed up right in front of us. We had run straight into their arms. We were once again fighting for our lives. I struck out with my staff and slashed with its blade, but we were outnumbered by the Lupus soldiers. I could hear Secuutus yelling in defiance somewhere to my left, a brief blur to my right showed Silĕre was still alive and fighting, but we stood little chance. Suddenly a massive blow to the back of my head turned the world black and I knew no more.

I awoke sometime later, my head hurt with an intensity I had never experienced before. I forced open my eyes and the world about me blurred as I again descended into the peace of unconsciousness. I don't know how long I lay there before I sensed rather than felt I was being dragged, the sensation fading as I slid into darkness again. Somehow I knew I was alive, but couldn't state that fact for certain. The world around me swam each time I briefly rose to consciousness, before the blinding pain in my head caused me to thankfully retreat again into oblivion. The sensation of being dragged had stopped but still whenever I forced my eyelids to part, the world swirled in a blur about me.

After what seemed an eon, the pain in my head eased to that of a severe hangover and I carefully opened my eyes to just mere slits, preparing for the worst. Aside from the brightness of the daylight, the world was stationary and no lights exploded behind my eyes. I could see I was lying on the forest floor on a bed of pine needles. The normal sounds of the forest reached my ears and I failed to sense any apparent threat from animals or soldiers. Taking this as I good sign, I attempted to sit up, a mistake, a bad mistake I realised as my head erupted and I once again submerged into an ocean of black.

The next time I awoke, the headache had subsided even further into the background and I summoned up the courage to open my eyes. As my vision cleared I discovered the world had stopped spinning. I looked about me as best I could without moving my head too much, just in case. I didn't want to fall back into unconsciousness.

I found I was still lying on the forest floor but now I appeared to be covered in something, what it was I could not tell without lifting my head and I sure as hell wasn't going to risk that just yet. Greenery sprouted around my resting place so I surmised I was hidden in the undergrowth, but how the hell did I get here? And where the hell was *here*? As I appeared to be safe for the moment, I slowly and cautiously began checking my limbs for damage. Clenching the muscles of each limb I found no injuries, I then gently moved each limb, only slightly at first but when I felt no pain, I risked more movement. No, everything appeared to work, except my head. I lay there for a while longer, wondering if I had the strength to lift my head, risk the possible agony and take a better look at my surroundings.

Suddenly a hand was placed on my chest and a face loomed into view. The face belonged to Silĕre and she was holding a finger to her lips, a gesture that ensured my silence. I was relieved to find I was not alone but any questions would have to wait as my ears also picked up the sound of voices passing near to our position. Silĕre appeared battered and bruised but otherwise alive and healthy, I wondered how Secuutus had fared in the fight against the Lupus soldiers. Hang on a moment I suddenly thought, how the heck had any of us survived? We were grossly outnumbered and should have stood no chance at all of survival. I prayed my friend Secuutus had made it, the fates would indeed be cruel if he had been dragged away from his home kingdom, only to die here in this strange land.

The voices drifted away and Silĕre finally removed her restraining hand, moving it under my shoulders now to aid me to sit up and take stock of my surroundings, and more importantly, my injuries. I found I had been laid on a bed of some kind of browning fern, the colour of the plant fading as the season changed. Another pile of leaves from the age old plant, shrub or whatever the stuff was, was placed over me. I realised the reasons straight away, firstly as marginal protection against the elements but mainly as concealment. Camouflaging my body as it lay on the forest floor. A very good idea I thought.

The world swam again as I finally reached the vertical sitting position, but this soon passed and I could see about me. There was nothing to see, we were deep in the forest undergrowth and alone, just the two of us. Where was Secuutus? I looked around again, fear growing inside me, but still no sign of the huge Ursidae. Silĕre saw and understood my actions, and placing a hand briefly on my shoulder to get my attention, she mimed her hands tied and her head bowed.

'Secuutus?' she nodded. 'Captured? Again she nodded.

There then followed a conversation of mime, gestures and questions as I pieced together what Silĕre was trying to tell me. It appeared that as our plight became desperate, Silĕre had managed to get away and hide in the forest, dodging her pursuers for many hours before they gave up. When the coast was clear, she had circled back and found me covered in blood and face down in the dirt. There was so much blood that at first, Silĕre considered me dead but upon closer examination, she discovered I was still breathing. The blow I had received had been hard enough to knock me so deeply unconscious that the Lupus soldiers assumed I was already dead and wasted no more time on me.

Silĕre had then searched for Secuutus but could find no sign of his body. Tracing around the site of our encounter with the soldiers, Silĕre found tracks leading away from the area, and in amongst the footprints, she could see where something large had been dragged away. It was obvious that in a war between the Lupus and Ursidae, finding Secuutus in their territory would be a matter for investigation. Secuutus had been taken prisoner.

This game of mime and charades was taking its time, but Silĕre persevered, struggling to make me understand the events following my clout on the head. In a break from the pantomime, she had offered me water and meat, I finished the water first, then chewed slowly on the meat while Silĕre went off to fetch more water from a stream. Once I was refreshed, she continued her story. Not able to help the ex-rider, Silĕre had turned her attention to me. She had dragged me deep into the forest and placed me where I now lay, under the trees and covered in ferns. Then she had retraced her steps and with the aid of a branch, she had erased all signs of our escape.

Next, she had examined my head wound and luckily for me, discovered not all the blood covering my body was mine. I raised an eyebrow at this and with a smile, she used her finger and thumb to show there was only a small cut but then formed a fist to indicate the size of the lump on my head which was the size of a large egg! To me it felt like an ostrich egg! No wonder I had been unconscious for . ? I realised I didn't know so with an assortment of gestures I asked the question of my new ally, least I hoped I had an ally. Silĕre pointed at the sky in the direction of the sun, then moved her finger across the sky once. One day.

For the next hour I rested, Silĕre remaining close but alert, occasionally she would sneak off to investigate a sound or fleeting movement but we were alone. I rested uneasily, wondering on the fate of my Ursidae companion. If he was captured and considered a spy, he would surely be tortured before the inevitable horrific death. I had to try and rescue him, but where to start? Getting to my feet might be a good place I decided, and with Silĕre standing near to offer support, I finally managed to stand. Immediately my head began to pound again and for a few moments, the world swam in focus again.

Nonetheless, soon my sight cleared and I was able to function somewhat normally again, though the headache remained and I wished the birds would not sing so loud. While I stood trying to remember how to use my legs, Silĕre broke camp, such as it was, scattered my makeshift bedding and then to my surprise, she handed over my staff. I was amazed, I could only assume the Lupus soldiers had considered it worthless. It was worth the world to me. I patted my side and found with further delight that the evil knife remained in its hiding place at my waist.

Finally, we were ready to move, but where would we go? The answer was obvious, we would follow Secuutus, find where he was being held and take it from there. I was responsible for him being here, I was responsible for his safety, so I had to go to his aid, somehow. We moved off with Silĕre leading the way, following the route taken by the soldiers. We set off to save Secuutus, or die trying.

Chapter Four: Help

We stopped constantly for the first couple of hours, the pain in my head making walking almost unbearable. Silĕre had managed to rescue or steal two extra water bottles scattered during the fight and at each stream we replenished our supply, not through lack of available water, more to the fact I was guzzling it by the gallon. I had not drunk since being struck down and now I desperately needed to rehydrate. I remembered many drinkers supped water after a drunken session to aid the recovery from a hangover. As my head hurt so much, I thought I'd try the same remedy. Gradually the water and the small amounts of food offered by my Tigris femina companion began to restore my strength and lessen my headache. By noon that day, I was feeling almost hu . . . hah, I can't say that any more as I'm not human. Let's just say I felt more myself and was eager to find my friend before his time ran out. We were a day or more behind his captures and had no way of knowing how far we had to travel before reaching wherever they were taking him.

My spirits grew with each movement, relishing the return to the magnificent health and strength of my Tigris body. I had almost forgotten the weakness and limitations of my past human form, almost forgotten but not quite. I followed Silĕre through the forest as she tracked our prey and companion. I could not help but marvel at her skill as she followed the tracks over hill and down dale relentlessly.

As my mind and body improved so other feelings stirred and I began to admire the figure walking tall in front of me. I walked in bare feet as all animan did and I was tall, edging towards seven foot tall perhaps and Silĕre stood only inches shorter. Her lissom body swayed gracefully and seductively as she made her way through the trees, gentle curves combined with wiry muscles made her the perfect athlete and woman. Okay, so she wasn't human but nor was I. Since my time on this world, I had become accustomed to the slight animal features of the animan, these features being so subtle that they could have been applied by a makeup artist, giving just a hint of the beasts they evolved from. After all, humans no longer strongly resemble apes, well most of them anyway, and so it was with the animan. Instead of using the term, species, perhaps if one thought in terms of a different race; that may be a better explanation. Nonetheless, however one described the animan, the one striding out in front of me was damn attractive.

Without warning, Silère fell to the ground, gesturing with her hand for me to follow suit. I easily obeyed her command, I simply collapsed into a prone position. Though my strength was returning rapidly, we had walked several miles and I was feeling the strain. I noted the direction in which Silère focused and did the same, eyes, ears and nose all attempting to identify what had caught her attention. It didn't take me long and I wondered how we had managed to get so close. At the foot of the hill we were descending was a large clearing in the forest, and there in the middle stood a stockade.

When I say a stockade, I really mean a stockade. There in front of us stood a structure including palisades, buildings and watchtowers. I was amazed at first but then I reasoned if one lived in a massive forest, the one commodity in abundance was wood. From our elevated position, I saw a square shaped structure with palisade walls and appeared to be elevated walkways behind them, constructed of wooden poles attached side by side like a huge fence. Each pole had its top sharpened and to my human television accustomed mind, it appeared to resemble an early Roman, Greek or even a Wild Western fort. Guard towers loomed over the structure on two diagonal corners and a wide gate stood as the only entrance and exit. This gate was heavily guarded, two guards stood sentry on each side and a patrol of four more guards paced to and fro outside the entire length of the front palisade and gate. Inside I could make out a long building that I assumed to be a barracks, situated against the east wall. To the north stood one building, perhaps the mess house I thought. Several smaller buildings lined the west wall and an even smaller building stood against the south wall and near the gate, a guardhouse I suspected.

To find such a structure after travelling so long through a maze of trees, gave evidence to the organisation and structure of the Lupus military. If Secuutus was held in this place, he was definitely in trouble, we would need an army of our own to rescue him. I could see figures moving about the stockade, I considered it too small to be classed as a true fort, though in our situation, it might as well have been. I glanced over to Silĕre and received a shrug in return, indicating she had no ideas either.

We decided to withdraw carefully and consider our next move. We retreated into the forest, staying amongst the undergrowth and avoiding any paths or trails. It had been pure chance that we had not encountered a patrol or Lupus scouts on our journey here, the discovery of a stockade in the middle of nowhere had come as a complete surprise to us both.

Concluding an animated conversation between myself and Silĕre, it was agreed we should wait for nightfall and then attempt to get a closer look at the place. I was worried, I could not see how we would achieve any of the three objectives on our list. First, we had to gain entry, second was locating Secuutus, if indeed he was actually there, and third was escaping with our hides intact. Easy! Yeah right!

Nevertheless, later that night, when all appeared quiet, Silĕre and I crept down the hill for a closer look. Sometime later we returned to our hiding place in the forest, crestfallen and tired. We had found no other means of gaining entry to the stockade so another plan needed to be devised, and quickly. We decided to wait until morning, scheming with a tired mind could only lead to failure. The night was cold and it would be too dangerous to light a fire, no matter how small. So we slept sat with our backs against a tree, our knees pulled up tight to our chests and arms folded tightly in an attempt to retain our core heat.

Despite the cold I slept well, exhaustion from the recent events plunging me into unconsciousness quickly. A hazardous state to be in when in such close proximity to an enemy, and the added risk of wild animals biting chunks out of me while I slept. I rested easy though, I knew Silĕre was close and would rouse me if danger approached.

The next day dawned bright and clear as we breakfasted on the last of Silĕre's supplies. I felt much improved for the few hours' sleep and my cognitive abilities and movement had returned. We moved within sight of the stockade again, remaining low in the concealment of the forest edge. Noises and activity had caught our attention so an investigation was paramount. The reason for the bustle of activity soon became apparent as we watched a figure, an Ursidae figure being dragged from one of the buildings by the soldiers. It was Secuutus, it had to be. With his hands and feet bound, he was forced across the stockade courtyard, half carried, half dragged to a waiting single horse pulled cart. Without ceremony or care, Secuutus was thrown into the cart by six Lupus soldiers; it took six of the slimmer, smaller Lupus because Secuutus was certainly not slim neither small. A thin blanket was thrown over the Ursidae either as a gesture to the cold weather or simply an afterthought. I didn't know.

To one side, an officer stood issuing orders, the Lupus soldiers now mounted their steeds and lined up behind the cart. With its sole cargo of Secuutus, the cart driver led the way out of the stockade and turned east, away from the border with the Ursidae controlled territory, travelling deeper into their own lands. Seeing this I began to panic, if Secuutus was moved to a stronger location, any hopes of rescuing him would surely be dashed. We had to think of something.

With only a brief moment's hesitation, I set off in pursuit of the cart, keeping out of sight in the trees while remaining parallel to the track. Silĕre followed though I wasn't sure why, she had no loyalties to Secuutus so why run the risk? In truth though, I was grateful for her company, an extra sword in such capable hands was appreciated. We followed the cart as best we could while racking our brains for a rescue plan. We managed to keep up with the horse drawn cart and its accompanying patrol by slipping through the trees at each bend in the road, taking any short cuts we could. I was pleased my strength had returned, the pace set by the cart was not fast but still required effort to keep it in sight.

Finally came a moment or two of respite, for at noon, the patrol and cart halted to rest the horses and allow the soldiers to answer calls of nature and take refreshments. While the patrol sat around nibbling on rations and sipping at water bottles, I noticed poor Secuutus was not offered any food or water, he remained trussed up in the cart like a sack of spuds. I sought a way to let him know we were here but saw no chance so it was up to me. I would need to react to any advantage that came our way. That night we found one.

I had no idea how far away it would be or how long it would take for the patrol and their captive to reach their destination, so I had to act fast. Night fell and Silĕre and I watched as the patrol made camp. A fire was built and food prepared but still no one offered even a sip of water to the Ursidae who remained prone in the cart. My anger grew as I witnessed such cruel treatment of a prisoner, the Lupus not once glanced at the cart as they supped and prepared their beds about the campfire. Seeing this lack of attention, I had an idea. Drawing away from our position out of reach of the fires weak glow, I led Silĕre further into the trees to outline my plan. Later that night, we put my plan into action.

As softly as cats we approached the now quiet camp, Silĕre from one side, while I crept closer from the other. One soldier sat against a tree with a blanket around his shoulders, he was obviously on guard duty but lulled by the sense of security at being in the territory of his Cast, the guard's head nodded, sleep overpowering him. Following plans made earlier, Silĕre won the battle of who would deal with the guard. I watched as she crept towards the slumped figure of the guard past the sleeping soldiers. Her footfalls were positive and confident, her actions soundless. If any one of those guards awoke, our plan and possibly our lives would be forfeit. I watched enthralled as she crept up behind the dozy soldier in absolute silence. She's very good I thought, submitting to her persistence was the best concession of mine that day.

At a signal from Silĕre as she positioned herself in readiness immediately behind the guard, I began to move almost as stealthily towards the still bound figure in the cart. I approached the cart whilst keeping the vehicle between myself and the prone soldiers, I did not trust my skill as much as those of Silĕre. My first precaution was to place a hand over the mouth of Secuutus, a cry of surprise would ruin everything. As my hand clamped down, Secuutus instantly awoke and wide eyes stared straight at me. I waited until realisation pierced his sleepy brain before using my knife to cut his bonds. Once I was sure he would remain silent, I removed my hand and allowed him to straighten aching muscles and cramped limbs before looking over at Silĕre and giving a small wave. Without hesitation, Silĕre grasped the guard from behind, her hand securely held over his mouth as her other hand slipped a knife into the base of his skull and then tilted it up into his brain. The sleepy guard died instantly and silently in the arms of his assassin.

Silĕre held the guard still while I gestured for Secuutus to move, offering my hand to aid him to climb quietly from the cart before helping him creep away to the trees. There I sat him down and after motioning for him to remain still, I crept back to aid Silĕre. My plan was simple. I had noted the guards paid no attention to their prisoner and a small deception may gain us a few precious minutes to make good our escape.

Making my way silently around the camp, I grasped the dead guard's feet, Silĕre placed her hands under the guard's arms and we gently lifted him up and very slowly and quietly carried him over to the cart. There we laid him out in a resemblance of the position Secuutus had previously occupied. I then covered the guard with the blanket, before laying the ropes I had cut off Secuutus over the body to ensure the deception of a prisoner fooled the soldiers for as long as possible. When satisfied with our work, we made our way back to Secuutus and between us, helped him to his feet and stole away into the forest. I prayed my plan would work, the soldiers would certainly discover one of their members missing in the morning. However, as they had paid scant attention to their prisoner, I based my plan on the fact that the cart would be the very last place they searched. They would be able to see a body, but would any of them bother with a closer examination? If not, they might assume the soldier had absconded during the night and simply continue on their journey. Least that's what I hoped, but time would tell.

Once Secuutus had recovered full use of his limbs, we increased our rate of travel through the trees to place as much distance between the guards and ourselves. It was difficult trying to move quickly and quietly through the forest in the darkness of night, more than once my attention strayed, only to be brought back into focus by slamming my face into a tree I had not seen. Secuutus and I followed the silent figure of Silĕre as she navigated west, how she knew which way to go I could not say. After a couple of bruising hours, Silĕre gestured us to stop and rest. I prayed we were far enough away from the guards but felt confident in our guide. Dawn was now lightening the small glimpses of sky above the canopy, so we rested while waiting enough light to search out a hiding place for the day. We all needed rest and sleep, food would have to wait. We would hunt when safe to do so, until then we fasted.

As it turned out, the site Silĕre had chosen for us to rest provided good concealment so we slept until early afternoon that day. Now rested and with Secuutus fully restored, Silĕre and I searched the vicinity for prey. It didn't take long in this land of abundance before we returned to the hiding place with a couple of rabbits and a squirrel, effectively caught by Silĕre of course. My hunting skills still required some work.

While we hunted, we had both taken the time to scan the area for signs of pursuit or danger. We hadn't detected any sounds or sight of a threat, the forest lay still in the late sunshine, with only the bird's song breaking the silence. I knew from films back home that if the birds fell silent, then we should worry, but for now, their song was reassuring. That's assuming the film directors knew what they were talking about, I had my doubts now. With no sign of danger close, we decided to risk a small fire and not long later, we were satisfying our hunger. The meal was meagre and we all knew that our next priority must be replacing our rations. Water was no problem, small streams crisscrossed the forest, allowing us to keep our water bottles full.

The next day we moved on and the obvious direction would be west, away from the Lupus. It was hoped that Secuutus's Cast, the Ursidae would be more welcoming to one of their own, however, caution remained the objective of the day. Secuutus had recovered but as yet had not spoken of his capture and incarceration in the stockade. Eventually, my patience ran out and I questioned him directly.

'Nothing happened really,' he began. 'We were all fighting those soldiers when I saw you go down. You collapsed to the ground like a felled tree when that soldier hit you, I think he used a club of sorts as he wouldn't have been able to hit you so hard with just the pommel of his sword. I tried to reach you but I too was beaten down to the ground. I looked for Silĕre but she had disappeared. I thought I was dead meat but no blades were used against me, I knew then that I would be taken prisoner and questioned. We three know I am not from these parts, but of course no Lupus military animan would believe me. I resigned myself to a long painful death as it was certain none would believe my tale, the truth.'

While Secuutus paused to take a breath, I interjected. 'Hmm. I was only clubbed down as well, so obviously they wanted us alive, seems you were the preferred victim and I was left discarded. Silĕre found me with a cracked skull when the soldiers had gone, taking you with them. I think they were on an intelligence mission, looking for prisoners to interrogate so clubs were used rather than blades. We were lucky.'

Silĕre had been listening and now she nodded in agreement, gesturing that she had also reached the same conclusion.

'What happened in the stockade?' I asked, 'did they question or torture you?

'No, they did nothing. I was thrown into a cell and virtually forgotten. From snippets of conversation I learned the Lupus officer in charge of the stockade was but a low ranker, he did not have the authority to decide my future. To be honest, I think my capture surprised them more than it did me. I don't think they had discovered the bodies we left at Silĕre's cabin and were not actively seeking us. I was a bonus but they just didn't know what to do with me. They couldn't decide why a lone Ursidae should be wandering about in their territory. In the end, the officer decided to send me to another Lupus outpost commanded by a higher ranking officer. I was being palmed off to someone else. No one did anything to me, I remained locked up in a small storeroom and given meat and water once a day. No one spoke or cared, I was no longer their problem. Once the cart arrived, the officer couldn't wait to get rid of me.'

'Yeah, we noticed their distinct lack of care for your wellbeing when we caught up with you.' I commented.

'The soldiers were told to have no interaction with me and they took the instruction to heart. I wasn't offered food or water and I'm afraid when I needed to empty my bladder, I was simply told to piss myself!' Secuutus gestured at his trousers with some embarrassment. 'I'm sorry if I stink, I had no choice. I promise I'll jump into the next water source we find.'

I laughed, 'Never mind Secuutus, to be honest, we hadn't noticed anything different.'

'Yeah go on, make jokes. How would you feel if it happened to you?' growled Secuutus as even Silĕre struggled to contain a silent chuckle.

'It's okay my friend,' I grinned. 'We understand and we were happy to oblige. Silĕre helped free you, now you can help us, the sooner we find a river or lake, the clearer the air will become.'

Happy that my fellow ex-rider and companion was back safely plodding beside me, we continued our journey west. The weather had now developed quite a chill, causing Secuutus to grumble all the more about this foreign land and expressing his wish to return to the warmer and drier climes of his home kingdom, Regnum. Secuutus was not alone, I too began to feel the cold biting at my skin, the faint fur that covered all animan was no defence against the weather. We managed to trap, spear, club or catch prey as we travelled but the depth of cold was now an important constant in our lives. Every night we risked a fire, to cook our meat of course, but mainly to avoid freezing to death in our sleep. As the miles and the days passed, the temperature continued to fall until one morning, the inevitable snow arrived. As the first flakes fluttered down from the grey sky, the next hour of our time was spent trying to explain snow to an angry Ursidae who had never even heard of snow before in his life, let alone have it land on his head.

We continued our travels, though slower now as the snow settled on the ground amongst the trees, hiding paths and obstacles alike. Our mood was buoyant though our bodies shivered with cold. The snow became deep and walking difficult, we needed shelter soon so a theoretical discussion arose concerning where, how and when to achieve this goal, theoretical because of course, none of us had any knowledge of our whereabouts. Whatever plan we may devise, whatever direction we chose to follow, our priority now was to obtain warm clothing and blankets. Just how we would gain such items was not known, but as we climbed over a ridge, cold and hungry, the trees thinned a little. As the wall of trees gave way to patches of sky, our view of the world increased in distance. And once past the trees, we could just make out that there in front of us, spread out faintly under a falling curtain of snow in the whitening valley below, was a town.

Chapter Five: Indutiae

There in a huge clearing sat a small town, wooden structures of all types and sizes, but no domed houses I noticed. Back in Regnum, all the buildings were domes, even the palace was constructed with one huge dome in the centre of numerous smaller domes ringing it like a flower petal. Here the buildings were the more familiar box-like shapes, all constructed of wood, some with tiny gardens, others with penned areas holding cattle, pigs or sheep. Some appeared to be businesses, there was even what appeared to be hotels. All this we saw from the hilltop on which we stood, staring in amazement. The questions raging in our minds included, is it safe? Can we get food? Can we get warm clothing? Moments passed before I noticed the large fort half a mile from the town. 'Oh crap!' I thought, 'here we go again.'

'I think we need to take a peek at this place,' I muttered to my companions, 'we need food and supplies.'

'Yeah, I'm sick of feeling cold. How do these animan manage living in such a bleak place?' grumbled Secuutus while Silĕre simply nodded in agreement.

I took a few more minutes to work out the lay of the town, forming a plan on how to gain entry without bringing soldiers down on our heads. I would have liked more time but a nudge in the ribs from Silĕre suggested it was time to move. I suggested the direct approach, we would walk right into town just like any other traveller would. A furtive attitude is bound to bring on suspicion. Clambering and occasionally falling down the hill, the three of us tried to remain in plain sight, making sure our approach did not set off any alarm bells amongst the residents and thus, bring the military to investigate.

Drawing nearer the town, things moved into sharper focus and with a shock, we witnessed both Ursidae and Lupus moving about the streets, along with the odd Leo and even a couple of Tigris. The town rested under a white blanket of snow and from what we could see, it also rested in harmony. No one fought or attacked one another, Ursidae and Lupus could be seen greeting and talking with each other and not one weapon was drawn. What happened to the war zone?

At last, we reached the valley and made our way onto what appeared to be the main thoroughfare through the town. Two Tigris and an Ursidae strolling in from the hills roused only minor curiosity amongst those who witnessed our arrival. Several animan nodded or smiled in greeting as we walked further into the town, a very pleasant welcome and quite a change from most previous encounters with populated areas on this world. I quickly noticed many of the inhabitants did not carry weapons and moved at ease as they went about their business. Even two Ursidae soldiers paid us little heed as they passed by, another surprise. I didn't know whether to be pleased or insulted by the lack of attention we received, I expected some form of questioning at least. As we walked, I glanced at my companions and saw similar disbelief on their features. Certainly, this was not what we had expected, even our local inhabitant of this land, Silĕre peered at her surroundings in amazement. Strangely I found the sight of a confused Silĕre comforting, it indicated I was not becoming paranoid, this serene town did actually exist.

The town itself resembled those from the old Wild West, wooden business premises lined the main street while an assortment of homes and smaller traders spread out over the landscape. I admit to searching for the Lone Ranger or Wyatt Earp but no joy, just peaceful looking animan from all the four Casts, going about their daily lives. Horses and carts littered the roads, children played and animan plied their trades, all in peace and harmony. It was nothing like I had encountered in Regnum, or Manchester for that matter. Something had to be wrong, but as yet, I couldn't place my finger on it.

'A publican,' came a single word of huge meaning from my disgruntled bear-like friend, and in mutual agreement, we headed off the street and followed him into the establishment. Inside we found a pleasant but rustic interior, again reminiscent of those cowboy films I devoured as a young boy. Tables and chairs dotted the floor and a long bar stretched the length of the back wall, ending at a staircase which indicated one other level at least. Still no one sought to question us, smiles, nods and polite greetings were all we encountered. Silĕre chose a table and sat at it, Secuutus quickly followed suit and quickly discovered the round was on me. I hoped my Regnum coin was accepted here, I had nothing else of value. My coin was good and in minutes I joined the other two at the table with three glasses of something in my hands. I had no idea what the drink was, I had asked the barkeep for something to warm us up, and this was what I received. Secuutus beamed in joy as I set the glasses down, Silĕre looked dubious and as I took my first sip, I understood why, but I bravely persevered and downed the fiery liquid.

There were several other clients sat about the place and it was not long before Secuutus managed to strike up a conversation with a grizzled old Ursidae in exchange for a drink, which I duly purchased. Soon the information about the town was coming thick and fast, with more emphasis on thick I noted. The town was called Indutiae and lay precisely on the border between the Ursidae and the Lupus territories. The main street itself straddled the border. The old Ursidae polished off another drink, at my expense, before explaining that this town was held as neutral by both sides, an agreement gained in blood and stretching back decades and so far, honoured by all.

It was the main town for the area and both antagonists purchased their supplies here, a form of trading centre. It was in no one's interest to attack or attempt to gain control over the town as both parties would inevitably lose out in the long run. Here Ursidae traded with Lupus and the Lupus sold and bought from the Ursidae. Without this trading place, here in the middle of a huge snow covered forest, life would be a struggle, only a mad animan would seek to destroy it. As the old animan spoke those words, I wished he hadn't. One learns never to tempt fate as fate loves a challenge. Still pondering the old animan's words, I ordered three bowls of what I took to be stew and paid for two rooms, one for Secuutus and me and one for Silĕre. It didn't seem appropriate to bundle all three of us in one room together. But now at least, we would be fed and have a bed for the night, a luxury I had not anticipated at the start of the day.

Relaxed, fed and warm, I slept well in the first real bed I had used since waking up in this strange world. Although the sheets and blankets were well worn, everything appeared clean and bug free. Even Secuutus's thunderous snoring failed to disturb my slumber, though I discovered later that a few other guests, including Silĕre, had not managed to sleep through the noise as well as I. The next morning we were greeted with a large hot breakfast by a mature, motherly like Lupus host. As she served us, the problem of supplies and clothing arose to which, with directions and advice, our host advised us on the best places to shop and obtain what we needed. I left a good tip at the table when we left, in gratitude for her service and friendly manner. At least that's what I thought I had done, but a few moments after leaving our table, the motherly figure came after us, calling that I had left some coin behind. I did try to explain the concept of a tip but was soon made to understand that the animan simply did not offer any gratuitous payments for services rendered. What one received was what one paid for, nothing more, and nothing less.

The same applied at each of the retail stores we visited, the price you saw was the price you paid, no haggling or bargaining, just pay the price. It was not long before we were wrapped in fur garments, a contradiction I thought, the animan wearing fur over their own fur, but I had to admit, it felt nice to be warm. Silĕre took charge of supplies while Secuutus checked out the weapons on show. As it turned out, his own sword was a far better quality than what was offered and I certainly had no use for a sword.

Eventually, we were all well clad and brimming with supplies, a fact I registered glumly as I felt the lightness of my coin purse. Our final stop was to obtain transport in the shape or shapes of horses, but once again the honesty of the townsfolk shocked me. At the stables we were informed in a manner of a teacher instructing a young pupil, that horses were of little use in such deep snow, and instead we purchased three pairs of snowshoes. I noted the snowshoes were very similar to what I had seen on the telly in my world, of course I'd never actually used any before.

If it snowed in England, the country simply stopped.

For the next few days, we remained at the publican and enjoyed the friendly atmosphere of the town. We spoke to several of the inhabitants and discovered many things about this land that even Silĕre didn't know. It appeared this land was once ruled by a Leo family, as is often the case on this world. There was no Leo ruler now, the last king failed to produce an heir and his remaining family of siblings all managed to kill themselves while attempting to gain the throne. The last of the royal Leo Cast died from his wounds some time ago. Since then, the country had experienced war, as no other eligible king stepped forward and the two Casts of the Ursidae and the Lupus fought each other for the right to rule.

This land was densely populated by Lupus and Ursidae, and the war centred on these two, both Casts wanting to be the rulers. Gradually the country had divided into two, one half being the territory of the Ursidae, the Lupus possessing the other half. And so the war raged until it stagnated. Neither side had yet gained overall control and apart from minor skirmishes, any actual fighting or battles were now rare. An uneasy peace reigned, a peace that was to come to an end soon if I knew anything about the greed for power. Actually I didn't but history is littered with those seeking power over others, so in my opinion, this peace could not last. I was right.

Our stay at the publican had continued for more a week when one morning our breakfast was interrupted. A commotion out in the street drew even Secuutus away from his food as we went to investigate. Standing just outside the publican's front entrance, me still munching on a piece of bacon, we watched as a large troop of Lupus soldiers marched into the town. None of the residents showed any signs of alarm, calm in the knowledge that Indutiae was a neutral town. These soldiers were simply on their way to some military manoeuvres or perhaps even a period of leave. The local animan continued with their day, content in their lives. At a shouted command, the soldiers halted in the town centre but did not break ranks. They just stood in formation in the silence of a bemused town. The residents paused to watch this unexpected diversion to routine, I watched with a feeling of detachment, for once it wasn't me the soldiers were after, or at least I hoped so. I looked forward to the military entertainment.

The peace was momentarily disturbed by an officer shouting orders as he marched to the front of his troops. In response one soldier stepped forward, a drum of sorts held by a strap hung from his neck. At another command from the officer, the soldier began to beat the drum in a loud regular rhythm. Boom, boom, boom, the thud of the drum echoed throughout the town and out across the valley. Within moments, the intrigued residents, Lupus, Ursidae, Leo and Tigris alike spilled from buildings and the surrounding area, converging on the town centre.

Shouts of confusion and whispered questions rippled along the street until the officer shouted for silence, glaring at anyone who felt tempted to ignore his command. At a signal from the officer, the soldiers all drew their swords and moved into a fighting formation. The town now fell into a complete hush, only the occasional whimper of a small child could be heard as the townsfolk waited for the officer to speak. What he said brought an even deeper silence to fall over all those present, a stunned silence.

'I hereby announce that this town of Indutiae is now under the control of the Lupus army, commanded by General Crudelis. All Ursidae must leave this area within six days, fail to do so and you will be arrested and suffer the consequences. Other Casts may remain but must abide by the orders of the General. Any who attempt to defy these orders will be dealt with. This town is now under military curfew.'

Now a fearful silence followed his words, animan from all four Cast stared at the officer as if he had lost his mind. At first, these words were treated to laughter and derision, but soon the arguments began. But the military officer would not back down and aggression rose as tempers flared. Shouts of neutrality and indignation, questions and accusations fired to and fro amongst the growing spectators. Inevitably a large crowd gathered as more and more animan came to investigate the drum call. Farmers, smallholders, wood collectors and herdsman trickled into the town, boosting the numbers of animan surrounding the officer and his soldiers.

Inexorably, a scuffle started between the local animan and the soldiers, there was pushing and shoving and bravado as testosterone levels soured, residents of the town began to fight with the soldiers, but the soldiers were armed, the townsfolk were not. The scuffle became increasingly violent as the townsfolk protested this outrage by the Lupus general. The scuffle became a fight and suddenly there was a body on the ground.

One of the younger soldiers had drawn his weapon in anger and used it in haste. The body lying at his feet was that of a young male animan, a farmworker, and a local lad barely in his teens whom everyone knew. Abruptly the arguments stopped, all movement stopped and a shocked stillness fell as it dawned on the crowd that this was no joke, no military exercise. It was real, and one of their own lay dead on the street. An intense and hostile unease fell over the town, not even a bird broke the silence.

The quiet calm didn't last long. Standing on the porch of the publican and watching the events in the street unfurl, I began to hear a muted rumble, a rumble that grew into a growl and in turn, the growl became a crescendo of voices, voices raised in anger, shock and disbelief. Slowly the crowd began to edge forward, encircling the soldiers and the officer, hostility and hate lining their faces, violence in their posture. The officer immediately barked an order and the soldiers rapidly moved to form a defensive circle around him. The Lupus officer stared back at the crowd with arrogance and defiance in his eyes. At first, the attack was verbal, until the first rock was thrown.

The crowd surged forward, all Casts including those of the Lupus and Ursidae, moved as an incoming tide towards the military. With cries of anger, the surge flowed forward, the crowd acting as one they tore into the soldiers with their bare hands. In seconds the soldiers were overwhelmed, caught in a battle they could not have anticipated, literally torn apart by those they wished to control. As I watched, some of the crowd reached the officer, who stood either petrified with fear or bravely rock solid, I could not tell. A few townsfolk were now armed after having taking the weapons of the beaten soldiers, and suddenly the officer found himself facing these swords.

At this stage the crowd became quiet once more, an uneasy silence settled over the animan as if a decision was being made by a majority consensus. Moments passed and nothing happened, the crowd encircled the officer who remained rigid and composed. I had to admire the military animan, faced with that situation, I'm sure my bodily functions would have gone into overdrive long ago. The moments stretched into minutes, the atmosphere surrounding the tight group of animan grew in its intensity, and still not one word was spoken. I found myself holding my breath, waiting for an outcome I could not foretell, one soldier, an officer, stood like a statue amidst the very depths of hate.

My eye caught movement, movement without haste or indication as four armed animan moved up to the officer, a Lupus, a Tigris, a Leo and Ursidae all with determination in their eyes. I barely noticed the slight nod from one of the Lupus before the four townsfolk thrust out their swords as one, every sword simultaneously penetrating the unmoving officer, each blade delivering a mortal blow. The swords were withdrawn and the officer simply dropped to the ground, his life gone, his dying, brave.

The silence continued and not one animan moved, all remained in a circle around the four executioners and their dead victim. I could see remorse and sadness bloom on faces in the crowd, I saw fear and hate but I saw no signs of regret, a fact that shocked me at the time. Animan, male, female and even some children of puberty age stood silently in the street. Finally one of the killers, a Lupus, held his sword high for all to see, the blood still dripping from the blade. Every eye there, including mine, focused attention on the raised weapon and then the animan who held it. A stern looking, well built Lupus male, dressed in the garb of a farmer with just the beginnings of grey appearing at his temples. Slowly the sword wieldier turned, turning a full circle while his eyes sought to catch the gaze of all those present. A moments continued silence and then the animan spoke.

'We must prepare,' was all he said.

Movement towards the rear of the crowd caught my attention then. One of the soldiers was still alive and being dragged to his feet by two Indutiae Tigris males. He was hauled to the centre of the crowd and forced to kneel beside his dead officer. The Lupus farmer, who I considered the leader of this defiant town, looked down upon the soldier before pointing at the body. Again he spoke. 'Tell your general, we reject his command.'

The soldier was then hauled back to his feet and ejected from the crowd while being encouraged to deliver the message with kicks, punches and insults to ensure he got the message. As the soldier fled the town hobbling from his injuries, the crowd began to disperse, animan quietly moving off and making their way home or to some other destination. The body of the young local vanished away within the crowd. And still the silence remained as the street emptied.

I turned to look at my companions for the first time and received a look of confusion from both in return. What the heck had just happened? One minute this was a peaceful town filled with polite and cheerful animan. The next moment a troop of soldiers had been torn apart and their officer cut down in the street right in front of us. I didn't fail to understand the significance of the kill, four different Casts. No individual Cast could blame the killing on the other. It was a combined execution, a defiance and a statement of solidarity between the Cast inhabitants of Indutiae. Immediately I was reminded of the Roman Emperor Julius Caesar, stabbed to death by multiple blades so no one senator could be held responsible.

The three of us quietly returned to the interior of the publican, and I found myself wondering how the military general would react. I feared the response would be violent. Soon the street was empty, everyone had disappeared, even the Lupus spokesman or leader, I still wasn't sure what he was, had disappeared. Secuutus, Silĕre and I sat back at our table in the publican and stared down at our cold breakfasts. Silĕre and I pushed our plates away, our appetites gone, but Secuutus dived right in as nothing had happened. The publican had been empty apart from us three and the publican himself, but it wasn't long before other animan began to drift quietly in. First to enter was our old talkative friend, making his way straight to the bar in silence. His first drink disappeared in one gulp as with a raised finger, he simultaneously ordered another. Two drinks down and his posture appeared to relax, his shoulders slumped and he slowly shook his head. A simple gesture the publican seemed to understand as he reached out and placed a hand gently on the old animan's shoulder.

We remained in the publican for another hour, watching as the town slowly came back to life. The snow was cleared from doorways, shops reopened for business and the town of Indutiae resumed its routine as if nothing had happened. No one spoke to us though the publican was busy, we were not ignored but nor were we invited to join any of the whispered conversations that hovered around the tables and the bar. The old animan had left after his two drinks, his head bowed and a glistening in his eyes. We never saw him again.

I had been watching the town's inhabitants for some time before I realised there was something different about them. At first, I could not identify what it was had caught my attention, but as another customer quietly entered the publican, the penny dropped. Every resident of Indutiae was now armed. Males, females and even those in their teenage years now went about their everyday lives bearing the added weight of swords and knives hung about their person. This once pleasant and peaceful town was now armed to the teeth.

'Maybe it's time we moved on?' muttered Secuutus. 'This place looks like it's going to get very dangerous, very soon.'

Silēre simply shook her head, she did not agree with Secuutus and I could understand why. 'How can we travel anywhere in this weather?' I asked, 'Besides, where would we go?'

'I don't know, I love a fight as much as the next animan, but this doesn't involve us. We could find ourselves in further trouble if we stay.' Secuutus replied.

'Yes but you're forgetting, we *are* involved, because of you.' I retorted.

'Why me?'

'Because we're in a land where the Lupus and Ursidae battle for supremacy.

You are an Ursidae, you've already been captured once. If we moved on we'll be on our own and you would be most at risk. Even if we crossed the border into Ursidae held territory, we could not count on our safety. A strange Ursidae suddenly appearing could be viewed as suspicious and we may end up in deeper trouble. At least if we stay here, we'll have a chance, a slim one I admit, but there are other Ursidae here, and they appear at peace with the Lupus.'

Again Silĕre was nodding as she stared at both Secuutus and me in turn, leaving neither of us in any doubt of her wishes. I could understand Silĕre's reluctance to move on, aside from having found a refuge from her shame, she also knew my coin purse was growing lighter by the day. I had enough for one, me, to live comfortably for some time. However, paying for three was tripling the decline of my wealth far faster than I liked. I didn't mind paying for the other two as well as myself, but it was risky to use our only coin now as we could not know where or when we would need it again.

Silĕre had been astute enough to realise this fact and following a quiet exchange with Secuutus, they had both previously sought out temporary work to help tide us over until the weather improved. Silĕre had immediately found a job, here in the publican, as a barmaid. Very demeaning for a Tigris warrior but needs must. The publican himself was delighted to have such a capable animan working for him, and more to the point, one so capable of protecting his property. Secuutus too had found employment, his strength and size meant he was snapped up by one of the local blacksmiths. Though both jobs were only short term and just a few days a week, the extra income took the strain off my resources.

It was the first time since her 'shaming' that Silĕre had felt useful, only a simple barmaid but it made her feel better about herself. She did not want to leave and become just a disgraced warrior again, least not yet. Secuutus moaned and complained about working, but Silĕre and I both knew he was secretly enjoying himself. Being paid for using his brute strength was a dream come true for the huge Ursidae, but of course he would never admit it. Consequently, I began to feel guilty so I too joined the search for employment, so far with no luck. Who the heck wants an

English science lecturer in this land? That's the excuse I told myself, in truth it was the fact that I was a Tigris warrior that frightened prospective employers away. No one wanted their customers confronted by a hulking, lean, mean Tigris. Secuutus finally relented and we decided to stay in the town and take our chances, waiting out the winter in comfort. And perhaps war.

The rest of the day passed uneventfully until that night, a meeting of the townsfolk was called, to be held in the publican. Although not invited, as paying guests of the establishment, no one could object to our presence. More and more animan packed the bar that evening, I realised I had not appreciated the number of residents in the town of Indutiae, animan filled the bar to bursting point while others crowded around the door and filled the street outside. Secuutus, Silĕre and I perched on the stairs, all chairs, tables and floor were quickly occupied, and looked down at the proceedings about to start. The low hum of expectant voices reverberated through the bar as each animan present whispered his or her concerns and ideas to those beside them. I was growing bored and wanting my bed, until the same Lupus from earlier pushed his way forward and climbed up to a clear spot on the bar surface, ensuring as many as possible could see him. My attention returned and with a surge of excitement and anticipation, I eagerly watched the scene before me unfold.

From the greetings I heard as the man had entered the room, I discovered he was called Pugnator, a strange name I thought as my mind immediately went back to the cute little dogs called a Pug in my world. However, I'm sure that here, it had another meaning, but I didn't care enough to give it any more thought. Once the room had settled and became quiet, the animan leader called Pugnator began to speak. He was quite a striking figure, one of the tallest Lupus I had seen so far, no fat but certainly solid in his build. Long black hair tinged with grey fell from a finely chiselled face onto broad shoulders. If he was a descendant of the wolf, I'm damn sure he was the Alpha. He was dressed in the garb of a farmer, however, seeing him stand ramrod straight with confidence oozing from every action, I decided farming had not always been his career of choice. He appeared more soldier than a farmer, and someone used to taking command and giving orders.

'Most of you know what will happen after our slight disagreement with the Lupus military and I'm sure we all know what General Crudelis will do next.' He began in a clear and crisp voice. I was beginning to like this guy.

'Nonetheless, we have seen and fought it before and won. We will do so again. Our town has remained neutral for decades. Here animan can mix and socialise, trade and live without fear of warring Casts. We all hold this town and what it stands for in our hearts and we will fight to keep it. This morning a regrettable incident occurred, some pumped up little soldier wants to take control of our town. Nonetheless, what happened proved to us all that we will not roll over and concede our way of life to anyone. It was not one individual that stood against the army today, it was the animan of Indutiae who fought as one. Now we will protect our town, our families and our lives, as one!'

These words from Pugnator instantly brought a reaction from those gathered in the publican and those who strained to hear from outside. Even I was impressed and I was a stranger here. Growls of agreement and cheers encouraged Pugnator to continue.

'We cannot seek help from the Ursidae, else they too attempt to take control of our town. There are not enough Leo or Tigris warriors to call upon for aid so we must fight ourselves. Those of you who remember the last battle for Indutiae, begin your preparation. Other Casts among us may choose to offer aid or flee, no one will give blame. If you wish to stay, please do so but you may find yourself entangled in this situation against your wishes, so be aware. To the townsfolk of Indutiae, I say, prepare, prepare to fight. Draw your weapons, secure your homes, and rebuild the barricades of old. We will stand, we must stand, for our homes, our lives and our families. We will fight, and we will win!'

Blimey! I thought, this guy can sure work a crowd, a thought backed up by the cheers that roared from the crowd. Swords and weapons of all kinds were waved in the air, even the odd farm tool joined the fray, held by those who possessed no other weapon. Lupus, Ursidae, Leo and Tigris bellowed their support for this single farmer who had stepped forward to lead the town. Above this clamour, the chosen leader could still be heard shouting for those who remembered past events to lead, any that didn't should follow, especially the young and any newcomers.

He gave order after order to the fervent gathering, erect barricades, move livestock into barns and stables, gather water ready to fight fires and to quench thirst. The list went on, sharpen weapons if you have them, blacksmiths forge more swords swiftly, women prepare bandages and salves to treat wounds and all children to be secured into safety. At each command, a group of animan would leave the crowd, off to ready themselves and organise to save the town. As I watched and listened, I realised this was no mob, no disorganised gathering of fanatics, the animan knew what they faced, and they were ready.

Chapter Six: Defiance

The next day, Secuutus, Silĕre and I sat in the warmth of the publican, still amazed by what we had witnessed. It had snowed again overnight but not enough to seriously impede travel by foot. The town of Indutiae shone bright white in the clear light of a new day and buzzed with excitement as each resident went about preparing themselves, but below the excitement lay a thick layer of fear.

This fear began to grow as the morning wore on, building tension as the realisation of their actions weighed on their minds. Every animan in the town knew they had brought this on themselves, instigated by the military perhaps, but it was their actions that would bring retaliation and violence. The three of us watched from a window, not wanting to step onto the path taken by the animan of this small town. As I watched I wondered, I had seen the fort not half a mile away, so why was it taking so long for the troops to arrive? Finally, I approached the publican himself with this question. I noticed he wore no weapon though his hand was never far from a heavy cudgel kept under the bar.

'Oh that old fort is no longer used by the soldiers, we now use it for keeping livestock and storage. There hasn't been a soldier in that place for a long time, ever since this war began,' he answered while his nervous gaze kept drifting towards the doors, fear written on his face as he pictured in his mind, the sight of Lupus soldiers bursting into his establishment.

'Why was the fort abandoned?' I questioned further, 'it seems a prime defensive location to me, why would the Lupus give it up?'

'Lupus? It wasn't a Lupus fort, it was an Ursidae outpost. But being so close to the Lupus territory, the Ursidae command considered it suicidal to post any of its soldiers or even civilians there. It was vacated soon after hostilities began.'

By now, Secuutus and Silĕre had joined me at the bar, their interest in our conversation peaked by the information offered by the publican. It was Secuutus who asked the next logical question.

'So why didn't the Lupus take control of the fort? Surely it would be a prime position for defence?

With a slight cynical laugh, the publican replied, 'For exactly the same reasons the Ursidae left it, it's too close to the border and would be attacked constantly, making it and our town vulnerable. I daresay the Lupus command didn't care about Indutiae but strategically, it had to be considered. The enemy could use the town as a stepping stone to the fort, or hiding any hostile approach. The fort has good visual aspects over the surrounding land, but the town provided a blind spot from which an enemy could strike.'

It all made sense to me, even though my military skills were only at a level of disarming students, relieving them of the assortment of weapons they felt compelled to bring into the university each day, and those were just the Primary Care students! War and military strategy was totally alien to me, however, common sense was something I did have. Why the fort had been built so close to a neutral town puzzled me, but what did I know? The publican appeared to read my mind, short story version, and continued with a brief history of the fort.

'When the old king was alive, this country was united and the fort was constructed as a defence for the town but mainly as a recruiting and training venue run by veteran Ursidae soldiers. No one expected our land to be split by warring Casts upon the demise of the heirless ruler, and the fort was not considered with a strategical view, it was more for attracting new soldiers into the king's army, his united army. Now it lies empty apart from a few cattle, sheep and pigs. With the fort being situated right on the border, it meant it would be a prime target for either side.'

'So where is the nearest Lupus military?' I asked, stopping the publican as he attempted to move off, obviously ill at ease in offering so much information to three strangers.

'The military base is roughly a day's good ride from here, far enough away from the border to avoid constant attacks, but close enough to defend this part of the border if the Ursidae should attempt to invade.'

It was apparent that was all he was going to tell us, for the moment he finished speaking, he quickly moved away, making a pretence of checking his barrels at the other end of the bar. It didn't matter to me as I already had enough local history for me to wonder what the hell I was doing here. I turned to my companions with an enquiring look, hoping they could shed some light on our next move. I was out of luck, Silĕre gave a small shrug, indicating she had no ideas while a low grunt from Secuutus confirmed he had no suggestions either. It was clear that any plan was down to me, and I didn't have a clue. I had hoped that Silĕre may have a suggestion or two as she was a resident of this land, but as I looked over at her again, she lowered her gaze, her meaning clear. I decided it was time for some drastic action, so I bought a round of drinks, returned to my seat and contemplated our future over a glass of the local battery acid.

As I took my first sip and awaited the fire in my throat, the door of the publican opened with a blast of cold air and in strode a group of four local animan, led by Pugnator, and they headed straight for our table.

'May I join you?' he asked in a deep rich voice.

Both Secuutus and Silĕre nodded their agreement so I responded, 'Make yourself at home friend.'

I had barely spoken the words before everyone stopped and looked at me in bewilderment. What the hell had I said wrong now I wondered, feeling slightly annoyed.

'I'm sorry, I don't wish to make the publican my home, I simply wish to sit at your table,' replied the rich voice in a puzzled tone.

Quickly I realised my mistake and explained. 'I apologise, I am not from this land and sometimes I use terms not familiar here. I simply meant you are welcome to join us. Make yourself at home is a form of welcome where I come from. Please, sit with us.'

'Thank you. I too am sorry for misunderstanding your words. It is a delightful statement of welcome, to be invited to feel as one does in one's own home is a beautiful concept. I readily accept,' replied Pugnator with a smile as he pulled a chair from a nearby table and sat down, his gaze encompassing the three of us.

Pugnator's three companions remained standing as our table was already feeling quite crowded, least that's what I hoped was the reason. All were armed and appeared very much like bodyguards for the town leader. I gave the matter no further thought as I introduced my companions.

When I got to Silĕre, I explained that during a recent battle, her throat had sustained damage and she would be unable to speak for some time. I offered no further explanation though, I saw no reason for anyone else to know Silĕre's shame. I received a grateful smile from Silĕre in return, followed by a faint nod from Secuutus to show he understood. Our table guest then introduced himself, though we were aware of who he was before he turned to his three companions and explained they were leading figures in the town and now part of the defence team, or local militia.

'We are setting up our defences; hence the formation of a town militia, and we are seeking the help of all out of towners such as yourself,' he continued. 'Others of the Tigris Cast and a couple of the Leo Cast have opted to stay, at a price of course. The others are leaving and I don't condemn their decision, it's not their fight after all. A reprisal attack from the Lupus military is imminent, so now I come to you and ask if you will aid us in our hour of need or will you too, be moving on?'

'You mentioned a price?' grunted Secuutus.

'Yes, I did. We have offered free food and lodgings plus a small bag of coin to all who stay. I'm sorry we cannot offer more but we are only a small town and it is the folk who live and work here who will be paying. I must point out that it is only our town that is under threat, our surrounding neighbours remain at peace, so the offer is open. Accept or decline, the decision is yours.' Pugnator sat back in his chair and folded his arms to signify it was now up to us to choose.

I looked at the others, I honestly didn't know what to say, or which choice to make. I could see Secuutus felt the same confusion, we were strangers here, ripped from our lives by a small jade box. How could we decide on the fate of others, we didn't even have a choice of our own. I had opened that damn box and been taken from my home in Manchester and my employment as a university lecturer, and dumped in the kingdom of Regnum whereupon I met Secuutus. When I finally got my hands on it again, I had opened the box once more, hoping it would send me home again, but it didn't. It sent me here along with Secuutus who was stood beside me when I opened the box. He had no say in his destiny and nor did I in my own, so how could we form a decision on the affairs of a land where we did not belong. Secuutus and I looked at each other, both of us needing some direction, so we turned to look at Silĕre, she at least was of this land. Suddenly our beautiful Tigris femina found herself at the centre of attention, not only Secuutus and myself staring at her, but also Pugnator and his town militia.

Several moments passed while she glared at me, I could tell she was thinking hard. She knew Secuutus and I would not have any idea on which choice to make. However, she also had her own life to consider, she was a shamed Tigris warrior and if discovered, she would be outcast again. Then her eyes dropped and in a single movement, she slammed both hands down on the table top and left them there as she looked at all around the table. I was puzzled at first until I noticed Secuutus nodding as if in agreement.

'You wish to stay?' I asked her. A nod of her head as she looked back at me indicated her answer was yes.

'I think we should stay,' muttered Secuutus. 'I like it here.'

I looked up at Pugnator and after another moments thought, I gave him my answer. 'It seems we have reached a decision, and as none of us has any place we need to be. We'll stay, we'll fight for this town.'

'Thank you, thank you all,' replied Pugnator with a smile. 'If you need anything, weapons . . ?' he finished while deliberately switching his gaze from the swords of my companions to me and my staff. It was clear he too was fooled by my heavy iron banded wooden staff, an advantage I had used many times. Not many knew of the hidden blade that would protrude from the tip of the staff at the press of a concealed button. More to the point though, only Secuutus and I knew how damn useless I was with a sword!

'I think we have sufficient weapons, thank you.' I said as I watched his brow frown in puzzlement. 'However information would be helpful, we're strangers here and our knowledge is limited. We'll need to understand how we fit into any plans that are devised concerning the defence of Indutiae.'

'Of course, of course. We'll sort out a local animan to fill you in on any details and I'll make sure you are all kept abreast of the situation. It's important that if any of the defences in the town require your services, you'll know where to go and what to do. I'll send someone over to assist you if that's acceptable to you all?' Pugnator stood while resting his gaze on each of us, in turn, to be sure we agreed.

'Good. We're pleased to have the assistance of two Tigris warriors and an Ursidae fighter. Now, if you're not too busy, there are barricades to be erected and plans to make. I'll send someone over immediately so you can get to work.' Then with a parting smile, the town leader and his militia left the publican and us.

Pugnator was as good as his word for within the time it took to finish our drinks and regain the ability to speak, a young Leo strode into the publican and made directly for us. The animan immediately introduced himself as Adserviŏ and asked us to follow him out into the town. Our guide was a character of few words it seems, but we followed him into the cold, each of us had no idea what to expect but we had made our choice. Adserviŏ showed us the locations where a twenty-four hour watch was being set up, mostly on the roofs of buildings, allowing a clear view of the surrounding area. A good idea I concluded, during daylight hours at least, but in the darkness of night, these sites would be almost useless. I decided to mention this to Pugnator when I could, I certainly didn't want a Lupus soldier sneaking in and removing my head in the night.

Catching a moment, I asked Adserviŏ. 'How long do you think it will be before we can expect an attack from the military?'

'I don't know,' he replied thoughtfully. 'The soldier who survived had no horse to ride so it would take him maybe two days, maybe longer in the snow, and that's if he hasn't been eaten already. He would have no chance of foot if he encountered a lynx or a Gulo gulo.

Also this close to the border, our Lupus messenger may even encounter an Ursidae patrol and I wouldn't think he'd survive that meeting either. So we may have a few days left yet perhaps, before the soldiers arrive, that's if General Crudelis is quick off his backside.'

'What if the soldier messenger didn't make it?' asked Secuutus.

'Doesn't matter,' said Adserviŏ. 'The patrol will soon be missed and another sent out to discover its whereabouts. Either way, we can expect more soldiers arriving soon to attempt to take control or looking for their missing comrades. A patrol may even be on its way as we speak so we must hasten.'

Our guide painted a dismal picture for that lone soldier we had sent back to his base to report the defiance of the townsfolk. The worrying prospect of coming face to face with a local carnivore or yet more soldiers, albeit Ursidae, reinforced our decision to remain in the town of Indutiae. We had all had enough of the cold and snow without including the further threat from wildlife or soldiers. In the decision of war and peace, warm beds and hot food won us over.

Our tour continued and our guide pointed out all areas of interest for defence or offence, though in all honesty, there were very few sites for an offence. The area around the town had been cleared for livestock pens and small allotments and working areas. Once past this clearing, the forest encircled us, the dark foreboding shadows under the trees could hide the entire Lupus army and have room spare. Defending this town was going to be difficult I suspected, very difficult indeed.

'I assume the soldiers will arrive on horseback and not by foot,' I enquired of a now bored Adserviŏ.

'Perhaps, they do have horses but I'm not sure what advantage they would be in this snow. Travelling on foot would take slightly longer but might be easier through the forest. Marching, the soldiers would be exhausted and require rest by the time they reach here but it may be the preferred option to horses. So I can't say what the general will decided. Why do you ask?'

'Just a thought, but are there any defences being set up at the tree line? Once the soldiers come out of the trees, they'll have a clear run at the town and we could be swamped in no time.' I answered while scanning the area thoughtfully. I was no military strategist but even I could see gaping holes in the town's defences, oversites that could swing the advantage to the oncoming enemy. I needed to talk to Pugnator before it was too late.

'The town is open and ripe for defeat, the way I see it,' growled Secuutus.

'I don't think we put any form of defences that far out,' replied Adserviŏ as my line of questioning awoken the dawn of realisation in my companions and our less intrepid guide.

'I think we need to find Pugnator quickly, else the Lupus army will be able to stroll unhindered into Indutiae. Now please Adserviŏ.' I commanded.

He finally understood the urgency and led us off in search of the town leader. As we walked at a fast pace, Silĕre grabbed my shoulder and pointed. She was indicating yet another weakness in the town's defences, bales of hay and straw stood in piles against several buildings that I took to be stables or some kind of animal house. If these were to catch fire, the flames would quickly jump from building to building, burning the town to the ground. The settled snow may slow down the growth of flames, but not for long. I acknowledged my attractive companion and added it to the list for Pugnator. This town was going to be hard to defend without us making it easier for the oncoming soldiers. I did notice one thing in the town's favour as we hurried along behind Adserviŏ. In the centre of Indutiae was a well, and it looked in good working condition, a female Ursidae was drawing water from it as we passed. At least we wouldn't be hindered by thirst and had some means to fight the inevitable fires I thought.

Eventually, we caught up with Pugnator, the town leader and his group of local militia officers. Initially, the Lupus leader attempted to shrug off my concerns until Adserviŏ added his weight, stating in a loud and clear voice that he too had witnessed the holes in the town's defences. My opinion of our guide changed for the better as I realised his loud comments were reaching the attention of other townsfolk. Many more animan began to question the militia's plans for defending the town, and very soon Pugnator was given no choice but to listen. Listening was all he could do because I decided as my hide was on the line, I needed to take action of my own. While Pugnator and his cronies conferred, I grabbed a wooden box and stood upon it, making sure I was easily seen by the gathering crowd.

'My name is Harry,' I roared out, bringing all talk to a halt. 'I am a Tigris warrior as you can all see. I am used to battle, as are my companions. None of you know me but I'm telling you all, this town will not survive an attack by the military unless we act now.'

Several of the town's militia began to move towards me, perhaps to silence my attempt to override the authority of Pugnator or to remove a crackpot from the street, I neither knew nor cared. I wanted the town to survive because I was in that town and I was in danger. I remained standing on the box as Secuutus, Silĕre and even Adserviŏ moved to position themselves between me and the militia, all had drawn their weapons. Seeing a huge Ursidae, a Tigris femina and a Leo standing firm, the militia had a change of mind and became still.

Questions erupted from the crowd as Pugnator moved to my side and whispered, 'What do you think you're doing?'

'I'm trying to save your town, that's what I'm doing. Now support me or back off!' I growled down at him, glaring with animal ferocity directly into his face.

Pugnator took a step backwards, an action that didn't go amiss from the eyes of the gathered townsfolk. 'All right, we'll listen to you. Then I'll decide what to do with you and your friends.'

I resisted the battle cry of every Mancunian, "Yeah right! Bring it on!" Instead, I turned away and ignored him as I began to address the animan around me.

'I have noted areas about the town that need to be addressed before the soldiers arrive. These need to be amended now. First, I need a small group to set up traps along the treeline, I know you can't protect the whole area but hopefully, we'll stop a few of the soldiers. Trap lines to trip any horses, pits, sharp stakes and iron caltrops to hinder the enemy should do for starters. Next, we need all the straw and hay bales removed from buildings, I realise some are wet with snow, but not all will be, one good fire arrow and this town will be ash.'

As I spoke I could see small groups, pairs and even individual animan peeling away from the crowd to undertake my instructions. Pugnator also noted this fact and nodded to each who caught his eye, indicating his agreement.

I continued my commands even though shock at my bold actions was threatening to make my knees jelly and my stomach evacuate its contents. I had never taken such a stance before in my life, yet here I was issuing commands like a born leader. How I had changed since my life as a lowly science lecturer. The list of defensive actions continued as both Secuutus and Silĕre pointed out issues of concern. Literally in Silĕre's case, she simply touched my arm and pointed, relying on my understanding of what she pointed at. Secuutus just growled at me to attract my attention to a weakness he had spotted.

'Talking of fire, I want every single barrel or bucket filled with water and placed about the town in easy reach. We make also make use of the snow, pile it up near your properties and use it if the water runs low. The military are bound to use fire against us and we must be ready to protect homes and property from the flames. Take care where you place the barrels and buckets, they must be in plain sight and easy to reach.'

I paused for breath and to control my urging stomach for a moment before giving my last order. 'We must set up a night watch, not from atop buildings, we need pairs of capable animan watching all entrances into town. Sadly there will be little sleep until this is over, your lives depend on you being alert to any threat at any time. Daytime the watch can be set upon roofs and high places, but at night it will be difficult to see anything from high, eyes need to be on the ground and moving as they watch. I realise many of you will already know what I am saying, but a reminder never hurts, especially when our lives are the prize. Protect yourselves and your neighbours, this will affect us all. No one can say it doesn't concern them, it does. Please heed my words and though I offer my apologies for my rude intervention, I wish like the rest of you, to simply remain alive. That is all I have to say. Thank you all and good luck to each of you.'

I stepped down from the box amidst much shoulder and back clapping as those around me congratulated me on my strategies. Even Pugnator smiled as he apologised for failing to see what we had seen. Then he stepped up on the box and reiterated my commands, making sure all who heard that my plans had his full backing. Soon the streets were busy as animan rushed to help in any way they could. I saw a group of farmers heading off to the tree line, a blacksmith fired up his forge to make the caltrops and water barrels were appearing everywhere. The town of Indutiae was preparing for war.

The planning done, Pugnator stepped down from the box and joined me and my companions. 'Thank you for spotting those areas of weakness, I'm afraid I'm more of a fighter than a planner. With that in mind, maybe I could count on you for advice? It's obvious you three are, shall we say, familiar with the ways of war?'

I was astonished, firstly that Pugnator bore me no resentment for taking over his theatre of war, almost shouting him done in fact. But then to be asked to advise on matters of defence and the forthcoming battle. Me! A lowly university lecturer who had never held a lethal weapon in his life until arriving here. All I knew about warfare came from too many hours sitting in front of a television. Nonetheless, it appeared the box in the corner of the room proved to be a most effective teacher. I had never been in a war, and to be fair, this was hardly a real war, it was a fight between the local military and the town of Indutiae. War, battle or fight, it didn't matter. It was happening and I was in the thick of it. So maybe I had no military training, but I did have a history of cowboy films, World War two films, even fictitious films like Star Wars and The Lord of the Rings. All this media training was now being called into real life use, how else could I explain my awareness of defence weak spots?

'We'll help wherever we can,' I replied with a glance at my companions. 'Though we're strangers here, a fight is a fight wherever one is.'

'Thank you,' said Pugnator. 'Could I ask that you take a look around the town and bring to my attention anything that requires improving? I am happy to bow to your experience but, as you say, you are strangers here and many of the townsfolk may resent you giving them orders. Therefore it may be for the best if you let me know what needs doing and I will see it done. Is that a fair arrangement?'

The three of us agreed before we left the town leader to go about his business while we went about ours, still accompanied by Adserviŏ who appeared to have attached himself to us. We began by walking around and examining the town's perimeter, offering suggestions here and there and trying to build confidence in the growing unease that was plain to see in the townsfolk. In fairness, few were warriors, they were shop keepers, tailors, farmers and labourers. A few, those from the Leo and Tigris Casts, had a good grasp of what to expect, but too many in the town had never raised a weapon in anger. I wondered what difference me and my companions could make, not a lot, I suspected.

It was during our walk around the town and its 'perimeter' that we were greeted by other Tigris warriors, mainly drawn I think, by the presence of the beautiful Silĕre. One particular Tigris persistently tried to chat up my female friend. However, when getting absolutely no spoken reply to his advances, I could see he was getting suspicious regarding her total silence. I could see trouble coming here but in truth, I had no idea what to do about it. I looked over at Secuutus and then had a thought.

'Do you remember how we fought that Lupus sorcerer?' I loudly asked a startled Secuutus.

'Yes, of course I do. He's the reason we're here! We should have killed him instead of letting him escape,' he growled in reply.

'Yeah I know,' I continued, seeing our conversation had caught the interest of the suspicious Tigris warrior. 'I do miss Janiz though, but I think he'll be a great king.'

'Yes, I miss Janiz and the riders, all of them. This land is strange and cold. How did we end up here? I don't like it, and I don't like snow!' This last statement was spoken with emphasis, clearly Secuutus had no idea what I was doing, but unwittingly he was playing along nicely.

Now we had the full attention of the Tigris, his curiosity had taken his attention away from Silĕre as he listened to a tale he could not understand. I had noticed his interest peaked at the mention of a sorcerer so I decided to take my scheming a bit further. I turned to look Secuutus straight in his eyes and continued, hoping he would understand.

'I wonder where that damn sorcerer is now, he needs to undo his magic before he dies. At least the magic that stops Silĕre from speaking, that would be a start.'

Secuutus eyes glinted, he did understand. 'I never really believed in magic until we fought that sorcerer, he nearly killed us all. Raising demons, which you banished, boiling the pond water and all that stuff, then taking Silĕre's voice. I wish we had killed him.'

'What sorcerer?' interrupted the inquisitive Tigris, 'I've never heard of a powerful sorcerer, who is he? And who is this King Janiz?'

'Ah, you will not know him. We come from a far off land, the land of Regnum. There we fought a sorcerer who wanted to rule the kingdom. But with Prince Janiz, we caught the sorcerer and cut out his tongue. Sadly not before he cast a spell and took away Silĕre's voice with magic, he would have done the same to us if we hadn't quickly sliced out his tongue, but he still used his magic to escape. If we ever find him . . . !'

It appeared my explanation, with a few untruths in it, had worked, the Tigris now looked at Silĕre with no suspicion, though I wasn't happy that it was replaced with a look of admiration as well as lust. A little while later and with some help from Adserviŏ, we managed to shake off our amorous friend and continue our examination of the town defences. Along the way, we caught glimpses of the randy Tigris and it appeared, as I'd hoped, that he was retelling our story to all he came across. If the town believed the story then Silĕre could walk tall and free, her shame hidden in the lies of a true story. Our beautiful female companion offered both Secuutus and me a huge smile in gratitude, her poise straightened and her head lifted, for now at least she could be a proud Tigris again.

Chapter Seven: And so it begins . . .

The next two days were taken up by building and rebuilding the pitiful town defences. A hasty palisade had been erected around some more open parts of the town but with such limited time, I doubted it would hold up to any persistent attack. Everyway in or out of the town was blocked off with a manned barricade, especially the two main routes which followed the direction of East to West. The barricades were constructed of anything that came to hand; carts, furniture and fittings, rocks and tree trunks obstructed any passage.

The snow had ceased for now and the ground turned to slush, but Adserviŏ warned us that more snow was inevitable but for now, mud and slush soon covered everything. Having made our presence felt, the townsfolk gradually began to accept us, though suspicion remained. Eyes followed us wherever we went, especially Secuutus. The tension amongst the inhabitants of Indutiae was overwhelming with tearful, wide-eyed children and silent fearful adults.

Everyone knew the military would respond but none knew how or when.

Pugnator had sent out a few of the remaining Tigris warriors to scout the surrounding forest and search for any indication that General Crudelis's troops were approaching. Silĕre and I did not escape this duty and soon found ourselves creeping with all our instinctive feline stealth through the dripping trees. Our companion Secuutus, had been conscripted into organising those Ursidae who remained into a semblance of a fighting force. Most were simple farmers or traders, shopkeepers or labourers. Some had previous battle experience but none could match that of Secuutus, most could not even match his size.

Pugnator trained with the Lupus, proving his own experience in the art of war, and causing a few raised eyebrows amongst the townsfolk as he whirled and slashed, jumped and stabbed with his wooden practice sword against terrified opponents. Being naturally skilled fighters, the Tigris warriors and Leo masculus practiced amongst themselves, no animan had stepped forward to assume the role of leader of either Cast as yet. I realised quickly with some concern, that all the Casts appeared to be training within their social structure, Lupus with Lupus and Ursidae with Ursidae. I made a note to have a word with Pugnator, all Casts needed to train and practice together. Our fighters needed to be as one under the banner of Indutiae.

The uncertainty of the next days was becoming tedious for me, all those about me warned of doom and gloom, but here was I, prowling through the peaceful forest while in the company of a striking Tigris femina. Silĕre moved with all the grace and flowing actions of a cat but it was her curves and bodyline that impressed me the most. I had no idea how males and females interacted here. I had witnessed affection between animan as in humans and the rough and ready approach by that lovelorn Tigris warrior, but no courtship. I certainly wasn't going to make the first move, she'd probably kill me! Also, I feared to upset our existing companionship, the bond that had grown between us, not just between Silĕre and me, but with Secuutus as well. We were a close team, companions, and I had no wish to destroy our circle. So I kept my feelings hidden and settled for admiring the lithe form that walked beside me.

Silĕre paused briefly before efficiently manhandling me to the ground. Then suddenly, I thought my luck was in, until I saw the focused set of her features. Slowly I turned to face the direction in which Silĕre stared so intently. I could see nothing through the screen of trees but I could hear. I could hear the clinks and rattle of metal, the sound of weapons, then came the unmistakable muffled thud of many feet upon the forest floor. Neither Silĕre nor I needed to be told who approached. Soldiers were marching through the forest, the military was beginning its campaign against the town of Indutiae.

Silĕre and I sank into the undergrowth, it was too late to escape back to town, all we could do was wait until the soldiers passed and hope we were not discovered. All my senses were alive at that moment, the same moment a line of marching soldiers emerged from the trees and into our vision. First in line and riding a huge jet black horse was a portly figure whom I assumed was our local military commander, General Crudelis. His tight fitting green uniform more elaborate than those of the troops behind him. I could see no medals or other expected military adornments other than a beautifully crafted and bejewelled sword hanging at his hip. Perhaps the animan don't go in for campaign or bravery medals or all the insignia that those in the armed forces at home do. The Lupus General sported a round face with bushy grey sideburns, giving even more width to his features. He rode tall in the saddle, tall for one of the lupus Cast at least, and his wolf lineage interacted with a pose of arrogance and cruelty. Although the general carried more bodyweight than his soldiers, his posture in the saddle gave no hint of weakness, a posture that indicated hidden strength. He looked for all to see, a formidable foe.

As the troops passed by only yards away, I counted twenty soldiers and one general, not much of an attack force I thought. A troop of just twenty would pose little threat to Indutiae, maybe the general has come to apologise I wondered? But no, I really couldn't take that thought seriously, something else must be afoot. My suspicions were immediately proved correct, as in the wake of the initial twenty soldiers came yet another twenty, and another then another until I lost count. Hundreds marched past where we lay hidden, well trained, well equipped and heavily armed soldiers on their way to Indutiae. Hundreds of Lupus infantry on route to attack the town of Indutiae. The townsfolk boasted a few warriors but most were peaceful folk and not trained killers. From what I could see, it may be a very short skirmish indeed.

In time no more troops stomped past us and when we were sure no further troops were bringing up the rear, Silĕre and I set off back to town, moving as swiftly as possible on a parallel route to the military. I knew we would be too late to warn the town, but I prayed at least one of the other scouts patrolling the forest would have witnessed the arrival of the military and warned the town. I could only run and hope my wishes come true.

Marching at a set pace, the troops would likely arrive before us, even though we both ran like the wind, we still had to remain out of sight, often taking the longer route. Finally, as we burst from the line of trees while carefully watching for and avoiding all the traps we had set, the general was already addressing the townsfolk over a barricade, his soldiers remaining stationary behind him. I was gratified in a selfish way to see a good number of soldiers already lying injured after falling foul of our crude defences. I just hoped I wouldn't follow their lead and blunder onto a set of caltrops or fall backside first into a pit of stakes.

Silĕre and I ducked down to the ground again, fearful we may be spotted and no way to get past. How I wished for a gun, an AK47 would be great right now. Having to rely on close-quarter combat made things difficult, even a bow and arrow could do some damage when behind the enemy as we were. But there was nothing we could do as we watched the scene unfold before us.

It was evident the general had already begun with the threats. ' . . . we will be forced to take this town through violence and many will be hurt or killed. Surrender now Pugnator, surrender the town to me and no one will suffer.'

'You lie General,' Pugnator spat back from atop a barricade. 'We all know what will happen to us under your occupation. We will be forced to fight for the Lupus, our town will become a battleground on the front line. How can you say no one will be hurt or killed? Of course they will! Once the Ursidae discover you have taken the town, they will attack in force and we will be caught in the middle of your war. Your war, not ours.'

'I cannot guarantee the Ursidae will not attack, but never has there been any guarantees from either side. Now it is time to take a stand, it is time this town was brought under martial law and all those Lupus who hide within your homes must be made to fight for our cause. You will let me in!' The general was shouting now, obviously patience was not one of his strongest traits.

'What about the Ursidae that live here, or the Tigris and the Leo? What will happen to them if we allow you in? Will you promise the safety of all Ursidae here?' replied Pugnator in a calm voice.

'Of course, no one will be harmed,' the general lowered his voice to a pacifying tone before building up to a roar once again. 'The Ursidae will be given a day to leave or risk imprisonment. The other Casts may do as they please, I care not. I do care about the likes of you and the other Lupus who hide from your responsibilities behind these barricades. It is your duty to fight against the Ursidae for our land. There will be a Lupus king, I promise it!'

'We don't care who wears the crown, all we wish is to be left alone. Indutiae will take no sides in a war not of our doing. We'll fight for our town and General; we will win!' These last words from Pugnator were shouted out as he pumped one fist into the air. Immediately the voices of Indutiae rose in support of their leader.

'We will win! We will win! We will win!'

The general's grey appearance began to turn red, angry at this defiance, defiance of his orders boiling his blood. 'No! No you will not!' he screamed back at the town.

His face still red with anger, the general turned back to his animan and began issuing commands. Immediately soldiers, whom I took to be officers, began running and shouting orders at the gathered troops. Soldiers were assigned to clearing the treeline of caltrops, pits and stakes, gathering them all up and stacking them in a pile them for the town to see. Guards were chosen to patrol the perimeter while others began erecting tents and building cooking fires.

The camp took shape at a distance outside the reach or arrows or spears and apart from the roaming patrols, the army took no further notice of those watching over the East facing barricades and the palisade of the town. It was obvious the general was planning to remain in force. As the attention moved from the town, Silĕre and I found ourselves cut off from easy access back to Indutiae. We had to travel quickly and deeper into the forest as soldiers appeared, searching for and destroying traps and collecting wood to feed the fires. All we could do was remain out of sight until the activity died down. The town of Indutiae was under siege.

We watched from the safety of the trees for the rest of the day, there were too many eyes and too much activity for us to try and return to the town. Though it was cold and my hunger grew, I didn't mind. I was in the constant company of Silĕre, a very attractive companion to spend any time with. While my testosterone and male urges rose, Silĕre remained firmly focused on the job at hand. Although she could not talk, she managed to communicate through gestures and drawings on the forest floor. Silĕre had a plan, we would wait until sleep blanketed the camp and keeping clear of any guards, make a wide circle of the army camp to reach the town. There we would attempt to avoid or silence any patrols and seek a way back inside. We could of course simply cut and run, leave Indutiae to its fate, but that choice was quickly dismissed, Secuutus was still in there and we had given our word. So we waited and watched, and more importantly, we studied the army camp, the guards and the patrols, searching for clues to the general's plan of action. Finally, we both concluded the general was in no haste to order the attack, in contrast, he appeared to treat the whole event as a distraction, a holiday from routine. He was enjoying himself.

The camp was laid out like the spokes of a wheel, at the hub stood the much larger tent of the general while the smaller regulation tents, each sheltering six Lupus soldiers radiated out from the centre axle. I could see no sign of a mess tent and assumed each soldier carried his own supplies. The general had his own cooking fire and probably even his own cook, while the troops sharing fires and preparing food where they could.

The hustle and bustle to and fro the surrounding trees for firewood had continued for much of the day, soldiers gathering enough wood to cook with and provide heat overnight. While the camp scurried about him, the general sat outside his tent and issued orders from his campaign desk. His personal aid keeping him supplied with food and some form of wine, a routine only interrupted after his noonday meal when he retired to his tent for a nap. Least that's what I assumed he was doing for no one entered or left the tent for that period. If not for the activity of the soldiers and the tents laid out in uniform lines around him, one could easily assume the general was on a winter vacation.

Night eventually arrived, a cold and very clear night that only winter can bring. The moon shone its silver light over the landscape, reflecting on the snow. Any other time, it would have been a night for being home by a cosy fire, with family or even seduction, wrapped tightly in each other's arms, but not this night. Waiting until we could hear the rumble of snoring, farting and sleep mumbling, we crawled stiffly from our hiding place in the forest and moved down nearer to the camp perimeter. We had both witnessed the soldiers on guard duty patrolling the camp, however, the general must have not been unduly concerned about an attack from the town as the guards were few. Keeping low and using all our feline stealth, we skirted the edge of the camp and prayed we were not seen. Slowly we made our way under the light of the moon, even crawly on our bellies at times as sentries came near, but we remained undetected. It was the first time since arriving in the land that I welcomed winter, its long hours of darkness giving us time to circumnavigate the camp.

After several hours of crawling, with the fear of being caught resting heavily on our minds, we eventually cleared the army camp. Now things could get tricky, for now, we had to be aware of those in the town mistaking us for enemy soldiers attempting to sneak into the town in the darkness, plus the added risk of being caught by the sentries. Our movements slowed, we kept to the sporadic patches of cover and keeping low, we crossed the No Man's Land between the camp and the town.

Now I began to know real fear, at any time an arrow might fly out of the darkness to bury itself in my back. I kept my eyes on the palisade and the barricades, watching for signs of discovery. The soldiers in camp slept, confident they would not be attacked, but the same could not be said about the townsfolk of Indutiae. I could see shapes moving about against the moonlit sky. Torches flared and the sound of muted conversation drifted in the still night air. I suspected almost half the town remained awake, fear pumping adrenaline through their bodies, making sleep impossible. The residents of Indutiae had no idea when the military would attack, they had not seen the General at his ease as we had.

Silĕre and I continued crawling in the scrub undergrowth, now reaching the North side of the town, No Man's Land behind us, now it was only the townsfolk we had to worry about as we searched for a way in. There was no way we could scale the palisades and most of the barricades were either too high or too wide to climb so we kept going. Out from the night we heard shouts of alarm, we had been seen and arrows and spears were aimed at our prone figures. Slowly and with our hands raised to the sky, Silĕre and I stood up, letting everyone see us, and hopefully restrain from killing us.

Standing tall in the moonlight while facing the prospect of a shower of lethal projectiles raining down on me, I could not help but wonder how I had got myself into such a mess. A few more moments of holding tightly to my bowels when a voice finally shouted out, cutting across all others in a command to halt. Then came the sound of something being thrown from a roof before the end of a rope came into our vision, dangling in front of us.

'Climb up!' ordered a voice I recognised as Pugnator. Silĕre and I happily obliged.

Once back in the warmth of the publican and sat with Secuutus and Pugnator, I explained what Silĕre and I had seen of the army camped outside. As I spoke I began to realise the town of Indutiae, no matter how brave, could not fend off the advances of General Crudelis and his Lupus soldiers for long. The town had never been designed to withstand an attack. That was its deliberate strategy, to remain neutral, it had to show itself as open and welcoming to all. The town could now be destroyed, burnt down and for what? The ambition of one animan, one arrogant general? There had to be some way of saving the town and its very existence other than full-scale battle. I kept my thoughts to myself at first, wanting to gauge the intention of Pugnator and his followers, I had no wish to be vilified as a traitor or coward just because I didn't believe Indutiae stood a chance.

While my brain pondered on the defensibility of the town, I concluded my debriefing on the military camp and then offered up my thoughts of the General's actions. I began tentatively, not fully certain of my deductions. 'To be honest,' I began. 'I don't think the army will attack immediately, old Crudelis appears to be making a holiday of the whole affair. He doesn't seem worried, possibly he's so confident of success that he's just playing the game.'

'Perhaps he'll attack at dawn?' offered Secuutus.

'That would certainly be the normal military decision, however, I think he may drag out the start of any conflict.' I replied.

'But why?' questioned a confused looking Pugnator. 'Why wait if he's so confident in his ability to conquer our town?'

'It's possible he's trying to avoid the loss of life, both amongst the townsfolk and his soldiers or perhaps avoid damage to the town he wishes to control. He may be hoping that the sheer presence of the troops will frighten us into submission. Personally, I stand by my conclusion that he's having fun, one more military action before he succumbs to age.'

None of the three animan sat at the table appeared to believe this, and doubt creased their faces as they considered my words. As I waited for a response, another thought occurred to me and I voiced my thoughts to the others. 'Why didn't the General simply move into the nearby fort? He could easily attack from there while safely ensconced in the secure purpose-built fort. Why set out a camp?'

'That's a good point,' muttered Secuutus. 'It's freezing out there and more snow is likely, why is that daft General not hiding in the shelter of the fort?'

After a moment's thought, Pugnator responded. 'I think I can answer that. The old fort has been used for years by the townsfolk for sheltering livestock, storing supplies and food. If the General wished to occupy it, he would first be forced to clear it out. I believe there are even a few beggar families living there, so not an ideal venue for a self-important General and his troops.'

'Also it would take time, setting up camp can be done in a couple of hours but restoring an old fort to military standard could take weeks. Besides, I expect he's enjoying a break from military forts and all that is associated with them, drilling troops, parades and the like. I think my original assessment stands, he's having a holiday.' I concluded.

'We'll soon know,' said Pugnator wearily, 'but it's been a long night and day is not far away. Best we all get what sleep we can so we're . . . . . '

A shout from outside interrupted Pugnator's good night wishes. A shout soon echoed by more cries of alarm. Suddenly an Ursidae shopkeeper burst into the publican shouting, 'We're under attack! The army is attacking!' Then he disappeared as rapidly as he arrived.

'Well, it seems there'll be no sleep tonight after all,' sighed Pugnator before leading the rush to exit the publican and shouting, 'To arms! To arms! Awaken everyone. To arms!'

'Well I'll be . . . The old General is actually attacking at dawn!' I grinned at Secuutus as we followed the town leader out into the frozen street.

Outside, the town was in chaos, animan running to guard the barricades, or staggering from their homes, some still in nightwear. Torches flared in the darkness, lighting up frightened faces all around me. Horses reared and children screamed, animan shouted and some sought to hide. I saw all this as I made my way the main barricade at the end of the street, Silĕre and Secuutus right beside me. I had lost sight of Pugnator in the confusion but I could hear his voice, powering over the babble, giving orders constantly as he tried to organise the town's defences.

I reached the barricade expecting a full-on assault but found peace and bewilderment, there was no attack at the barricade, what was going on? I wondered briefly before shouts alerted us to the other end of town, there the

168

fighting was furious. The army had crept around the town and caught us by surprise. At a run, Silĕre, Secuutus and I sped towards the west barricade, but several steps later I suddenly stopped, a growing suspicion had entered my head. My two companions barrelled into me, my coming to such a rapid halt catching them unawares.

'What do you think you're doing?' shouted Secuutus. 'Don't stop now or the fighting will be over before we get there.'

'Hang on . . wait a minute,' I gasped as I turned my gaze back to the east barricade. 'I'm not sure about this. Why move troops around the town to the west when the main forces are camped right outside the front? Somethings not right. Come on, let's head back to the east barricade, fast.' Without waiting to see their reaction or explain further, I retraced my steps and picked up speed.

Within moments we could see those defending the east barricade were now fighting desperately for their lives. It was soon evident that the east barricade was indeed the focus of the main assault, the commotion at the other end of town was just a diversion, it was here that the real attack came and with only a handful of guards and now us to repel it. Screaming at the top of my voice in an attempt to alert Pugnator, I threw myself into the fight. My staff whirled at any head that appeared within reach over the barricade. Alongside me Secuutus roared insults at the Lupus soldiers as his sword cut and slashed, Silĕre's blade darted and stabbed in a blur of speed as she matched my body count.

The barricade was holding but I could see it wouldn't last long. If Pugnator and the town animan didn't reinforce our tiny group, we would be overrun very soon. In a brief lull, I flicked the hidden switch in my staff which released the blade, I now had a spear. Using the extra reach, I stabbed at a Lupus soldier, catching him in his right eye before withdrawing and smashing the butt of the staff into another opponent who sword pricked at me. Both went down but there were plenty more attacking soldiers and the numbers of our little group began to fall as the unexperienced animan of Indutiae fell before the army blades.

More and more enemy soldiers rushed at the barricade, more and more lethal blades glinting in the bright moonlight. If Pugnator did not realise our plight soon, all our troubles would be over, for good. A fleeting thought entered my head, why did that small green jade box insist on sending me to places in conflict? Was the damn thing trying to get rid of me for some reason? I couldn't answer my own questions but nor did I have the time as yet another Lupus soldier reared up in front of me. All I saw was his sword, grasped in both hands flashing down towards my head. Terrified my head was about to be split asunder like a watermelon, I brought up the staff and just managed to deflect the blow. However, my opponent was fast, very fast and already he was powering forward in a strike to my stomach. I blocked the strike but not before his blade had cut a thin red trail across my gut. Again he moved swiftly into another attack, all his focus centred on taking my life, which was weirdly fortunate for me because he didn't see the other blade coming until too late. Standing at my side, Silĕre had stabbed her sword through the soldier's neck as he concentrated on dissecting me. The soldier dropped, his neck shredded as he slid off Silĕre's blade. I had just enough time to nod my thanks to her before another attack forced me back into the fight.

'Need any help?' came a voice from behind me. I daren't turn my attention away from the line of green uniforms attempting the scale the barricade and decapitate me in the process but I knew the voice, Pugnator had arrived at last. Within moments the tide of Lupus soldiers was being turned by our increased numbers and new strength. A huge hand grabbed my shoulder and pulled me back, a fellow Tigris warrior then took my place at the barricade, growling at me as he swung his sword at an unfortunate soldier. 'Take a break, you've earned it.' I was only too happy to oblige and moved out of his way. All who had protected the barricade were now being relieved by those who had initially rushed to the west barricade, fooled by a diversion ploy by the General. Now they pushed back at the soldiers, forcing them off and away from the battered barricade. Weapons flashed, blood flew and screams intermixed with growls of hate and fear. As I stood at the rear with Silĕre, Secuutus and the other original defenders, my eyes registered the scene around me. And it was then that I saw it.

There in the midst of the melee, something caught my eye, something I had not assumed to see again, something common back in my world. Amongst the struggling bodies of animan, I saw a set of dog tags! Those small round metal plates that contain a soldier's details, name and number. They were hanging from the neck of a Leo masculus who was presently engaged in chopping down a Lupus attacker. I stared in shock, the significance of those tags was immediately obvious to me. I was looking at a soldier from my world, a fellow twenty-first century human. The glance was only fleeting and I instantly made my way back to the barricade in the hope of finding the Leo animan again, but my hopes were dashed as I was quickly engulfed in the battle once more. Lupus soldiers were now attacking the barricade in a frenzy of swords and spears, shouts roared out in battle cries and pain. Pale grey light of the oncoming day was pushing back the dark of night as we fought on, our only advantage was the position of the barricade. Situated at the end of a street with buildings at either side meant the mass of soldiers were forced into an impotent funnel, the general was not able to use his superior numbers in the small gap between buildings. It was the perfect defensive position, a handful of townsfolk could hold of an army, and indeed that was what we were doing.

Finally, through the cold morning air, a horn sounded, one long wailing note that cut through the noise of turmoil. Surprisingly, the soldiers were withdrawing, moving back towards their lines, leaving a grisly pile of mutilated dead and dying in their wake. But it was not only the soldiers who had lost comrades, as the fighting ceased, the scale of loss amongst the town defenders quickly became evident. I realised the barricade had deepened during the attack, it had been reinforced with the bodies of the dead and even the wounded. Defenders had fallen where they fought, dropping at the foot of the barricade as other bodies piled atop them. Unwittingly, we had continued to fight while trampling on corpses, literally standing on the bodies of brave individuals who gave their lives for Indutiae. It was then that I realised my feet were covered in blood, glancing around I saw I was not alone. The blood was not mine, it was the blood of the unfortunate souls who now lay trampled and crushed at the barricade.

Leaving a few sentries on guard at the barricade, the rest of the defenders wearily trudged back to homes and loved ones, grateful to be alive or grief-stricken. With no home or anyone waiting for our safe return, we headed back to the publican. The sounds of war had died and now arose the cries of anguish as mothers and fathers, wives and children discovered their loss amongst the bodies. Those who survived were too exhausted to feel pity at that point, and the mourners were left to their grief. I joined up with Silĕre, Secuutus and Pugnator and a few moments later Adserviŏ appeared. At least the few animan I called friends had survived, a fact I was grateful for as we made our way along the street, leaving the sorrow and tears behind us. We gathered in the publican, too tired to eat, the publican himself had walked in a moment behind us, his blooded appearance bearing witness to his contribution to the defence of Indutiae. Soon others drifted in, most still in shock from the recent events, others frightened and seeking comfort. I recognised many of the town leaders and several traders but many that wandered in were strangers to me.

Slowly those gathered began to mull over the fight, many called it a battle but Pugnator quickly but gently warned them that it was no battle, no war and barely even a real fight. It would get worse. Moans of fear and anxiety mixed with expressions of disbelief rippled around the animan in the room. To be honest, I had expected more from the general but I could hardly be classed as an expert. A life in education, in a classroom, does not nurture one's battle skills. Nonetheless, I had expected the town to fall under a full-scale attack, not just a skirmish at the barricade. I wondered why the General had chosen this course of action, surely with his vastly superior numbers, conquering Indutiae should have been fairly simple. The ripple of moans, groans and whimpers were threatening to become a flood, an outpouring of fear and grief, threatening to turn into hysteria and panic before Pugnator staggered tiredly to his feet.

'Quieten down please, this is not helping,' he began in a soft voice. 'This attack was just a demonstration, the first punch so to speak. The general is fully aware his forces could squash us and our town like a fly, but he chose not to. At first, I could not understand his reasoning, but now I think I do. He still carries the hope that we will surrender, bow to his command. He attacked the east barricade, not to gain entry to the town, but to give all of us a taste of the misery, of death and despair that will befall us if we continue to stand against him. You have all now witnessed what our defiance will cost, many more will die, and Indutiae will face destruction.'

Here Pugnator paused, giving those who heard time to digest his warning. Sure enough, voices began to raise, some calling for surrender to save lives, others demanding the town fights for its freedom. Many simply wept. I remained silent, it was not my town. I had no ties here so in fairness, my opinion didn't count. I was wondering why the hell I had volunteered to remain, a glance over at my companion's testified to their own doubt. In truth, I knew why I remained, the choice was simple, I had nowhere else to go. Here at least I had friends, I had shelter and I had food. I knew if I left,

Silēre and Secuutus would follow me but where would that lead? To be torn apart by wild animals, murdered by bandits or starving to death in a land alien to me. I had chosen to stay and after a moment of contemplation, I felt justified in my choice.

Pugnator was speaking again, attempting to calm the fear of those in the room. 'Our paths are simple, it only rests on which direction we take. We can concede to the general and allow our town to be controlled by the Lupus army and see the Ursidae driven from their homes. We can stand by as all our male Lupus are conscripted into his army, wives losing husbands, children losing fathers. We can allow our free trade to diminish as other Casts inevitably leave our town and we lose any business with the Ursidae across the border. These are our choices, but there are many more to consider.'

'What if we fight the general? What will happen to the town then?' cried a frightened voice from the onlookers.

I had not noticed the room filling with more stunned townsfolk as Pugnator spoke, I had been preoccupied with my thoughts but now I saw the gathering had become a crowd, filling the room and spilling out onto the street outside.

'If we wish to remain neutral in this land, the fight to win it back will be difficult, lives will be lost and livelihoods destroyed. That will be the cost of defying General Crudelis. I'm sorry but that's the truth,' replied Pugnator as uproar ensued. Animan of all Casts shouting their fear, their defiance and their right to life. One familiar voice pierced the babble. All eyes, including mine, turned in the direction of the voice as silence fell once more.

'What can we expect from the general's attacks? What will come next?' It was the publican who voiced the questions, questions that lay at the back of everyone's thoughts that day. All eyes switched back to Pugnator but it was a Leo masculus who now stood to address the room. A glance at Pugnator received a nod of acceptance in return, the new speaker had the floor.

'I am called Veterator. Some will know me, others not, but I can tell you what the General will likely do next. First, he will attack both the east and the west barricades simultaneously as well as any other weak points in our defences. He will encircle our town with soldiers in a crushing manoeuvre, pouring all his resources into an all points attack. I can tell you now, we will be hard pressed to defend ourselves then, we will need every animan to give their all to survive. It may not be enough.'

Veterator paused as the sound in the room grew, drowning his voice in a tide of despair, fear and desolation, anger and aggression, all gave voice to their own emotions. Before things became uncontrollable, Pugnator stood and glared at the townsfolk, silencing them almost instantly with his sheer force of will. I was impressed, this was an animan who could lead a nation, given the chance.

'If we repel that attack, the following will be far worse,' continued Veterator. 'Then he will use fire. He will burn down Indutiae and all those in it!'

Chapter Eight: A lost soldier

The room now fell deathly quiet, the words of Veterator stilling each voice and filling the minds of those present with futility. Not even Pugnator rose to speak, no one had anything to say, no one could offer hope. As I looked at those crammed into the publican, I saw tears run from downcast eyes as all contemplated the end of freedom and neutrality in Indutiae. The spirit of the town was broken. Finally, a voice broke the despondent silence just as the sound of shuffling feet became audible, the townsfolk moving as one to return home to their families and make plans for their new future.

'We may be able to withstand the next attack,' began Veterator again, 'but when the fires start, that will be a different matter. We need some ideas, a new strategy to protect the animan of this town. No one should leave until we have at least attempted to examine all the options available to us.' The shuffling stopped as the animan turned to Veterator once more.

'But what can we do?' asked a quiet voice from the crowd.

'How can we fight the inevitable?' cried another.

Pugnator stood and held up his hands to silence the crowd. 'I agree fire is a problem, but first we must deal with the next attack. Veterator is correct in his analysis of the situation, however, I do not share his vision of hopelessness. This town has stood neutral between the lands of the Lupus and the Ursidae for longer than most of us can remember. We have fought many battles to ensure our way of life but now the greed, ego or power lust of one animan, one general in the Lupus army is threatening all we have. We cannot allow ourselves to fall at the feet of such a tyrant. We can win this fight but we need help. It is time. We must send word to the Ursidae. We need their help.'

A shocked silence followed Pugnator's words, but it didn't last long before every voice in the room raised in acceptance or denial. I and my companions, Silĕre and Secuutus were the only ones to not contribute. Looking around the room in the publican and at the jammed doorway, everyone I saw appeared to be shouting, trying to make themselves heard over the cries of their neighbours, all bar one. It was the Leo defender I had seen at the barricade, the same animan who wore dog tags from my world. He remained silent, standing amongst the baying crowd and surveying the room until he noticed my gaze upon him. Being of the Leo Cast, I would have expected a degree of arrogance, of superiority in his eyes, but not this one. In instead he lowered his eyes to the ground and fidgeted nervously for a moment before moving back deeper into the crowd of animan.

I pondered on his actions, I could not discuss my suspicions with my companions for they may think me mad. I had tried to tell Secuutus and Silĕre that I was not of this land, I had explained about the green jade box, Secuutus had even experienced its power, but I knew they didn't really believe me. I think Secuutus still believed it to be magic, a spell cast by the sorcerer whom we defeated. So I wondered about the Leo on my own, determined to seek him out and discover his secret. The sight of his dog tags had raised suspicion in my mind, but I needed to be sure. I had met two other animan who had been transported to this world by the jade box. My friend

Sophos and the fake sorcerer, including myself that would be three ex-humans who now live in an animan body. I was convinced the dog tag wearer was one of us, a human. I needed to find him and discover if my deductions were correct. But for now, that would have to wait, for Pugnator had stilled the confused crowd and was now issuing commands for the next defence of Indutiae.

As I listened to the plans being laid out for the defence of Indutiae, I knew they would struggle to make them work, we needed an edge, something to help swing the battle in favour of Indutiae. With this in mind, I managed to get away from my friends and sought out Adserviŏ. I needed some local knowledge for a scheme which may assist in the fight for Indutiae. The mysterious Leo masculus had stirred a memory from my meeting with the fake, and now mute, sorcerer I had encountered in Regnum. I knew what I contemplated would be dangerous, not only for me but for the future of the animan themselves, nonetheless it was too good an idea to dismiss. I was going to make some common human weapons but I didn't know how to acquire one of the ingredients. I had already remembered the infamous Molotov cocktails and knew I could use whatever the animan filled their lamps with, or that rocket fuel that passed for alcohol in this land. But something stronger would also be required, I set off alone while the townsfolk prepared themselves for the next attack.

The day had reached noon as I sneaked away from the publican, giving a call of nature as my excuse to leave my companions. I already knew Adserviŏ had not been at the meeting as he was still on guard duty at the main barricade. It didn't take long to find my helpful friend, but describing what I sought was another matter. Finally, using simple terms he understood and led me off to one of the agricultural traders. It took some persuading for the storekeeper to open up for us, he too had manned the defences during the attack and was attempting to catch up on sleep. Finally our persistence won and he grudgingly opened the door. The agriculture trader was an Ursidae called Commeatus and when I said what I required, he gave me a strange look.

'You don't look like a farmer. You're a Tigris and that Cast doesn't farm, they fight. Why would you want such a thing?'

'Never mind why I want it,' I replied firmly but politely. 'My question was, do you have it?'

'Of course I stock it. It's not exactly an expensive item and is easily obtained, we have sack loads of the stuff out back. The farmers use it on their lands, it helps the crops grow. So, how much do you want?' The Ursidae storekeeper still eyed me with suspicion but Adserviŏ nodded his encouragement and, after I had informed him of my order, the storekeeper disappeared through a door at the back of a rough plank counter.

'Anything else?' he growled on his return, his arms full with my order.

'Yes, do you have any er . . . carbo I think you call it?' I asked.

'Of course. The blacksmiths use loads of it. How much do you want?' Again the storekeeper vanished through the back door after I had given him the amount. I had what I needed and thanked him, passing over coin as Adserviŏ and I left carrying our goods. Back on the street snow was falling lightly, the temperature had dropped and the ground was hardening with ice once again. I pulled my furs in tighter as I turned to Adserviŏ with my last request.

'What?' he exclaimed. 'What could you possibly want with that place?'

'I need something they have in abundance,' I told him. 'The older the better.'

'Oh come on, that's just strange. Why on Terra would you want that?'

'You'll soon find out,' I replied with a grin. I was being as careful as I could without offending Adserviŏ. What I was planning must never become common knowledge or it would change the lives of the animan forever. The responsibility for a change for the worse, of such consequence, was not what I wanted hanging on my shoulders.

Still mumbling about the state of my sanity, Adserviŏ led me round the back of a stable, with the equesters permission. There I dug down into the straw and muck that had lain there for years, digging at the very bottom layer with a crudely made spade and placing it into sacks provided by the owner. Finally with all my supplies obtained, Adserviŏ and I returned to the publican, but instead of entering the front door, we made our way around to the rear of the building. There stood an old shed, or shack, unused for years and in a state of noticeable disrepair but secure and dry. It would do nicely I thought, I had offered the publican coin and now the shack was mine until further notice. The publican and my companions all thought I was mad, why would I want an old broken down shack? I didn't let on.

Having placed my strange supplies in the shack, we returned to the warmth and company of the publican, greeting those who choose to fortify their courage with some of that rocket fuel. I soon found Secuutus and Silĕre but was surprised to also see Pugnator in their company. I was updated to the fact that he had been busy organising the town's defences and had noticed my absence. I apologised and joined them at their table. Secuutus offered me a drink and I accepted, I still have a penchant for self-destruction it seemed.

'How inflammable is this stuff?' I asked when my breath return following the smallest sip of the drink.

'Oh it's very inflammable, it'll burst into flames in strong sunlight, the stuff's lethal. Why d'you ask?' answered Pugnator.

'Just a moment, I'll tell you soon but first, do you have any glass bottles?'

The other four sat at the table peered at me in confusion before Adserviŏ replied in a tone one might use on a child. 'No, glass is much too expensive to use on bottles, only the finest vinum is stored in glass. As you can see about you, our ale is in jars made of pottery or animan skins. Come on, what are you planning? These questions are either strange or stupid.'

'Have you ever heard of a Molotov cocktail?' I asked innocently.

Within moments of my description and instructions on how to make the favourite weapon of angry mobs on my world, Pugnator was up and running, Adserviŏ close behind as they sped off to assemble this new weapon. As I watched them leave, I could see it had started to snow, big delicate flakes floating down from the dirty grey sky. Suddenly I was reminded of Christmas, a memory I quickly squashed. This was hardly the time for mistletoe and wine or to be dreaming of a white Christmas. I had just introduced a horrible weapon to the animan, it was certainly not a present in keeping with the Christmas tradition of human kindness.

My thoughts were suddenly interrupted as another animan entered the publican, it was the Leo masculus who wore the dog tags. This time I would not let him escape. I had to know one way or another if he was from my world. As he made his way to the bar, I stood and followed him. My companions made to rise also but I gestured for them to remain in their seats. If I was correct, none of what I was about to say would make any sense to them.

Reaching the Leo's side, I leant against the bar and said quietly, 'Army, navy or air force?'

The reaction was immediate. The Leo spun round to face me, his hand darting towards the sword at his waist. Behind me Silĕre and Secuutus shot to their feet, reaching for their own weapons as they rose. However, I had been paying attention, my hand flashed out and clamped down on the hand of the Leo, pushing down hard and halting the drawing of his weapon. For a moment he stared at me, fury lining his face. He was caught and he knew it. Between myself and my two friends, he didn't stand a chance. Still glaring at me, he slowly released his hand from the sword hilt.

'What do you want?' he growled menacingly.

I gestured for Silĕre and Secuutus to return to their seats, the threat of their presence had already achieved its purpose. The Leo stranger knew I was not alone. Equally as slowly, I release my grip and stood back, resting one elbow on the bar. The Leo before me stood just a few inches shorter than me, not as muscular as other members of his Cast but that could be down to the fact that he looked half starved. His dull yellow hair was unkempt and long and he was in need of a wash. He was dressed in simple homespun trousers and what I assumed to be a leather jerkin under a long fur skin coat that reached down well past his knees. After my brief appraisal of the Leo, I replied, keeping my voice friendly and non-threatening.

'I see you're wearing dog tags, my friend. I assume they are your own?'

'Yeah, what of it? How to you know about dog tags? He growled again as realisation lit up his eyes.

'I know that dog tags are used in the forces, so I ask again. Army, navy or air force?'

This time the Leo did not answer immediately, instead his eyes bored deep into mine before drifting over my countenance, making his appraisal of me.

'Army,' he finally replied. 'USA.'

'Ah,' I responded with a grin. 'Did you find a little jade . . .'

'Box!' he finished for me. 'Yes I did, why?'

'So did I. That's how I'm here. I'm from the UK.'

Suddenly his whole demeanour changed. The threatening pose and frightened stare disappeared. He turned away from me and slumped on the bar, his shoulders sagged and for a brief moment, I thought a saw a glistening of tears in his eyes. I signalled for the publican to bring us both a drink and waited while the Leo gulped at his. After a few moments, he straightened up and turned to face me once more. Then he held out his hand and introduced himself.

'My name is Eustace and I'm from Montana, or at least, I was. No idea where I am now. No idea what I am now,' he finished with a swallow of sorrow.

'Nice to meet you Eustace. My name is Harry and you're on Totus-

Terra,' I answered as I led him over to our table.

I introduced him to the other two and then ordered a meal for us all, outlining the story of Eustace while we waited. I couldn't explain much to Silĕre and Secuutus, so I simply stated that Eustace came from the same land as I so he has little knowledge of where he is now. As we chatted, it came to light that Eustace had been a private in the US army until he awoke and found himself on the forest floor on the outskirts of Indutiae. He had managed to 'obtain' some clothes and a weapon and survived by doing odd jobs and finding work where he could. He had remained to help with the defence of the town simply because, like us, he had nowhere else to go. He didn't know where he was but he knew he wasn't in Montana. We filled in some of the missing parts for him but both Eustace and I avoided any mention of humans, it would only cause Silĕre and Secuutus to become more confused than they had been when I attempted to explain how I had arrived in this land.

I ordered more food for Eustace, he still looked like he could eat a whole gazelle, and I needed him on my side. The conversation soon returned to the defence of Indutiae and when the use of Molotov cocktails was mentioned, the golden eyes of Eustace immediately turned to stare at me. In reply, I simply shrugged my shoulders, a gesture that every human understood. Soon Silĕre and Secuutus grew restless and excused themselves, stating they would be at the main barricade when I was ready. With a brief word to Eustace, the pair left the publican, leaving Eustace and me alone.

I remained silent as my fellow ex-human finished his second meal and we contemplated each other. I couldn't tell what he was thinking but my mind pondered on trust, could I place my trust in this ex-army man? I decided I had no choice and as the last mouthful of food disappeared, I began to outline my plans. I needed his help but would he agree and at what price? I knew he was in the same situation as myself and all the inhabitants of Indutiae, but I also understood that as a complete stranger here, his loyalties as yet had no foundation.

'So, providing we don't end up dead in this town, what plans do you have for the future?' I asked the now sated animan.

'I don't know, I really don't know. I would like to get back home, home as a human I mean, but first I have to find a way. Until then I suppose I'll hang around here and do what I've been trained for, fight.'

'I intend staying, for a while at least.' I replied, 'I too have nowhere special to be. I did manage to get hold of another, or it could be the same, jade box back in a place called Urbem Regiam. I opened it but instead of sending me home, it sent me here. Seems the box has a mind of its own and we have no say in where it sends us. I have made friends here, I am learning about this world, but still, I would like to go home to Britain. I think I miss the rain.'

'That's another reason why I'm staying here,' began Eustace in reply. 'I've heard there is a jade box around here somewhere. My source wasn't very clear, mainly because he couldn't understand my interest, but I did discover someone of authority in this region has a box in his or her possession. I just have to find out who it is.'

'Well, if I can help in any way, let me know. Perhaps we can both return to our former lives one day. Though for that to happen, it would help if we remain alive to find the box, and in order to achieve that, I could use some help. What d'you say?' I had an idea but I needed his cooperation. Being a fellow human and a soldier, he would certainly understand what I intended to do, and it would avoid the danger of the animan learning what sulphur, potassium and charcoal can do.

Several hours later found Eustace and me producing the first batch of readied ingredients, working in the draughty shack at the back of the publican. We had not put the ingredients together as neither of us wanted to put ourselves at risk of dismemberment just yet. Outside the snow was falling heavier amidst a howling wind and increasing darkness as night fell. We could hear the town readying itself for the next attack which Pugnator suspected would follow the usual format of just before dawn, if the weather didn't worsen. I found myself wondering what kind of animan the general was, to stage a siege in the winter months and with snow on the ground, hindering the movement of freezing soldiers. I concluded the Lupus general had either an abundance of confidence, or a screw loose.

With the onset of darkness, Eustace and I decided to halt our production line, the light was now too dim to see and lighting an oil lamp in the shack would not be the wisest move. After securing the shack as best we could, we made the short but cold journey back to the publican and warmth.

Back inside we found the place almost deserted, the majority of the townsfolk being busy with guard duties, seeing to their families or simply preparing to defend their homes against the soldiers if they breached the barricades. A couple of old Ursidae animan were sat in a corner of the publican, nursing their rocket fuel and reminiscing over old battles. They both looked up as we entered but lost interest after a brief nod of acknowledgement. Eustace made himself comfortable at a table near the roaring fire while I ordered hot food, if it was to be a long night, I at least wanted to face it on a full stomach. I had barely pushed the fork into my meal before the door burst open and my two companions rushed in, a blast of cold air following them.

'Where have you two been all afternoon?' enquired Secuutus. 'We've been trying to build the defenders confidence and your presence would have helped. The townsfolk need to see they have the support of Tigris and Leo. Yes I know, before you interrupt, there are other Tigris and Leo's here but you Harry, you're already gaining the reputation of being somewhat of a hero. So where in Terra have you been?'

As Secuutus and the silent Silĕre dragged chairs nearer to our table and the warmth of the fire, I paused before replying, not knowing how much information to offer at this early stage. If I outlined my plan, expectations would rise, but if it failed, what then? In the end, I decided on an explanation more fitting to my animan friends.

'Hello to you two as well! Is it cold outside by any chance?' I began light-heartedly. All I received in return were two low growls, I keep forgetting British humour is somewhat of an acquired taste, so to speak. 'Sorry. Anyway, we've been trying to copy some of the sorcerer's magic, remember him?' I asked Secuutus with a raised eyebrow. I received a grunt in reply before continuing, 'I don't know if I can get it to work so I'm not going to say any more about it just yet. Eustace has been helping me as there's lots to do and interruptions or distractions could be fatal, and I'm too young and good looking to die.'

Again, my attempt at humour fell as flat as a politicians face when asked to pay from his own pocket. Eustace managed a slight smile, he being the only other animan in the room who may have appreciated my jokes, but I don't think he did. Secuutus made to speak even before I had finished. As always, when you tell someone you don't wish to talk about a subject, they immediately begin asking questions. I managed to fend him off by first asking one of my own.

'What's happening outside? Why did you come bursting into the publican in such a hurry?'

For a moment confusion lined the face of my Ursidae companion and ex-rider as his mind attempted to switch from one subject to another. 'We've discovered some news that may be significant. Signs in the snow show footprints leading away from the Lupus army camp.'

'And?' I enquired.

'Well each set of footprints lead off in different directions, indicating, or so Pugnator believes, that some of the Lupus soldiers are deserting. Pugnator thinks the general has made a huge mistake coming out on a campaign in such lousy weather, and his animan are not happy and some have decided to leave. If that's the case, maybe his numbers will drop enough that he will be forced to forego the siege and retreat. What d'you think?' finished Secuutus.

'How many tracks have you seen?' I asked.

'At least six, maybe eight,' replied Secuutus. 'I know it's not much when compared to the hundreds that remain but we can hope for more.'

Until now, Eustace had remained silent, but with a shuffle nearer to our table, he spoke. 'It's not the fact that soldiers are deserting that's interesting,' he began. 'But the evidence of low morale amongst the general's troops. If morale sinks too low, and it well might in these conditions, any confidence we can show may be a deciding factor in the next attack. If we can spread the word that the Lupus soldiers are reluctant to fight for a lunatic general, it may boost our fighters and lessen the cloak of fear that covers the town. That's what I think anyway,' he concluded.

A brief pause in the conversation followed as each of us digested this new interpretation of the recent observations. As a human, or ex-human, I was well versed in battle strategies thanks to countless John Wayne and John Mills films depicting the two World Wars. Admittedly, I had never faced a life or death situation until waking up in this strange land, however, my short time here had brought me up to speed, fast! Eustace though, he had been a soldier and this meant his input could be crucial. After some thought, I could see the advantage of Eustace's plan. 'Okay, I agree. I suggest we find Pugnator and see if he can use this new propaganda to the benefit of the town.'

'Does that mean we have to go out in the cold again?' grumbled Secuutus.

'Yes, sadly it does,' I replied.

'I'll leave you to it,' said Eustace as we rose to leave the table. 'I'm gonna hit the hay if that's okay?'

'Yeah that's fine. You got somewhere to stay?' I replied while avoiding the inquisitive eyes of Secuutus and Silĕre. 'I could probably get you a room here if you wish?'

'Nah its okay, I've got a small place. I'll start again at first light.'

'If you're sure? I could do with some sleep as well after we've spoken to Pugnator. Actually, as you came up with this, wouldn't it be better if you spoke to him yourself?'

'Nah, you know what to tell him, I'm not much for plans and strategies so I'll leave that to you, I'm sure you'll manage,' he finished with a grin. With that, Eustace made his way out the back door while we exited the front and went off in search of the town leader, Pugnator.

The town had been busy, though everyone was hindered by the cold and snow, each animan worked at their allotted tasks. Reinforcing the barricades, sharpening weapons, filling buckets and barrels with water as a precaution against the inevitable fire threat and seeing to horses and livestock. Older children were kept close to parents while they completed their tasks, or were snug indoors blissfully unaware of what the future may hold for the town of Indutiae. Elderly animan took charge of any children who had lost their parents in the first attack along with those whose parents were otherwise occupied keeping watch or grabbing what rest they could. Fear was plain to see on the adult animan faces but not on the very young, to them it was a new game, they didn't understand it and therefore didn't fear it.

Secuutus, Silĕre and I drudged through the snow towards the main barricade where we knew we would find Pugnator. Sure enough, there he was, silhouetted by the flames of oil soaked cloth brands that flickered in the falling snow. For a brief moment I was again reminded of Christmas, a snow covered landscape with animan rushing to and fro, illuminated only by the feeble light from burning brands. The thought was quickly shattered by reasoning, it was not Christmas and the townsfolk were not rushing to purchase last minute gifts or a plump turkey. Here the hustle and bustle was driven by the most important gift one could have, life.

A sudden movement on my right caused my ponderings to end abruptly, Secuutus, my huge Ursidae companion had accidentally blundered into a small figure wrapped in furs against the cold, a large bucket of water grasped in each hand. Secuutus immediately apologised and offered to carry the buckets and I could see why. The figure had removed a face scarf to shout at my friend and in doing so, revealed a rather plain but not unattractive Ursidae femina. Secuutus's gaze lingered on her face as he stammered his offer of help. With a shy smile, the female Ursidae agreed and following a glance back at myself and Silĕre, my huge companion shuffled off in the figures wake. Silĕre looked up at me and smiled, we both knew what our friend was up to and who could blame him, or her. In these current times, everyone welcomes the company of another, even animan. As if sharing my thoughts, Silĕre gently slid her arm around mine and moved closer. I said nothing and of course, Silĕre couldn't say anything, so on we walked, arm in arm as the snow fell around us.

Chapter Nine: A New Weapon.

Pugnator turned to face us as we approached, one raised eyebrow his only acknowledgement of the apparent closeness of Silĕre and me. But the moment was over and we parted as I explained what Eustace had said, pointing out over to the army camp that was rapidly becoming buried under snow. All traces of footprints leading away from the camp had now been obliterated by the new covering of snow, a minor point as Pugnator knew exactly what had happened and needed no explanation. As I looked out at the camp myself, something odd struck me. Then I had it, there were no signs of the movement expected in an army camp, few soldiers could be seen anywhere amongst the tents. Fires still glowed in the darkness but no activity other than a few guards.

'Is this normal?' I asked Pugnator, 'Do the Lupus army retire to their beds early and leave so few guards in place?'

Pugnator glanced at me with a wry smile, 'I've been wondering that myself. There has been little movement for some time and with what your friend Eustace has said, I wonder if our General Crudelis even remains in the camp!'

We both turned back to stare and ponder over the quiet rows of military tents until Silĕre tugged at my sleeve. I turned to her as did Pugnator and interpreted her meanings. It was not difficult, Silĕre was suggesting we take a closer look at the camp and I think she was volunteering the two of us. Nice of her I thought. Pugnator looked at us and then turned back to stare once more at the inactive camp. I looked at Silĕre standing by my side, though not so close now, a fact that disappointed me I will admit. As my gaze fell on her face, she looked back at me with a mischievous smile and I understood. Silĕre was a Tigris femina and like all able-bodied members of the Tigris Cast, she was a warrior. She may have failed one task which resulted in the removal of her tongue and being ostracised by her Cast, but her spirit and courage had not deserted her. I think she had grown bored waiting for the next attack on Indutiae and this was her escape. No need to drag me along I thought, but I knew I would go.

'That's a great idea Silĕre,' said Pugnator after some thought. 'I don't like what I'm seeing and I certainly don't trust the general. We have been so preoccupied with defending the town, we failed to keep a close eye on the enemy. Thinking further, I'm very suspicious of those tracks we saw, just how many soldiers have left the camp? With morale low, I wonder if the general has tricked us, deceived us in some way. Whatever it is, we need to find out so, if you two are willing to take a closer look, it would be very useful?'

Useful? I thought, that's an understated word to use for sneaking into a camp full of enemy soldiers in the dead of a black and cold night. However, before I could express any misgivings, Silĕre was nodded enthusiastically at Pugnator. It seemed my decision had been made for me, and I wasn't even married to the girl!

'Thank you both. If you need any further clothing or weapons, I'll provide them for you. What about Secuutus? Will he be joining you?' asked Pugnator.

'No I don't think so,' I answered, 'I think he's otherwise occupied. It'll be just the two of us. So what's the plan? Do we just take a peek . . .'

'What?'

'Sorry, I forgot. A peek is just another word for a look, taking a peek means taking a quick look, that's all. Anyway, do we just take a look from the perimeter of the camp or what?' I asked.

'I think take a . . . peek will do, don't get yourselves caught, we need you here just as much as we need the information on the general's activities. So be careful and come back, alive preferably,' said Pugnator with a very wolfish grin.

I didn't reply, I was way too worried about leaving the town and stealing over the crisp white snow to the camp. Our dark figures would show up like dog turds on clean white sheets, even in the darkness of night. This was going to be very difficult and I was rapidly scaring the hell out of myself as my mind brought up all the ways in which we could fail, and die. My mind continued to race as Silēre and I went off to prepare. In truth I didn't have a clue, prepare with what? Harry Potter's invisibility cloak would have been useful or some form of camouflage, but what sort of camouflage can one use in snow? I had noticed there was little or no white clothing around here, as in the middle ages of my own land, white was a colour best avoided. No laundrettes or fancy washing machines here, and from the underlying smell of the town, washing of clothes didn't happen that often anyway. So in uncertainty, I just followed Silĕre and waited to see what her plan was, I had none.

Turns out there was no plan, other than not getting caught of course. Silĕre did show me how to wrap any weapons with a cloth so they wouldn't glint in any light or rattle and create noise that might give us away. My staff, being made of wood and its blade retracted was safe, but I followed her advice with my knife. Extra furs were provided along with a form of thin material that Silĕre demonstrated, instructing me to cover my eyes with. The material was thin enough to easily see through but it would help to protect our eyes against the whirling and stinging snow. Finally, we were ready and I came to the conclusion we resembled two furry ninja's as we clambered over a barricade and headed out into the snow covered No Man's Land between the town and the tented soldiers' residence.

The snow was deep and crisp and even and made movement cumbersome, our footsteps crunching through the crisp snow crust, I instantly realised stealth would be difficult. Silĕre led the way and gestured for me to walk in her footsteps to reduce sound and give the false impression of only one animan if our tracks were discovered. I also suspected another reason might be to stop me falling flat on my face in the snow, which of course was always a possibility. But I was happy to follow and concentrated on my surroundings. The night had cleared and visibility for we two big cats was not a problem. Unfortunately, it wouldn't be a problem for the Lupus either. For the first part of the journey we simply walked, but it wasn't long before Silĕre gestured for me to lower my outline by crouching as we grew nearer to our objective. For the last stage, we dropped onto our bellies and slivered through the snow, Silĕre occasionally threw snow over her back so I did the same. The dusting of snow helping to lighten our dark figures. A simple form of camouflage I knew but I hoped it was enough.

Then in the darkness I saw Silĕre stop and push herself deeper into the snow. I followed her actions immediately, knowing she must have a reason. I was right, for a moment later I caught the faint sound of something coming towards us. I held my breath as I waited, rooted to the freezing ground as fear built inside me and prayed I was low enough in the snow to be hidden from all but a close scrutiny. Then, out of the darkness came the unmistakable figure of a soldier, a Lupus soldier walking stooped over and not ten yards from where I lay. The soldier was huddled within his uniform and his steps were careful. Fortunately his attention was on his movements and he passed by without noticing me lying prone only a few steps away. I made ready to move again as soon as he was out of sight but Silĕre, who lay right in front of me, halted my rise with a soft kick. A soft kick it might have been but it landed squarely in my face. Though it caught me by surprise, it was an effective method of quickly drawing my attention to another figure looming out of the night.

Lying freezing in the snow, I counted around a dozen soldiers pass me, spaced out with several minutes between them. Each soldier trod in the footsteps of the first, and I realised those single tracks we assumed to be deserters could have been made by a number of soldiers. What the heck was going on I wondered, soldiers don't desert their post in such a precise way, something else must be happening and I needed to discover what. Reaching out and getting Silĕre's attention by grabbing her foot, I indicated that we should follow the soldier's tracks and see where they were going. Silĕre hesitated a moment before nodding in agreement and we set off. Keeping low and carefully stepping into the footprints left by the soldiers, playing the same game as the military. Hopefully if discovered, we would be mistaken for soldiers and avoid further scrutiny.

Silĕre followed in my tracks as I in turn followed those left by the soldiers. We had been walking for some time before I realised we were heading in a direction that would take us around the town of Indutiae, faintly visible by the glow of brands and torches. I knew we could not be seen from the town and were at least safe from any lookouts, but I was beginning to form a realisation of what the general had planned. I trudged on through the night, my senses on high alert and anticipation growing within me. I felt sure I knew what was happening. Sometime later we were on the far side of the town, directly opposite the army camp location with the town of Indutiae sandwiched between us. We were heading up into the trees and I could hear faint voices, it was time to get off the track. Turning, I made to gesture at Silĕre but she was way ahead of me and already moving away. I followed the Tigris femina, moving through the night as quietly as the cats we evolved from. Silĕre lead me up to the treeline away from the voices.

Once amongst the trees, Silĕre stopped and turned to me, gesturing and pointing to where the sounds were coming from. I understood and followed as we crept nearer to the activity. Remaining quiet as we moved was easier now, we trod on a carpet of snow covered pine needles, the snow much thinner here beneath the firs. Moving quickly, it was not long before we discovered the reason for the footprints we had seen from the town. The tracks were not caused by individual deserters as we first thought, for there in front of us sat at least a hundred soldiers. All were huddled around small fires, the light shielded from the town by walls of snow. I now knew my suspicions were justified, the cunning general intended to attack both the front and rear of the town. A pincer movement I think the military types call it. This manoeuvre would completely catch the town unawares, all their focus was on the camp. None would expect an attack from the trees at the rear of Indutiae. The town was doomed unless we could warn them. But how?

In the darkness, Silĕre and I looked at each other, despair for the town in her eyes but my brain was working. Yep, it surprised me too. Leading Silĕre to the very edge of the trees, I communicated to her what I planned. It could be suicide for us but it was the only thing I could come up with at short notice. Catching on quickly she agreed and we set about my plan. We would build a fire of our own, a fire big enough to be visible from the town, a beacon of warning that I prayed Pugnator would understand.

Making a fire from scratch in the snow was far beyond my skills, but not Silĕre. She was a natural animan, not a helpless human in animan form. Following her lead, I collected twigs and forest detritus, placing a small pile on a patch of cleared ground. Most animan, including me, carry a form of tinder box and of course, Silĕre's was fully equipped. Within moments I saw a tiny flicker grow from the corner of my eye as I kept watch on the soldiers. I saw the flicker grow as Silĕre piled on more combustible material, the flames now covering Silĕre in a pale yellow glow that soon warmed the back of my legs. As the fire grew, so did my apprehension. If the soldiers saw us before the fire was big enough to be seen, our efforts would be for nought. Luckily, my fears remained unfounded, the soldiers either didn't notice our fire or assumed it to be more of their comrades trying to keep warm. Silĕre now had the fire roaring, hurriedly feeding it more fuel that sent sparks shooting up into the night sky. With crackles and snaps, the fire sent its bright yellow light out through the darkness, hopefully to be seen by the Indutiae lookouts.

With the fire blazing high it was time to go, with another armful of brush dumped onto the roaring flames just to be sure, we took off and broke from the trees at a run. We ran as fast as we could through the deep snow as shouts pierced the still air behind us, the soldiers had seen the fire. The voices grew louder as soldiers saw us breaking from the trees and began to pursue. Others rushed to extinguish the bonfire that lit our daring escape. The forest and the town were separated by only a few hundred yards, but in the deep snow, it felt like a hundred miles. A hundred miles with an enemy at our heels. I risked a look back and was rewarded with the sight of the fire, piercing the darkness like the beacon it was intended to be. Surely the town's sentries would see it, praying its significance would be understood. Suddenly a spear struck the snow just a few paces behind us, a sight guaranteed to make one run faster, it did.

The exertion of driving one foot after the other in the deep snow was bringing to tell on both Silĕre and me, our breathing became gasps and despite the cold, sweat ran down inside my clothes. My only consolation was that the soldiers would be facing the same struggle. But perhaps not the four soldiers who loomed out of the darkness right in front of us. A moment of shock dulled my reactions for a split second as Silĕre leapt at the first soldier, her sword flashing down to cleave his head open in one blow. My brain woke up and I quickly pressed the hidden button on my staff, releasing the blade, none too soon as two soldiers ran at me. I managed to sidestep one but the other was on me, sending me crashing down onto the ground. I shoved him away and scrambled a few feet to one side, narrowly avoiding the second soldiers attempted stab at my stomach. Leaping to my feet, I swung up the staff, catching him under the chin before lunging, blade first at the other. His sword deflected my blow but I kept my balance and kicked out, sweeping his legs from under him. Now the first soldier had recovered and charged at me, his sword held firmly out in front of his body. Almost automatically my staff swept up and mirrored his advance, piercing his gut with its longer reach. I continued forward, driving the blade deep, fury now taking my mind. Sharp pain in my side replaced the fury with fear, the other soldier had slashed at me from behind. I spun but I knew I would be too late, the soldier was striking at me again. I awaited the inevitable killing blow, as the tip of a sword suddenly protruded from the soldier's chest. He sagged to the ground, his face set in surprise, a surprise I shared until Silĕre came into vision.

'Thanks,' I gasped but Silĕre pointed quickly behind me before taking off at a run. I understood immediately and set off after her, blood pouring from my wound but the pain in my side forgotten as I remembered the pursuing soldiers. I knew they were close, too close. Our brief struggle had allowed our pursuers to gain ground on us and now they were only feet behind me. I may have forgotten the pain but I was still wounded and quickly realised Silĕre was drawing away from me, I could not keep up. Snow crunching footfalls were following close on my heels, I could almost feel the hot breath on my neck, my back tensed in readiness for a blade. I ran as fast as I could but knew my speed had gone, I was a sitting duck without a quack. Through a haze of fear and pain, I heard shouting but could not place its origin, I ran on, each step adding lead to my already heavy legs. Inevitably I fell, my face sinking into the snow as I slipped into oblivion.

'Harry? Harry! Wake up Harry, you're not dead. Wake up for Terra's sake!'

The voice cut through the comforting blackness and awareness crept back into my brain. I couldn't quite place the voice at first, certainly too gruff for my mother and my boss wouldn't be so polite, but I knew the voice. I slowly surfaced, waking to expect a hangover while my mind still whirled in confusion. Then it all came back, rushing into my head like a train escaping British rail. 'Shut up Secuutus,' I muttered.

Opening my eyes I saw I was lying on the ground a few yards inside the town defences. Silĕre, Pugnator peered down at me while Secuutus loomed to the fore above my face and appearing as if the mountain had indeed come to Mohammed. I made to sit up but a pain in my side warned me to do it slowly. Reaching out a hand I felt a wad of cloth covering the source of the pain. Slowly and oh so gingerly I achieved a sitting position and looked up at the faces about me.

'So what happened? How did I get here?' I asked.

Before anyone could answer, Silĕre moved to sit down beside me and examined the wadding. Satisfied she then almost shocked me back into unconsciousness as she gently grasped my hand and held it tightly. 'We saw the fire,' began Pugnator. 'It didn't take a Sage to understand its meaning so I rushed to see what was happening. It was Adserviŏ who spotted you entertaining the general's troops and he and your friend Secuutus led a small party of townsfolk out to help you.'

'How long have I been unconscious?' I asked.

'Oh not long, just long enough to get us to carry you over the barricade like an ancient,' replied Secuutus with a grin and followed by a knowing glance at Silĕre who still held my hand. 'You're not seriously wounded so if you've finished sitting around, perhaps you could get back to the publican? Or do I need to carry you?'

'How is my wound? Why did I pass out . . . sorry, become unconscious back there?'

'Blood loss and cold,' explained Pugnator. 'Your wound isn't serious and a medicus patched you up while you slept. It was the loss of blood combined with cold and exertion that felled you. You'll be fine after food, drink and a rest.

That's if you don't open the wound again. How are you feeling now? Can you walk?'

I cautiously rose to my feet, added gently by Silĕre, 'Seems I can,' I grunted as a wave of pain emanated from my side. 'Did the soldiers attack? There are about a hundred of them hiding up in the woods, I think the general intended to surprise you with a double-sided manoeuvre.'

'Yes we know, Silĕre managed to convey what you'd uncovered, but as you're awake, you can supply any further information while we walk to the publican.' Pugnator paused as I took the first faltering steps before gaining momentum.

'There has been no attack so far, their ploy became worthless as soon as it was discovered. And it would be a mistake in this weather I think. Without the element of surprise, the depth of snow would slow any charge to a crawl and allow us to simply pick off the soldiers when they came within spear or arrow distance. Even the general would not be stupid enough to send his troops against an alert enemy while his troops were hampered by the snow. We would cut them down easily long before they threaten our defences, especially with those *cocktail* things you told us about. We have quite a supply now, though I don't think the publican is too happy at losing some of his stock. I have assured him the town will pay if we survive. Now please try walking faster before we freeze out here.'

'Come Harry, we'll get you a good strong drink,' encouraged Secuutus while almost gently helping me to walk.

'Oh goodie,' I replied, my attempt at sarcasm wasted on the animan.

The weather worsened over the next two days, and I thanked it for my respite, my wound may not be life-threatening but it still damn well hurt! There was one disappointment however, as my condition improved so Silĕre became less attentive, reverting to her battle hardened self. Secuutus I soon realised, didn't do sympathy although he kept a close eye on me, between visits to his new female friend, visits that were growing in length each time. I was pleased my friend had found companionship here, far away from his roots back in Regnum. I had little success in attracting the opposite sex back on my world, and it appeared the same was to apply here. I had thought I stood a chance with Silĕre but I realised her moment of compassion was just consolation between two warriors. While I was happy for Secuutus, the unapproachable Silĕre remained on my mind.

Eustace came to see me and informed me he had managed to prepare quite a stock of the ingredients we had collected before, as he put it, my stroll in the woods. Eustace also informed me he had added fragments of flint to the mixture to act as shrapnel. He explained that a simple gunpowder explosion would not do enough damage to the enemy, but by adding shrapnel to each bomb, the area of effect would be much larger. Along with the killing capabilities, the shrapnel would also inflict major wounds, rendering many more assailants unable to fight. The glee in which he described the effects of flintstone as shrapnel worried me, but I had to agree he made sense. An impotent weapon would be almost as ineffective as no weapon at all.

So the following day, I joined him in the shack and we began the process of mixing, very carefully, the ingredients together. Eustace had also been busy around the town collecting clay pots in which we poured the final mixture. Each pot lid was then bound securely with leather strips and placed in an unused barrel in an attempt to avoid the attentions of noisy animan. Finally, we filled the smallest pot we had and prepared it for the demonstration we both knew would be needed to convince Pugnator and the town animan. Eustace, the American ex-soldier beamed with delight at the thought of the animan's reactions. I simply hoped we didn't end up burnt at the stake for witchcraft.

Leaving Eustace to prepare a suitable site, I went off to round up Pugnator, my two companions and the town's elite. With a little persuasion, I managed to lead them to the site chosen by Eustace and myself. The inconspicuous pot sat in a small clearing behind our shack, far enough away, of course, if the shack went up we would all go with it! A cord impregnated with powder ran from the pot, ending at the feet of Eustace. He had elected himself as the demonstrator, I think he eagerly anticipated the reaction our device would cause. In truth, so did I. At last with everyone standing in a semicircle at a suitable distance from the pot, I attempted to explain that what they were going to see would shock and possibly frighten them. I could see most didn't believe me so I told Eustace to go for it. With a wide grin, Eustace set a light to the cord fuse before running back to my side. At first, the animan were mildly surprised as the cord rapidly burned along its length, but nothing prepared them for what happened next.

Apart from Secuutus who had witnessed it when we fought the sorcerer, for everyone else it was the first time they had ever encountered the effects of - gunpowder! With a flash, a plume of smoke and a mighty bang, the little insignificant clay pot exploded, disintegrating and sending fragments flying in all directions. A second later all that remained was a fading cloud of smoke and a blackened pit in the ground. The initial alarm that ripped amongst the audience was swiftly followed by panic, each animan grasping for their weapons amidst screams and shouts of fear. Some of the town's leaders made to run, their flight only halted when their wits returned enough to see Eustace, Secuutus and I standing still and grinning at them, no fear on our faces. Then Eustace began to laugh, a laugh I imitated as the sight of the bewildered animan reeling in shock proved too humorous to bare. As the last echoes of the explosion faded and the shouting began. I readied myself for the onslaught.

'What in Terra's was that?' cried Pugnator.

'Sorcery!' came another cry.

Until now I had never heard an animan swear, but now I was hearing words of which I certainly had no understanding. It all made me feel more at home somehow. I held up my hands to calm the animan. The babble began to die down a decibel or two, falling to utter silence when Eustace appeared with one of the larger pots held carefully in his arms. Gently and precisely he placed the pot in the centre of the small blackened pit on the ground, his eyes never leaving the animan that surrounded him. The ex-soldier was enjoying himself immensely, an observation that formed questions in my mind as to the level of his sanity.

'You've all seen the power of just one small pot,' I began. 'Now please imagine what this large pot would do to your enemies. The pots are filled with a powder know only to Eustace and myself and we will not be passing on that knowledge. It's far too dangerous! So please don't ask.' Immediately several questions bombarded me so I repeated more forcefully. 'Please do not ask!'

The voices quietened instantly when Eustace laid out a new fuse cord, fear dumbing the animan. I smiled, I knew Eustace had no intention of lighting the fuse this time, the size of the pot and the powder it held would blow us all to the animan equivalent of Hell. Eustace then picked up a brand and now I admit, I too became scared. Was he really going to set off the charge? For a moment I thought he was until I saw the glint in his eyes, he was revelling in the animan's fear. That's it I thought, he's definitely nuts!

When my new American friend had sated his weird idea of fun, Eustace calmly extinguished the brand in the snow before retrieving the clay pot and returning it to the shack. Now all animan eyes were on me, wide with fear and suspicion. Some of the more timid town leaders were edging backwards, flight obviously upon their minds. I decided I had better explain quickly or the next thing I knew, I would be either dangling from a rope or torching my privates while tied to a stake on top of a huge fire. With slow and purposeful movements in case I startled anyone into rash action, I walked over and stood in the blackened circle. Once there I turned slowly, making sure I caught the eyes of everyone there before I spoke.

'Firstly I promise you all this is not magic nor sorcery. It's called science, it's a way of using what Terra has given us, but in a different way. There are no magic spells or demons, no wizards or anything that is not entirely natural. What Eustace and I have made is called gunpowder. You won't know what that means but it doesn't matter. What we have here is a weapon. A weapon that can be used alongside the Molotov cocktails that Pugnator has already produced, to swing the fortunes of the battle in our favour. However, I must point out that no matter win or lose, no more gunpowder will be made and none should try to copy what we've done. If we discover treachery in any form, Eustace and I will aid you no further. Is that understood?'

Silence.

'I repeat, it that understood?'

I waited till all had voiced their agreement and to be fair, I think they were all so terrified of what they had just witnessed, none would willing attempt to emulate our actions. But I knew time can overcome fear. Time, greed and a lust for power have dominated fear since time immemorial. I doubted the animan were that much different to the humans? I had to ensure that once the battle was over, all traces of how to manufacture gunpowder were obliterated. In this land where swords, spears and hand to hand combat reigned, gunpowder could be as powerful as the nuclear weapons Eustace and I were familiar with back home.

'One more warning,' I added as most of the animan made ready to leave, 'I will personally cut into little pieces anyone I find near this shack or trying to gain the secret of gunpowder. That is a promise. No matter who that animan is, I promise!'

I glared once more at all present, including Pugnator and even Eustace, radiating out my threat through my eyes and posture, leaving no one in any doubt of my words. Then I watched as the town leaders left, off to their homes with shock still lingering on them. As expected,

Pugnator, Secuutus, Adserviŏ, Silĕre and Eustace remained. Once we were alone, I calmed Pugnator and Silĕre, ensuring them I knew what I was doing and there was no evil intent. I explained my plans for how we would use the gunpowder and the *cocktails* to give General Crudelis the shock of his life.

Chapter Ten: Retreat

There was no attack from General Crudelis and his army that night, perhaps the failed attempt at a pincer movement had forced the general to take stock and devise another plan. Whether he knew it or not, a night without an attack proved more of a strain on the townsfolk than he realised. Many animan didn't sleep at all that night, most were wide-eyed with fear and expectation, anticipating an assault that didn't happen. In the darkest hours of the night, just before dawn, the smallest shadow or faintest sound threw the town into panic. The biggest threat that night was their own imagination.

Silĕre, Eustace and Adserviŏ and I made good use of the darkness, carrying out the plan we agreed earlier. It fell to Eustace and me to instruct the other two in what to do, each of us taking the utmost care to avoid detection by the soldiers. And trying not to blow ourselves to little pieces in the process. The plan was based on my experiences playing computer games. In the games, a device called a Claymore mine is used and it was these that gave me the idea. When our nocturnal activities concluded and we crept back into town, I couldn't help looking up at the black sky and wondering if the snow would destroy our plans. But there was little I could do about it so I headed for the publican and some sleep.

The next morning signs of activity increased within the camp, the weather had improved and I suspected the general was growing impatient. I knew he would attack soon but I didn't realise how soon. Breakfast was hardly over when the town lookouts called the alarm, the army was forming up and heading for the main barricade. I rushed to the nearest viewpoint, my staff tightly grasped in one hand, the evil knife in the other. Footsteps pounded up behind me and I turned to see Secuutus running to catch up with me. Shouted orders and commands told me the location of Pugnator but as yet I couldn't see Silĕre. I hurried over to Pugnator's side and looked out at the scene before me. Sure enough, troops were marching towards the town, the general leading the way, riding a huge charger. Everyone showed surprise, it was the custom in any battle to strike at dawn. But here was the enemy marching forward in the cold light of morning. I still hadn't swallowed my last bite of breakfast for Terra's sake!

I knew little of military tactics so had no idea of what to expect, and I knew the same could be said for the majority of animan standing at the defences with weapons ready. Fortunately, someone, probably Veterator or Eustace did understand military tactics.

Looking up I spotted figures moving about on the roofs of the buildings that formed part of the town's perimeter, it took me a moment or two to identify them as teenage children and female animan. As I stared I saw one young male bend down and lift a large rock, hefting it in his arms as he gauged its weight, an action quickly followed by the others. Then I understood. The battle experienced animan had been very busy organising the defences, any soldier coming too close the town would be met with a hail of rocks. Brilliant I thought, all we need now is boiling oil.

'Throwers to your positions,' called Pugnator as the soldiers drew near. I watched as about a dozen town animan ran forward, each clutching earthenware jugs with strips of cloth hanging from the rims. Behind them came other animan carrying more boxes and trays of the alcohol bombs, prepared and ready. I decided this was going to be a very interesting morning, made even better when Silĕre finally showed up and stood at my side. The Tigris femina had changed into something more comfortable, tight leather trousers, some form of woollen top and the briefest of waistcoats hugged her slim but firm body. Belts hung from her waist and over her shoulders, each holding either a sword or knife. I could see from a couple of her nicer attributes that she was feeling the cold. I must have stared too long because I received a sharp blow in my ribs from her elbow. I reluctantly returned my focus to the troops now forming into battle lines outside the town.

As I watched, the green clad figure of General Crudelis urged his mount forward and approached the town. He used no white flag or any such item to state his reason but in a situation such as this, it was obvious he wanted to talk. As he came nearer I could not help but admire the animan's nerve, he did not stop until he was well within range of spears and missiles from the town. This gesture did not go unnoticed by those watching, a brave ploy I thought, the general is showing all that he didn't fear the animan of Indutiae.

'Harken to me,' he called as his horse came to a gentle stop. 'Harken to me and hear what I say. I give you one last chance to surrender this town peacefully, one more opportunity for you to see sense and save your lives. Surrender to me and the town will be unharmed. You may go about your daily business, nothing will change. Eject the Ursidae and welcome my soldiers and you can continue to live in peace.'

'Peace?' shouted Pugnator in reply. 'Peace? How can there be peace? Once the Ursidae know you control Indutiae they will attack. They will bring their armies and raze the town to the ground, you and your animan will die with us. There can be no peace if Indutiae falls.'

'You are wrong! We, the mighty Lupus army, will protect you. The Ursidae dare not challenge my authority here, I will take control of this town and I will reinstate the nearby fort. This area will become a stronghold of the Lupus

Cast.' The general was fast becoming angry and it began to show in his speech.

'I will take this town, I will slaughter the Ursidae and you and your pitiful defences cannot stop me. Now, for the last time. Surrender and save your lives and your shambles of a town!'

That was a mistake I thought and sure enough, a moment later an angry rumble rose from the mouths of every Indutiae animan who heard the general. He had insulted the town in which they lived, a town they loved. With just those few words he had effectively buried any thoughts of surrender. Pugnator also heard the rumble, he turned his back on the general and hailed the animan of Indutiae.

'Do we surrender?'

'No!' came a barrage of angry voices.

Pugnator turned back to the general and gestured behind him at the town. 'There is your answer general. We reject your offer of surrender. We will fight for our *shambles* of a town!' said Pugnator quietly, his anger visible for the general to see.

The general stared at Pugnator for a moment before casting his eyes over the town's makeshift defences and the inhabitants of Indutiae. 'I am sorry. I am sorry for what will be your deaths,' he called to all who watched before turning his horse and slowly riding back to the lines of troops.

Pugnator watched the general's back, a frown upon his face. I could see a faint shadow of doubt on the Lupus town leaders face. But then, with a shrug, he shook himself together and turning, he shouted for all to hear.

'Everyone to your positions! Fighters to the defences. Throwers, make ready. Spears to your stations, fire watchers prepare water. Medicus, make ready your potions and bandages. The time has come to defend our town, our way of life and our freedom. Are you ready?'

His voice rose to a crescendo, 'Are you ready?'

The townsfolk of Indutiae screamed back their response, masculus and femina, Lupus and Ursidae, Tigris and Leo; all raised their voices in a shout of defiance. The town was ready. Hearing the roar from the townsfolk, I caught a brief glimpse of the general, for a second his ramrod straight back sagged, he knew he was facing a hard fight. But it was ephemeral, his posture swiftly straightened as he reached the front lines of his army, his long years as a soldier overcoming his misgivings. I turned back to the job in hand, wondering how a university lecturer had come to be here, facing an army of animan to defend a town of animan. It was then that I realised I had no place, no position to defend. Everyone in the town had a duty, a task to fulfil but what of me, where did I fit in? There were no answers so I did the only thing I could, I sought out Silĕre and took up a position at her side, Secuutus barely a step behind in joining us. We stood together and waited for the war to begin.

Then, in the stillness of the morning, a great roar erupted outside the town, the army was attacking. In a trice, my world was filled with shouts, screams of fear and the unmistakable sound of weapons made ready. I released the hidden blade and rushed to the nearest house the overlooked the battlefield, I needed to see for myself, my mind needed to see the truth of what I faced. From an upstairs window, I saw the lines of soldiers. I saw them charging at the town,

I could see their faces, I saw hate and fear, but in some, I saw anticipation and excitement. It seems even in the animan world, willing killers lurked. A vanguard of soldiers broke away from the main body of troops and rushed at the barricade. I left the house at a run and returned to my companions at the barricade, praying for courage as the first soldier reached the barricade. Others joined him as he began tearing at the structure, the plan was obvious; the soldiers intended destroying the obstacle and gaining clear access to the town. If that were to happen the town was doomed. With little thought, I scrambled over the barrier and leapt upon the soldiers in a frenzy of fear and fury. My feet caught the first soldier, knocking him down as I swung my staff at the head of another.

Instantly I was surrounded by Lupus soldiers, I stabbed and slashed with both staff and knife, spinning one way and another, striking with both ends of my staff. I kicked out using karate techniques and on one or two occasions I even managed to head butt an opponent. Every part of my body became a weapon as I now fought not for Indutiae but my very life. But it was hopeless, I was heavily outnumbered and I knew it, but there was nothing I could do but fight. With a primeval roar, I forced my body into a higher gear, trying to avoid the blades that flashed at me. I was aware that three shapes thudded down to the ground behind me, followed swiftly by shouts of something I could not grasp. I dared not turn away from the tide of soldiers facing me even though I knew my back was exposed. I fought on, expecting at any moment to feel the lethal pain of a sword piercing my body from behind. The pain did not come, instead visions of fury finally came into sight. It was Secuutus, Silĕre and Adserviŏ and a few other Tigris and Leo who were the shapes I saw earlier as they leapt from the barricade to my aid.

Now I was not alone, the surge of soldiers gradually halted, or rather they finally died. The group sent to attack and remove the barricade were quickly whittled down in number, their bodies now adding to the very blockade they sought to destroy. A horn blew, a signal from the Lupus army for their soldiers to retreat. A command happily obeyed as the few remaining would-be wreckers fled back to the safety of their comrades. Relief flooded into me and my strength flowed out, dropping my weapons on the ground at my feet, I hunched over, resting my hands upon my knee while my lungs gulped in air. Bodies littered the ground on which I stood, I could not believe the slaughter done by my hand even before my companions had joined me. How could any man unleash such violence I began to ask myself, before remembering I was no longer a man. I was an animan, an evolution of a Bengal tiger, a Tigris warrior. Suddenly from behind came a slap to my head. Upsurged my adrenaline in an immediate response as I spun to face this new attacker, only to find Silĕre glaring at me.

'How could you be so stupid?' demanded a very irate Secuutus, 'How could you put the town at such risk for your own entertainment?'

'What?' I exclaimed as I found all three of my companions glowering at me. 'I was defending the barricade. What the Terra is wrong with that?'

'Just think yourself luck our general is no military genius!' growled Secuutus. 'You gave him the perfect opportunity to wipe you out and destroy the barricade. If he ordered a charge while you messed around outside, he would have gained the advantage. Plus he now knows how desperate we are to protect that barricade; he'll throw all his forces at it and destroy our first-line defence in minutes. We had enough townsfolk guarding the fortification, we could have fought them off easily, but no, you had to leap into their midst and then need our help to get you out. Stupid!'

What could I say? I had no words to justify my actions, the build up of fear, anticipation and blood lust had all overcome me at that moment. I dropped my head in shame before returning to my position inside the barricade. The others followed me, anger in their posture, even the beautiful Silère stared at me with cold eyes. I pondered my actions but I knew I had let the battle lust grip me. My inner animal had risen to the fore. I had only thought to defend the important barricade, least that's what I told myself. My reasoning was to stop it being dismantled and laying the town wide open to attack. I had not given any thought or credit to the many town fighters or their abilities to defend their town. I could not label my actions as courageous or heroic, but perhaps I should lay the blame on arrogance and impetuosity. Or a basic inherent desire to kill. This was a lesson I needed to learn.

No more was said on the matter, though I did receive a glaring look from Pugnator, for at that very moment the general charged again. The ground shook as hundreds of soldiers began to run, battle cries and shouts of encouragement ripping through the cold clear air. The sound drew little whimpers and sobs of terror from behind me as I watch the charge approach. It wasn't the brave charge often seen on television, in fact to my mind it appeared somewhat comical. In the lead rode the general on his horse, followed by his Lupus army. However, the general could not gallop his horse else he would leave his troops behind. This time he sort of ambled, reining back his horse to maintain pace with his charging soldiers. Somehow the sight didn't quite fit, leading a military charge at a trot. Nonetheless, the army was attacking Indutiae and any humour was instantly replaced with apprehension, excitement and fear.

I tensed as the army reached the town walls and the battle began to rage. Swords flashed, spears flew and animan on both sides died. My position to one side of the barricade soon became a focal point for assault, immediately throwing me into the battle. A soldier had scaled the barricade and lunged at me, but I had seen him coming. As he leapt so I drove my bladed staff into his gut, his momentum carrying him over my head before sliding off my blade and landing at the feet of the furious townsfolk. An array of weapons rained fatally down on the soldier as I turned to face the next attack. This time two soldiers loomed over the structure in front of me. I thrust my blade into the chest of one before whipping the staff around to smash into the face of the other, knocking him backwards to fall amongst his comrades.

A brief respite but now the barricade swarmed with soldiers, plunging myself and fellow defenders into the fight of our lives. Standing with Secuutus at my shoulder, I caught brief glimpses of Silĕre as she whirled and danced, her blades cutting through the enemy like a scythe. Pugnator ran between areas of fierce fighting, issuing commands while taking his fair share of lives, Adserviŏ right at his side. Fighting now raged all around the town as the defenders fought and died to defend and repel the invaders.

I remained in position as the first line of soldiers faltered in front of the barrage of weapons that awaited them, animan died on both sides but the soldiers fared the worst. Bodies lay strewn at the perimeter, in some cases piled two or three high. Again the horn blew to signal the next assault as a new wave stepped forward in readiness. The remaining soldiers of the first attack staggered back from the defences. Relief at retaining their lives, they hurried away back to the safety of their main army. Some helping wounded comrades, others using their weapons as walking aids, many wept as they retired from the slaughter. The battlefield holds no joy, no future and no compassion for any individual, survival is the only goal. Those behind the walls and barricades did not escape the carnage either, bodies of loved ones, fathers, brothers and sons lay where they had fallen in defence of all they held dear. With a heavy heart, Pugnator called for the bodies to be removed, the town would grieve later, if it survived.

As soon as the exhausted soldiers moved out of the way, so the general sent forth the next wave of fresh Lupus troops, eager with the bravery of youth they charged towards the town. Again the townsfolk rose to defend their homes, Tigris and Leo standing against the enemy alongside Lupus and Ursidae. I stood once more with my companions, each watching over the other as the soldiers trampled their dead or wounded comrades in their commitment. Then we were fighting again, soldiers poured against the main barricade while others peeled off to assail the smaller defences. Pugnator screamed for more reinforcements to help fend off the attack while we defended the main entrance to the town. The fighting was vicious, no animan giving quarter, no pleas for mercy heeded. My arms began to feel the strain of wielding my staff, stabbing at one end, clubbing with the other. I was tiring and I knew my companions and those of Indutiae were also flagging as we fought soldier after soldier in a wild melee of survival.

The violence and loathing on both sides appalled me, even as I ripped open the stomach of a young soldier. I could never have envisioned such ferocity as I saw that day, my human side not believing what I saw, what I did. Another soldier reared up directly in front of me. I could see the terror in his eyes, the sweat on his brow even as he shakily thrust his sword at my gut, the terror replaced by horror as my blade slashed deep across his throat. All around me cries of hate mingled with those of despair and pain. Animan killed and animan died by the score. The futility of it all hit me, spurred by the look of desperation on the face of Pugnator as he fought furiously even while screaming commands at his defenders. We may not win this battle I concluded. I didn't want to die, I doubt anyone did, but I didn't want to die here, in this land, far away from my home. To add to my misery I then heard the sound of the military horn blowing. The general was calling back this second of soldiers as the third line of attackers prepared. My brief relief turning quickly to despair as I rested, knowing the next attack would be by fresh soldiers against the already exhausted defenders of Indutiae.

Amidst my misery I heard my name called.

'Now is the time Harry. Get ready.' The voice of Pugnator.

Oh, good grief! I thought to myself, I had completely forgotten the plan whilst otherwise occupied trying to stay alive. Quickly I made my way to a good vantage point to view the battlefield before me. 'Throwers to your positions,' I shouted, the command echoing around the town as it was relayed by the animan, ensuring everyone heard it. Of course there were no mobile (cell) phones nor any radios. Each command or order was repeated loudly by all who could hear it. A system I admit worked very well, it was not unknown in human military history, so I was not surprised to witness it here.

My mind snapped back to the job at hand as I heard the reply, 'Throwers ready.'

There was little time to waste, the new wave of soldiers were almost at the town walls. I just hoped our plan had escaped being trampled under the feet of soldiers as the third wave charged towards us.

'Light up!' I called.

'Throw!' I screamed and watched as flaming jugs and pots threw through the air like shooting stars. Within seconds a wall of fire erupted in the faces of the oncoming soldiers. Screams filled the air as the clay pots broke apart and released the liquid alcohol and ignited with a whoosh. The burning liquid splashed over all within range. A minute later I saw clouds of smoke and flame before the sound of explosions reached my ears. As the flaming liquid spread over the ground, it ignited the half-buried pots of gunpowder placed during the night. Each pot exploded, sending shrapnel shooting through the air, maiming or killing all within the deadly radius. The flames and explosions caught the wave of soldiers, blowing them to bits or removing limbs and leaving gaping wounds. I knew which way of dying I would prefer. Many of the screams were instantly silenced. As the smoke began to fade and the flames died down, dozens of black and torn bodies lay writhing in agony or lying still upon the cold ground.

The whole sequence had taken just minutes but the final result was devastating. With no casualties amongst the townsfolk, almost an entire platoon of

Lupus soldiers had been destroyed. Silence fell, disbelief taking its toll on the animan who had never witnessed the like before. Townsfolk and soldiers stood like statues, too traumatised to even move as the sound of explosions faded into the distance. I feared I had become death I thought, as Robert Oppenheimer once said back in the world of humans. Of course, his weapon is far greater than a few Molotov cocktails and a few pounds of gunpowder, but here, in this land, the result was the same.

The silence was broken by a single horn. The horn blew loud and long in the stillness, a note that called the Lupus soldiers back from the hell in front of them. A seemingly melancholy note that echoed horror and sadness. The animan world had changed today, and not for the better. No town defender cheered as the soldiers quietly withdrew, no one had the voice to give as they gazed upon the blackened bodies strewn upon the once white ground. I knew we had won the day but somehow I felt dirty, my soul as black as the burnt bodies. I turned from the wall and slowly made my way to the publican, I needed to put that potent and lethal animan alcohol to far better use. I needed a drink.

There were no more attacks that day, one lone soldier had approached the town and requested a truce. Pugnator quietly agreed, knowing the soldiers wished to collect their dead, and soon after a large group of unarmed soldiers silently removed the bodies under the sad and stunned eyes of Indutiae. The atmosphere in the town had changed, animan who saw me coming would step aside, and many avoided looking me in the eye. I sensed a fear growing within the town, fear of me. I felt their dread like a blow to my soul.

I had acted as I did to help protect their town and save lives, but now I was feared more than the enemy. Only Secuutus treated me as usual, no fear or worries appeared to bother my ex-rider companion. He had witnessed gunpowder before though not on such a huge scale, and he didn't care, he was alive thanks to me and that was what mattered. Eustace of course, being like myself, a human in animan body couldn't see what all the fuss was about. I realised then how callous and accustomed to killing we humans had become.

Several days passed and no more attacks, the snow continued to fall periodically and the town gradually began to heal itself. The animan still eyed me with fear but now they smiled as if finally admitting to themselves that my actions had been for their benefit. I had stopped the fighting and saved many of their lives. Though peace had returned, most of us realised it would be brief, it wouldn't last because the general had lost face and needed to restore his reputation. Plenty of activity had been witnessed within the quiet camp but none so far that gave evidence of another pending assault. Pugnator paced the publican restlessly, the frown on his face displaying his concentration. The days of peace had unsettled the town leader, I could see he worried how we would cope with further attacks. Eustace and I had been busy gathering the ingredients for more gunpowder, but now the general was aware of the weapon, what would he do next? He had to do something else he would lose the respect of his troops, and most likely his command. Pugnator worried, he worried over this respite and he worried over the general. Pugnator desperately sought information, he needed to know what the general was planning. Finally, after much more pacing, he arrived at a decision, one I knew I wouldn't like.

'I must know what steps the general will make next,' he began. 'Have we won? Will he leave us alone? No, I don't think so. I think he will - he must attack again but how? I am blind here, I can't make plans or form a strategy without information. Your *weapons* Harry, have changed the whole established methods of war. We have entered a whole new era of military tactics and quite honestly, I'm out of my depth. So I'm asking for volunteers to spy on the general and discover what he plans to do next. Harry, who will go with you?'

Huh? Have I just been volunteered against me will? It appeared I had. I didn't argue as in a way, this new situation was entirely of my own doing. Therefore, I was the obvious choice, like it or not. Before answering I had to think, Secuutus would be ideal but he now had interests within Indutiae or one interest at least. Eustace was required to continue the production of gunpowder so he was out, Adserviŏ was an unknown quantity and that meant I had but one choice left, Silĕre. My feelings for Silĕre were growing and I wasn't sure if I wanted to put her into danger. Of course I didn't say that, she'll kill me! But in truth, she was the obvious choice, a capable Tigris warrior with all the knowledge and skills to undertake such a task. It had to be her. I had to stop this human trait of trying to protect the little woman. This woman didn't need any protection from me. Indeed, the reverse was true, I needed her to protect me! My decision made, my eyes involuntary turned to rest upon her face, and discovered her golden eyes already watching me. As if reading my mind, Silĕre stood and nodded to both Pugnator and me, she agreed, as I knew she would.

'That's settled then. Silĕre and Harry will act as my eyes and ears and try to uncover the general's new plans. If Indutiae is to survive, we must know his next move. He has retreated for the moment, but it will not last long.'

Pugnator then turned to look directly at Silĕre. 'Get the information I need and if you can, keep Harry safe please, we may need his strange knowledge again. As a Tigris warrior, I charge you with this responsibility.'

I realised immediately what Pugnator had said. He had acknowledged Silĕre as a full Tigris warrior and given her a task, the first since her disgrace and mutilation. Silĕre now had the opportunity to regain her status, she knew it and so did Pugnator, along with Secuutus and me of course. No one else knew the real reason she couldn't speak. Pugnator must have guessed the truth and his words carried much more weight than the others present could know. The Tigris Cast are renowned fighters and thus they make their fortune, if they survive life as mercenaries, bodyguards and assassins. However, if one fails in their set task, the punishment for a failure is the removal of their tongue. An unmistakable sign to all potential employers that this Tigris warrior has failed. A failure with serious consequences would result in the painful death of the Tigris. With the loss of their tongue, a Tigris may live but would find getting employment very difficult, no one wanted to hire a failure. By setting Silĕre a task, even babysitting me, he had paid her the highest compliment, something she would never forget.

I just worried how I could concentrate with such an attractive babysitter in charge . . .

Chapter Eleven: At Risk

Silĕre and I left that night under cover of a dark leaden sky. This time we came across no tracks in the snow to distract us from the camp, and reached its perimeter with relative ease. If you could call crawling through the snow on your belly easy? The closer we came to the tented military encampment, the more we could see and hear. Again I noted how useful it was having the heightened senses of a tiger. I shadowed Silĕre, matching her prowess as we snuck past the first row of tents. She had made it quite plain that she was in charge and I should just shut up and follow. I smiled, I do like a dominant woman, or in this case, a Tigris femina.

Approaching voices caused us both to flatten further down into the snow, keeping our bodies outline at ground level. It was hard going, avoiding sentries, restless soldiers and the glow from cooking fires, aware our survival depended on it. The voices trailed off into the darkness so I unclenched my buttocks and kept moving. The army camp was as expected, tents erected in neat lines of the military, but the locations of fires appeared to be random. I had expected more order, more formality. It made our task harder as one wrong move would place us within a patch of illumination for all to see. I prayed Silĕre's skill was up to the task, I was relying on her entirely. My knowledge of sneaking around military camps in the dark was limited, to say the least. Not much call for that pastime in Manchester, besides the city had enough odd pastimes anyway. Stealthily we crawled on, keeping to the areas of shadow and darkness, the uniformed figures around us unaware of our proximity.

Before we left Indutiae, it was suggested we disguise ourselves by donning uniforms taken from the bodies of dead soldiers. A suggestion quickly rejected as neither Silĕre nor myself could ever hope to pass as a Lupus, we were much taller than any of the Lupus Cast and I'm sure Silĕre's curves would give her away to a bunch of soldier's very quickly. Soldiers were randy sods no matter what race Cast or breed, they could spot female shapes anywhere.

As night deepened, many of the soldiers were retiring to the warmth of their blankets, Silĕre and I lay in the cold snow and waited. In the darkness, a hush settled over the camp, the only noises came from the snores, grunts and farts common wherever males congregate. The footfalls and quiet greetings of the guards and voices coming from what I judged to be the generals tent were the only other sounds in the night. Raising from the ground, we made our way nearer at a crouch, dodging from tent to tent silently. We kept to the darkness and avoided any areas where the guards stood watch, a difficult task as sentry fires had been built up to combat the cold, sending out a dangerous flickering light. For some strange and random reason, the realisation that the Lupus army used no dogs came as a blessing. I had no idea why but I was thankful for the absence of even more canine noses.

Noiselessly we approached the general's tent, dodging the guards had been relatively easy on a cold and miserable night such as this. Anyone who has stood around for hours in the cold and dark will understand that concentration wanes quickly. The general's tent was situated in the centre of the camp, torches burning at each corner, lighting the perimeter and illuminating two guards who stood shivering at its entrance. The tent was larger and appeared far more comfortable than those of the poor regulars. The material was of better quality and thicker than normal army issue. I could see a pipe which I took to be a chimney from a campaign stove poking through the fabric via a leather rimmed hole. The general at least was warm, a fact further testified by the gentle pink glow that emanated through the material. I envied the general, jealous of his warm tent as I lay in the cold snow under a black sky.

Silĕre and I remained hidden alongside one of the lines of tents that surround the general, we couldn't approach any nearer because of the guards and the light of the torches. But now we were close enough to catch snippets of conversation. It became apparent that the general was holding a meeting with his senior staff officers. Most of the discussion was too muffled or quietly spoken for us to follow but one particular thread immediately caught our attention. The general was questioning one of his officers, asking when the reinforcements would arrive. Both our ears shot up, figuratively speaking of course.

' . . . . Runners have been sent back to base, from there they will forward your commands before procuring horses and riding out to notify other bases we require assistance. I anticipate less than a week before we see the arrival of reinforcements, the rest will arrive as and when they can. It's difficult to gain any speed of travel in these conditions, but I doubt the town of Indutiae will be going anywhere,' reported one of the officers.

'Good, good,' replied the voice of the general. 'I will not tolerate my commands being refused by those horrid Indutiae animan. Lupus living with Ursidae? It must not be allowed to continue. I want that town and all its inhabitants crushed.'

We had heard enough and rather than outstay our welcome, Silĕre and I slipped away and out of the camp with as much haste as safety would allow. I knew we needed to get back to the town and report our discovery as soon as humanly . . ., sorry, as soon as animanly possible. I forget occasionally. It still took some time for us to creep out of the camp. Although quiet, the guards remained on watch and it would only take one vigilant guard and our escape and our lives would be forfeit. Crouching low where we could, slinking on our bellies at times, avoiding the light of fires and cold guards as we stole through the night. Ultimately, and unbelievably, we crossed the boundaries of the camp and fled into the darkness. We remained cautious, we were not home safely yet. Keeping low, I followed Silère as she found our previous footprints and used the same tracks to return to the town. Any soldier coming across our tracks would not be able to discern which way the footprints led. A little confusion in the enemy ranks could only be a good thing I thought.

Without mishap or detection, Silère and I finally reached Indutiae. Pugnator and some of the town animan were waiting for us, eager for news. Yet when I informed him of the pending arrival of reinforcements, Pugnator's eagerness evaporated quickly.

'So we'll be safe from another attack for a few days,' he began. 'After that, we will face far greater numbers of Lupus than ever before. They have bases scattered liberally over this land, it won't take long to gather a huge force of soldiers, a force so large our defeat is guaranteed. We cannot defend against such forces.' Pugnator paused, 'We must surrender or all will be slaughtered.'

Even though I was not an Indutiae resident, I shared the fear and despair of those present, even Silĕre appeared defeated. We had to come up with another plan, even with gunpowder and alcohol bombs aiding the swords and spears of the town fighters, there was no perceivable way we could hold off a larger force. Indutiae was only a town, it did not have the population or the defences of a city. Indutiae would fall to General Crudelis. That was now certain. I needed to think, I needed to find Secuutus and Eustace. I feared it may be time we moved on. I know it sounds cowardly but in truth, it wasn't our fight. Me and Eustace were not even true animan, we were humans in a different body. Not human maybe, but Silĕre and Secuutus were my friends, my new family, I had to talk this over with them.

I left Pugnator and his fellow's and went off in search of Secuutus. I knew where he would be and that fact made my choice even harder. I had not asked Silĕre to follow me but she did, she was astute enough to know what I was thinking. I could see the same thoughts on her face. I was pleased she choose to accompany me, but I still didn't have any clue which way she would decide. Stay and help the doomed town or flee with me to safer pastures, I didn't know. I wasn't even sure which choice I would make, so I couldn't second guess the wishes of my Tigris companion.

Soon we came to the little house where I suspected I would find Secuutus. I hammered on the door and waited. After a short time, the door was open by an Ursidae femina, still in her nightclothes. I asked if Secuutus was there and upon receiving confirmation, I asked to speak with him. We were invited in and asked to wait while she roused her 'companion' who remained asleep. She was wrong and I knew it, for a moment later Secuutus appeared from just behind what I took to be the bedroom door, already dressed and more importantly, armed. Secuutus's life had not allowed undisturbed sleep, anyone who has fought as an outlaw would sleep with one eye open. I knew he would have woken even before we knocked on the door, it was no surprise to me to see him with a sword in his hand.

'Oh, er, sorry Harry, Silĕre. I didn't know who to expect. No one is supposed to know I'm here.' Secuutus sheathed his sword and gestured for us to sit, there were only two chairs available so I paused and looked at our host but she gestured for me to use the chair. As Silĕre and I took our seats, Secuutus introduced us to his new friend, 'Harry, Silĕre, this is Socium Vidui, we are . . .um . . together. She is known as Soci.'

When the introductions were complete and Secuutus had given Soci a brief account of our friendship, and I mean brief, the time came for serious talking. Soci supplied some drinks, a type of hot fruit juice, and a pleasant change from the battery acid served in the publican.

I began to explain the situation with frequent nods of reinforcement from Silĕre, I told Secuutus about our trip out to the army camp, news that caused some annoyance to Secuutus because he had not been invited. I pacified him with a simple glance at Soci, a glance that said he had someone else to think of now, and for once Secuutus understood. That out of the way, I continued to tell what we had overheard in the generals' tent, what Pugnator had said and then I told him what was on my mind.

'Leave?' he roared, 'How can we just run away and abandon Indutiae and its animan? We - I have made a home here, I can't leave! Surely you and Pugnator can come up with a plan? You always have a plan. What about some of your magic? The magic you call science, whatever it is, can't you find a way? You helped Janiz and his father the king, now help us.'

'That's just it,' I replied. 'I don't know how to help and I have no plan. We would need an army to . . . . '

'To what? What army?' demanded Secuutus as the eyes of Soci and Silĕre bored into me.

'I've just had a thought, hang on while I think. How far is it to the Ursidae side of this land?' I finally asked.

'What? What has my Cast got to do with the town? You said we need army so what have the Ursidae . . . . . Oh, I see.' Secuutus had joined my train of thought as he lapsed into a contemplative silence.

Secuutus was a stranger here as was I but Soci was not. The little Ursidae femina stared at Secuutus for a moment, muttered a few words to him and receiving a nod of approval. I could see her composing her thoughts before finally giving us the information required.

'The nearest Ursidae outpost is but two days from here, roughly the same distance away as the Lupus base. The distance was deliberate because if one Cast was closer, it would be deemed unbalanced and unfair. So a distance was agreed in order to maintain the neutrality of Indutiae. I have a brother there and occasionally I manage to get away and visit him. I know the location very well and can offer instructions. My brother is called, Fortis Maior. If you can get to him, he will be able to help.'

When Soci finished speaking, a discussion followed as to who should go, Secuutus obviously demanding it should be him. But Soci disagreed. 'If you were to be captured by the Ursidae, they would take you for a spy. You are not known and have no knowledge of this area, they would suspect you were in the pay of either Indutiae or worse, General Crudelis.' Soci paused a moment before adding, 'I don't want you to go, I don't want to lose you.'

Secuutus shoulders slumped in defeat, I knew he would not leave Soci now and in a way, I was pleased for him. He needed someone other than a fellow warrior and ex-rider, he needed a mate. And it appeared he had found one. Silĕre on the other hand was a different matter, I felt her tug at my arm and turned to find her nodding furiously while pointing at herself then at me. Her meaning was obvious, she wanted to go, and she wanted to go with me. In moments the matter was settled, Secuutus would remain here and help strengthen the defences while Silĕre and I went off on our travels again, this time to the Ursidae army. I still had doubts though, what if we didn't make it, what if we were captured by the Lupus or the Ursidae didn't believe us? There were too many 'ifs' in this plan, there had to be another way. Indutiae was just a small town, how could it defend against a united army of Lupus?

A Light Bulb moment occurred!

I had an idea and I quickly bounced it off the others. 'What if the animan of Indutiae took over the old fort?

It's not far and you could sneak the townsfolk over in small groups during the night while we go for help. At least there they would have a better chance of survival, of defending themselves.'

I was immediately but politely informed my idea was not the best I'd ever had. Why leave the town we were actively trying to defend? Indutiae was their home and although there was only one resident in the room, Secuutus and Silĕre made the argument for them. Upon hearing their views on my plan, I concluded they were possibly right. Nonetheless, I still considered the idea to be sound and asked Secuutus to talk to Pugnator, find out what he thought. I would have sought him out myself but our time was short, Silĕre and I had to get to the Ursidae army before the Lupus reinforcements arrived and sacked the town of Indutiae.

Following a full day's sleep and loaded down with supplies, Silĕre and I set off to find the Ursidae base that night. We had to begin our travels under the cover of darkness else we would never get past the Lupus. The general's messengers didn't have to avoid enemy detection in their own territory and they had a day's start over us. Silĕre and I moved as quickly as we could through the snow in an attempt to make up time, constantly watching for Lupus patrols and of course, the odd wild animal. I still hadn't forgotten the sight of the huge lynx Secuutus and I had encountered on our arrival here. While I hoped the Hyaenidae didn't roam in these parts, the lynx and the Gulo gulo did and I didn't want to encounter either of them. A light flurry of snow fell as the night grew colder, it seemed I was destined to be constantly cold in this land. What I wouldn't give to be back in the warm climes of Regnum, or Manchester for that matter. I know it sounds impossible but this place was even colder than the Mancunian city.

Once we gained some distance from the Lupus camp, we allowed ourselves to relax as dawn arrived, and now travelling in daylight, our speed increased. The area was thickly wooded and night travel had resulted in plenty of battered noses as one walked into a tree in the darkness. I must point out that the battered nose belonged to me. Silĕre it seems, managed to avoid such obstacles, she had, after all, lived in this area whereas I arrived via a small jade box. Our rate of travel was slow, even in daylight. Blundering through snow and forest undergrowth was definitely more a matter of endurance rather than speed. Roots and fallen branches snagged at our feet, unseen under the blanket of snow. Rocks tripped us, bushes blocked our way causing time consuming detours. Drifts of deep snow tricked us as we sank waist-deep into what we thought was solid ground and all the while, our senses were alert for danger.

All in all, it was an exhausting journey. I suspected the Lupus messengers had an easier time. I didn't doubt they followed established paths in familiar territory. Not so for Silĕre and me, we travelled a different road. We had to avoid Lupus patrols and as we neared the front line so to speak, we also had to watch for the Ursidae.

Finally to my relief night came and Silĕre indicated we should rest. I pretended reluctance but falling to the ground panting belied my charade. It was so cold we decided to risk a fire. We dug a pit in the snow and surrounded it with a ring of built up snow in an attempt to hide the light from unwelcome eyes. I heated some food while Silĕre gathered pine boughs for a mattress. Sleeping in such cold was dangerous, so by placing a barrier between our bodies and the frozen ground, we might survive the night. The meal consumed, we settled down to get as much sleep as the temperature would allow.

We both carried blankets of sorts but they were too thin to offer much warmth and it wasn't long before we were huddled together, combining our body heat. Now things became uncomfortable, for me anyway. I was lying under a blanket in close proximity to a stunning Tigris femina, a beautiful woman in any language. My body stirred, no matter how hard I tried to blank my mind, the form lying beside me was causing a reaction. Which was only to get worse.

Silĕre quietly sat up and removed her blanket before crawling under mine, huddling close, and using both blankets to cover us both. Now the proximity was overwhelming, basically we were in bed together. I understood Silĕre's actions, now we had each other's body heat and two blankets covering us. It seemed to be working because I was starting to sweat. I lay still as a rock, not daring to move lest I portrayed my feelings as Silĕre cuddled even closer. I felt her arm move over me and come to a rest just below my belt. I froze, if that's the right word, it was to avoid freezing that led to this situation. Silĕre began to move her hand downwards, down to rest on my groin. Feeling my hardness she gave a little squeeze, then another. Oh crap! There was nothing I could do, I was helpless.

I reached down and laid my hand over hers, pressing it down harder while my lust grew. I expected her to move away then, perhaps she hadn't realised what she had done? But Silĕre squeezed again. It was too much, within moments I had moved over to lay on top of Silĕre. I didn't know the accepted animan procedure for what I was going to do but Silĕre grabbed me tight and urged me closer. Silĕre reacted with the same passion I was feeling, a brief fumble with clothing and we were both naked from the waist down. The cold and dangers of the night were forgotten as Silĕre opened and I entered.

Dawn arrived to find us up and ready to move. Nothing was said about what happened, several times, during the night, Silĕre didn't appear to be the romantic sort and as I valued my wellbeing, I wisely kept my mouth shut. Soon we were travelling again, treading carefully over the snow covered ground. We travelled that day and the next before finally sighting what we hoped was the Ursidae army camp. Warily we remained under cover of the tree line and examined the area in front of us. On a small hill in a clearing stood a stockade, not a huge fort but it appeared a capable deterrent against an attack by any force smaller than a good sized army. Wooden palisades ringed the structure and four towers stood sentinel over a group of buildings nestled within its defences. From our hidden position, we watched as Ursidae figures went about their daily routines. Soldiers drilled while others patrolled both inside and outside the walls. From within the stockade rose trails of smoke indicated fires for cooking and warmth. Two long buildings suggested barracks, I could see what I assumed to be the commanders quarters and scattered about were several smaller buildings, blacksmiths and armoury probably accounting for two, others were stores and the like I concluded. All in all, it looked a well maintained and organised military base. It also appeared somewhat unfriendly.

We watched from the trees for some time, occasionally I would glance at Silĕre or her at me. Both of us hoping the other would come up with some plan that would avoid our being slaughtered on sight as soon as we emerged from the trees. It was cold and my muscles were growing stiff, if we didn't move soon, I feared I wouldn't be able to. However, the decision was taken from our hands as a voice suddenly sounded behind us.

'Get up and don't try for your weapons, you'll be dead before you can stand!'

With a whispered curse at being discovered, I did as bid, Silĕre also rising slowly, her hand well away from her sword. I had the sense of mind to use my staff to help me to my feet, hoping I could pass it off as a walking aid. It was a trick I had used before so it couldn't harm trying it again, could it? With both Silĕre and I standing, me leaning heavily on my staff, two soldiers moved in front of us, weapons held ready. Another stood right behind us, rested his sword on my shoulder with obvious intent while our weapons were removed. They found my evil knife but ignored my staff. Silĕre was none too gently relieved of her armoury of swords and knives. At first, I thought she was going to try to break free, but the soldiers were too thorough in their actions. I took the moment to examine our captors and saw the stocky build, stumpy legs and faint brown fur of the Ursidae. Heavily armed in their brown uniforms, their every action portraying professionalism and expertise. Any escape attempt would be immediately fatal.

The soldiers grunted for us to begin walking towards their base, nothing else was said. No threats or attempts at intimidation, no curses or snide remakes, just the one simple command to move. They didn't even give the obligatory shove to help us on our way. It was very unsettling, a silent enemy is far more frightening than one who yells and threatens. Silĕre and I did as we were told and headed for the base, with me limping as best I could. I had to keep the pretence up, if I forgot which leg I was limping on or showed any disruption in my stride, I would lose my staff, and most likely my head.

Leaving the trees, we walked across clear snow ground for a distance before the guards ordered us to move to our right. We did so without question but a quick glance from Silĕre mirrored my thought, why? Another fifty paces and we were told to move to our left. Now I understood, I concluded there were traps or something similar set into the ground and the soldiers knew the path through. It was a point I needed to remember, any escape would have to include these hidden traps. Unfortunately, it's one thing knowing the traps are there, it's quite another matter knowing where they exactly were. Under the covering of snow, these traps lay invisible and would be highly effective in hindering any attacking force, or two escaping Tigris.

A few more changes of direction and we were at the main gates, still no words from our guards other than giving direction. I hobbled and even managed a hopefully convincing stumble as Silĕre and I were led towards a small building. As yet, no one had asked who we were or why we were there. We had merely been disarmed and escorted into the Ursidae base. Other soldiers and inhabitants of the base stared as we moved across the interior but still no one spoke, no derisive shouts or cat calls, no sneers or even questions. It was all getting very damn un-nerving. I had at least expected some form of reaction, but there was none. Finally, one of our guards opened the door of a small building and gestured us in before securely locking it behind us. We were well and truly caught.

It didn't take long for our cat eyes to become accustomed to the dark of the room in which we had been imprisoned. Looking around I could see it was a wheat store and mill. Sacks of wheat were piled high against the walls and in the middle of the floor stood a crude but functional grinding mill. Scattered about the mill, the overspill of ground flour lay upon the ground. It seemed strange to me, why had we been locked in a milling room? Did the base not have a jail? Or more worrying, were prisoners not expected to live long enough to require a jail? One thing was for sure, we would soon find out as outside, the sound of footsteps approaching could be heard. Seconds later the door opened and daylight streamed in, making me blink against the sudden brightness. Four Ursidae soldiers entered the room, the deportment of one soldier indicated his authority.

'I am commander Aequus, I am in charge of this Ursidae military base. Who are you?' he asked.

I looked at him, trying to decide how much I should tell him. The stocky Ursidae was dressed in a darker brown than the soldier's uniforms, and some form of insignia glittered on his chest. I must have delayed my reply too long for one of the soldiers stepped towards me, his sword coming up in the first real threatening move I had seen since being captured.

'I am Harry of the Tigris Cast and this is Silēre, also of the Tigris Cast,' I responded quickly.

'I can already see your Cast and your names mean nothing to me. Why were you hiding and covertly watching our base? Are you spies? I must hear your reasons or you will go to your graves quickly, your purpose unknown and you forgotten,' growled the commander in a tone that let all know he meant his words.

'We come seeking your help' I explained. 'The Lupus army is holding siege to Indutiae, which as you will know, is a neutral town on the border between your two territories. As we are neither Lupus nor Ursidae, we were tasked to plead for your assistance in this matter. The matter of keeping Indutiae neutral for the sake of both sides.'

'And why should the Lupus be sieging Indutiae? The officer in commander, whom I believe is General Crudelis, knows Indutiae is not to be touched,' asked commander Aequus. 'Both the Ursidae and the Lupus councils agreed long ago and signed a treaty stating that Indutiae would be open to all Casts, why is Crudelis attempting to break this agreement?'

'I cannot answer for the general I'm afraid, he caught the town completely by surprise and demanded we surrender to his command,' I replied. 'He also declared there would be a Lupus king, so perhaps he needs Indutiae as a base for advancement into your territory. I don't know his reasons but that sounds the most plausible explanation.'

The commander stood just inches from my face, his eyes boring into mine. Although he stood at least a head shorter than me, his posture radiated strength and power. I wouldn't like to face him in battle I decided, but I knew the threat of a Lupus invasion would be the most likely hook on which to catch his full attention. But would he believe me I wondered? After several intense moments, the commander turned from me at stared at Silĕre.

'Do you confirm this report?' he asked my mute companion.

Silĕre stared straight back at the commander and gave one clear nod of her head.

'Answer me femina!' shouted Aequus.

I quickly interrupted, knowing what I had to say would shame Silĕre, but this animan would see through any lies. 'My companion cannot speak.'

'Ahh,' sighed the commander knowingly. 'So it is with you I must converse. But why have you brought a failed assassin? I thought your Cast shunned such animan?'

'She strives to regain her honour,' I said. 'Also her sword arm remains useful in a task such as this.'

'Can you trust her?'

'Yes,' I stated clearly.'

'Well, I hope your trust is not ill-advised. It is no matter, the actions of

Crudelis are of far greater concern. Come with me and tell me all you know of the situation.' With that, the Ursidae commander strode out of the grain mill with the three soldiers escorting Silĕre and me in close formation. Our plight, I concluded, was still to be decided.

Chapter 12: Escape

Silĕre and I were led to the commander's quarters where we were questioned, grilled and thoroughly investigated by Aequus and his senior officers for over an hour. Once they had gleaned all the information we had, we were marched, or in my case, limped back to the grain store and again locked in. We had been given no indication of the Ursidae plans or even if they believed our story, we were simply dismissed and imprisoned.

I was furious and from the agitated actions of Silĕre, I guessed she too was mad as hell. I wisely left her alone while I gave thought to our problems. If the commander didn't believe me or had decided not to put his army at risk by riding to the assistance of Indutiae, then we desperately needed to get back and let the others know. If Pugnator was relying on help coming, he would not formulate alternative plans of defence. General Crudelis would overrun the town in no time. Soon Silĕre stopped her pacing and sat beside me in the gloom of the miniature mill, both of us in despair at our inaction and helplessness. There was nothing we could do until we knew the commander's plans, if he intended aiding Indutiae or ignoring their plight. All we could do was wait.

After a couple of hours had passed, the door of the mill flew open and there stood the commander, again flanked by a guard of three soldiers. With a stern expression, Aequus entered the building and stood facing us, well actually, he stood facing me.

'I have decided to assist Indutiae against the Lupus army. Not for the townsfolk or the town, but because Crudelis has broken our treaty and must be put in his place. Left alone he would surely attempt to invade and conquer the Ursidae, and I refuse to allow that to happen.'

The commander drew himself up, straightened his shoulders and turned to leave. I made ready to stand and follow him but a soldier moved to block me. Seeing this, the commander turned back to me and said. 'You two will stay here. I will leave guards so please don't do anything to antagonise them, they will have orders to stop you, permanently if required. I'm sorry but I don't know either of you, and she,' he said pointing at Silĕre, 'has already been proved a failure, for what reason I don't know or care. However, it means I cannot trust you. You will remain here until this matter is sorted, then and only then will I consider your situation. Goodbye.'

With that the commander and his guards left, locking the door behind them. We were alone in the gloom again, broken only by a small oil lamp, its feeble glow barely penetrating the shadows. I hoped we would be given food and water, or it was going to be a long campaign of waiting for Silĕre and me. Also, if the Ursidae lost, then so were we.

Soon we could hear the sounds of an army preparing to move. Horses snorted and whickered, officers shouted commands and steel weapons rasped as they were drawn, checked and replaced into scabbards. Through the gaps in the crudely build wooden walls, we could see snatches of activity within the compound, soldiers running to and fro, horses being harnessed and the mess wagon made ready. The Ursidae army was going to war. Silĕre and I could do nothing but watch as the army marched smartly out the stockade, a silence falling as the sound of hooves receded into the distance. Apart from the two guards outside our prison and a few others going about their duties, the Ursidae base now appeared empty. A shadow suddenly fell over the door followed by an order to stand back, the door opened and two soldiers entered, one stood guard while the other carried a jug of water and a plate of meat and bread. At least we were to be cared for I thought, even if only rudimentary.

However well fed and watered, whoever the beautiful company, I knew we couldn't stay locked up while our new friends and Secuutus were fighting for their lives. Perhaps Aequus would be true to his word and help the Indutiae inhabitants, but maybe we were simply replacing one dictator with a tyrant. Pugnator needed to be warned very soon, Indutiae would be the filling of a military sandwich. I must get out I thought with some desperation, an emotion that surprised me, after all I had no ties to the town other than Secuutus. I wasn't even a real animan for God's sake. Yes I admit, I had gained close friends, hell I had even shagged one, but was this really my fight? Humans have excelled at not getting involved with the problems of others unless oil or another valuable resource is at stake, then the interference of America and Russia is guaranteed. One could invade a small worthless country and bomb all its inhabitants and no one would do anything other than a few political rumblings. Invade a country with oil or gas and the whole western world would descend upon your head.

However, like it or not, I was here and I had nowhere else to go, unless I could find the jade box of course. But so far I had heard no rumours of anyone possessing such an item in this land. I knew Eustace was also searching and he had been here longer than I. Finding and opening the jade box would not necessarily send Eustace and me home, him to America and me back to cold and damp Manchester. Nonetheless, I would continue to search for that green box in the vain hope that one day I may return home. A thought struck me then, I hadn't asked any of the animan if they knew of such a box. Yes, I had spoken to Eustace about it, but perhaps I should actively ask around. One never knows, Pugnator or Aequus or even Crudelis may know of one. I doubted the common animan would own such a thing, but an animan of wealth might. I promised myself I would make finding the jade box my second highest priority, the first of course, was staying alive.

I sat down on the flour covered floor in a despondent mood, Silĕre still peered through cracks and gaps in the wooden walls, watching for what I didn't know. I knew she wanted to escape, as did I, but how? There were two guards stationed outside our door, a door which appeared old but solid and locked. The walls themselves were firm and didn't budge a fraction if pushed or kicked, I know, I had watched Silĕre test all four walls, her anger growing. Silĕre was not a home chick, not one to sit around indoors all day.

When I first met the Tigris femina, she had a small cottage in the forest, well away from other animan. The interior of the cabin was sparse, giving no indication of a homemaker. Silĕre was a warrior and being held captive was not on her bucket list. In frustration, she kicked hard at the door, but all she achieved was a low growl from the guards outside. Silĕre gave up and sat down near me, her actions portraying her dejection.

'Did you see anything out there? Are there many soldiers still here?' I received a shake of her head in answer to each question, her head bowed in defeat.

'Could you see the way out?' I asked.

This time Silĕre nodded and pointed in the direction of the main gate. It was to our left. I fingered the flour as I thought, there had to be a way to break out. If the number of soldiers were few, now would be the best time to attempt an escape. We would have no chance at all when the other soldiers returned. Now was the time but what to do, how do we escape? I still had my staff, and I'm sure I glimpsed our weapons placed just outside the door under the watchful eyes of the guards. If we could get through that door, we would at least have a chance of arming ourselves. I was already armed with the only weapon I could use apart from that evil knife which remained out of reach. I had tried a sword but had quickly dismissed it, I would have been a greater danger to myself than any opponent. I continued to play with the flour on the floor while my eyes examined every single inch of the grain store.

As I played with the fine white flour, feeling the odd tiny piece of grit from the grinding wheel, I remembered visiting ancient flour mills during one of my few excursions during semester break back home. I remembered how many precautions were in place to avoid naked flame igniting the particles in the air. Anything will burn if ground fine enough and . . . . Suddenly I leapt to my feet and grabbed the small oil lamp, holding it up to my face for a closer inspection. In a second Silĕre was standing beside me, her curiosity stirred by my burst of action. I stared at the lamp before turning to the flour spill on the floor, I had a plan!

Gathering all I needed, I tried to explain to Silĕre what I intended to do. However, explaining a scientific theory to someone who can't speak is difficult. They can't ask questions to clarify a point so I carefully explained and mimed the whole process to her, careful not to allow the guards outside the door to hear. I was so glad that modern-day human use of CCTV cameras didn't apply here. I'm positive my actions would have been a hit on YouTube in no time at all.

Finally though, I think Silĕre understood, at least she knew her part in my plan, that was something. I picked up a discarded bucket and carefully began to fill it with flour, trying to avoid dust rising in the air. Once filled to a level I hoped would be sufficient without killing us both in the process, I placed it safely away from the lamp before removing the glass chimney to reveal a naked flame. The next part of my plan was trickier, we had to get the guards to open the door. Playing the old sick card wouldn't work, I felt sure, so some other method was required. And I knew what.

I conveyed to Silĕre exactly what I needed her to do. I could see she wasn't impressed but after some consideration, she reluctantly agreed. As I may have mentioned once or thrice, Silĕre was a beauty, slim but curvy in all the right places. Yes she was a Tigris and the guards were Ursidae, but just like humans of different colours and creeds, a beautiful woman could stir the interest of any race, or in this case, any Cast. I knew some animan had inter-Cast relationships and I prayed the guards were not racist. When we were in place and Silĕre knew her task, it was time to try out my plan.

Outside, the two Ursidae guards suddenly heard sounds of what appeared to be a fight in the makeshift prison they guarded. These noises were punctuated with my voice, growling or shouting, the meaning in my tone leaving no doubt what I was doing. Silĕre gave out a realistic cry, followed by whimpers. From outside it sounded as if I was trying to violently rape Silĕre. I was counting on the assumption that even males of a different Cast would run to the aid of a beautiful female, prisoner or not. I was right for abruptly the door burst open and in rushed the two guards. Before their minds registered that I was not physically pinning Silĕre to the ground and trying to rip her clothes off, it was too late.

The instant they entered the store, Silĕre threw the contents of the bucket into the air above their heads. I followed immediately by hurling the naked lamp at the wall above the door. The result was instantaneous, the flour particles in the air around the guards ignited in a plume of flame, momentarily stunning the guards into immobility, their eyes wide as they stared at the already dying ball of flame surrounding them. I immediately powered forward, swinging my staff with all the force I could muster, first at one guard, then the other. Both fell to the ground, one already unconscious, the other helped on his way by a vicious kick to the head from Silĕre. Without hesitation, Silĕre and I darted through the open door and out of the store. A brief pause as we retrieved our weapons before sprinting for the gate. No one shouted the alarm or made to stop our flight until we reached the gate itself. Hastily the bewildered gate guard stepped into our path, his sword held out in front of him in a stance I could not distinguish between defence and attack. It didn't matter, the butt of my staff outreached his sword and with my forward momentum behind it, the butt slammed into the soldier's stomach, folding him over. As he bent to hold his winded belly I raised the staff again and smashed it down on his head. The soldier fell like a stone, unconscious and no longer a threat. The whole action had taken place with barely a break in our stride and now we were outside the stockade and running. We made sure we followed the wide tracks left by the departing troops to avoid the traps we knew to be buried under the snow.

Though we were free, we would never reach the town in time to help. I realised we would need horses if we were to stand even the slightest chance of beating Aequus and his soldiers to Indutiae. Still no sounds of alarm issued from the army stockade so without breaking my pace, I turned and ran back in through the gate, past the prone figure of the guard. There were still no other soldiers in sight, soldiers were the same wherever they were found. The officer in charge was away, so it was time to catch up on sleep, gamble with whatever game they played here or generally try not to be busy. The Ursidae soldiers were no different.

Earlier, from a crack in a wall of the store, I had noticed a group of about five horses tied to a rail outside the stables. At a flat out run, I headed for the horses. Once there I untied all five but kept hold of two sets of reins, letting the other three horses wander off and amuse themselves. hopefully slowing any pursuit. Quickly I leapt onto the back of a horse before escaping at a gallop with another horse in tow. Through the gate again I slowed just enough to allow Silĕre to leap onto her horse, I handed her its reins and we both urged the animals into full speed away from the Ursidae military base.

After a mile we slowed the horses to a walk, it would be of little use tiring the beasts when we still had far to go. There were no signs of pursuit from the base so I concluded the three soldiers we had whacked remained unconscious and undiscovered. I knew it wouldn't be long before the alarm was raised so we both rode with one eye watching behind us. Nonetheless, we needed to pace our mounts, if we continued at speed, they would be blown in no time. When we reached the cover of the trees, I knew we were safe, if safe is the right word. Behind us, the tracks of the horse's hooves were plain to see, acting as a signpost to our direction. I turned my horse and veered off on a right-hand vector, hoping the undergrowth and thinner snow would throw off any followers long enough for our escape. We could get back on track later, but for now I led the way on a random path.

A short time later, with still no signs of pursuit, I turned my horse, who I had named Fred the third, back onto the main track in the direction of Indutiae and we increased our speed as much as the snow covered terrain and our mounts would allow. I was surprised at the ease of our escape but taking into consideration how we escaped, I suppose I shouldn't worry. If the ball of burning flour hadn't caught the two guards unawares, we would both be still locked up and twiddling our thumbs. Riding alertly along the road, I had noticed that whenever Silĕre looked at me, her expression changed a little. I hoped she didn't start thinking what I had done was magic, I had enough of that with Secuutus. Here on Totus-Terra, science was an unheard of conception. All animan understood the ways of the land and its animals, but other than the ability to forge steel, construct buildings and clothe themselves, the animan remained quite backward. I had compared this world to that of my own back in early mediaeval times. They had not invented gunpowder yet, thankfully, and the use of substances to achieve a goal were thought of like alchemy, sorcery or magic.

The Ursidae army had several hours start on us but I hoped we would make up some time along the way. Soldiers have a set routine when travelling, with set rest periods and meal times. Agreed we also had to ensure we rested the horses at regular intervals but as we had little food, meal times were short. We could do without much sleep if necessary while armies tend not to rush. So although I knew we might not catch up, I hoped we wouldn't be too late.

Our horses plodded on, both horses used to the military life so both were well behaved and gave us no problems. I wish the same could be said for the weather, it had begun to snow again and it looked like it was getting heavier. I was not sure how long we would be able to continue before seeking shelter. My only gratifying thought was that Aequus and his army would be experiencing the same conditions. After a couple more miles, I admitted defeat and turned Fred off the track and under the cover of the trees.

It was hard travelling with a mute companion, stunner though she was.

Though I could speak to Silĕre, she could not answer without her form of sign language. However, in a situation such as this, few words or even hand signals were required. It was cold, it was snowing hard, time to find shelter. Soon we were erecting a camp, or rather a temporary roof over our heads. Finding a branch loaded tree, we cut further branches from other trees and interwove them in the lower branches to make a sort of crude umbrella. There was no room to stand as the tree limbs were low, but we didn't intend standing during the night, we intended sleeping. It was obvious we wouldn't be travelling for some time, tomorrow at the earliest. Next, we piled snow around our small camp, building the walls as high as possible to protect us from the full force of the bitter wind. Lastly, a floor of pine boughs completed our shelter and a fire was lit. As cosy as one could be in the midst of a storm, we had done the best we could to survive. We had erected a basic shelter for the two horses, before feeding them grain from their saddlebags, thoughtfully provided by the animal's normal riders. Silĕre had recognised a few Cottonwood trees in the area and cut off several branches to supplement the horse's diet. Now they were munching happily. A dip was dug near the fire and a mound of fresh snow was placed inside. My idea was the fire would melt the snow mound enough to provide us and the horses with a drink later. It worked, sort of. I didn't ever say I was a skilled survivalist, lucky maybe but not skilled.

There were still a few hours of daylight left but we could do no more than huddle under our blankets and attempt to stay warm. It was no use, I was hungry, and with Silĕre beside me under the makeshift umbrella, I was getting horny. In an effort to keep myself busy, I crawled from the camp and began hunting around for food, any food would do. I intended searching for nuts and berries, though I had no idea what grew in this land or what could be harvested but decided it wouldn't hurt to find out.

It was a short while later as I was stood peering up at the tree branches to discover something edible when from a small hole near my feet, a tiny head poked out. I froze, not with cold this time but with anticipation. The head slowly emerged, brown eyes searching for danger, not realising the danger stood right above it. Keeping my movement slight and slow, I readied my staff then as the rabbit fully emerged from its burrow I slammed the staff down upon its head.

Recently a city dweller before being mysteriously transported to this world, the idea of smacking a defenceless rabbit on its head would have revolted me. But now, after my time here amongst the animan with no supermarket or mall to buy food from, catching a rabbit seemed perfectly normal.

I returned to the camp as the proud hunter with food for my mate, maybe some brownie points here I thought. Maybe not, for as soon as Silĕre saw what I held, she pushed me away from the camp and led me back the way I had come. Then she grabbed the dead rabbit and moved deeper into the woods. I followed, unsure of what she intended, fearing her animal side had surfaced and she was going to devour the rabbit herself. Now I may not be a true gentleman, but if she was that hungry, I would have gladly given her the whole rabbit and remained hungry myself. By the time I reached her, she was already in the process of skinning the animal, and under her deft hands, it didn't take long.

While I watched, still unsure, Silĕre removed the skin and all the unwanted parts of the animal and buried them deep in the snow. Then she gathered handfuls of snow where the blood had fallen, squeezed it into a ball and flung it as far away as she could. To my astonishment, Silĕre then turned to me and smiled, holding the skinned, gutted and headless rabbit carcase up proudly. Grabbing my arm she headed back to the camp, pulling me along after her.

I remained confused as Silĕre mounted the rabbit over our small fire. Then in her own remarkable way, she explained her actions. If I had skinned the rabbit in the camp, any nearby scavengers would smell the blood and come calling during the night. Preparing the animal some distance away may keep any hungry beasts from being attracted to our camp and chomping down on us. As it was, the smell of cooking meat may still attract a curious carnivore, but not as surely as the scent of fresh blood would. I still had a lot to learn it seems, killing food is one thing, keeping it and not becoming food for another is a different matter. I conceded my mistake openly and thanked her for her guidance and knowledge. I was grovelling I know, but one must do what one must do while in the company of a beautiful femina.

As night began to fall and surrounded us in blackness, we munched happily on roast rabbit. Silĕre continued her lesson in survival by instructing me to throw all the picked clean bones into the fire, burning all evidence of our deed, so to speak. A final check on the horses, a drink of cold melted snow and it was time to attempt sleep, hoping the weather would blow itself out overnight. There was no passion that night as we huddled together in our makeshift camp and tried to sleep.

I had become accustomed to the noises of the forest, identifying the creak of a bough, the scurrying of small animals and the falling of twigs. I could identify a rabbit moving in the darkness, or a fox crying for a mate, even what one owl was hooting to another. It seemed only yesterday I slept in a comfy bed surrounded by the sounds of the human city. Now I slept on the cold ground surrounded by the sounds of the forest. Not a choice I would have made willingly I decided as I finally fell asleep.

The next morning we were up before dawn, which didn't mean anything as the nights were long in winter. A drink of freezing water for us and the horse and we were on our way. The route back to the town was uneventful at first, no more snow had fallen overnight so we followed the main track with little difficulty. The day gradually grew lighter as we rode, dappled light piercing the canopy of trees and warming the air by almost a degree, least that's what it felt to me. I was feeling grumpy, fed up with my adventures in this land. All I wished for was to return to my human home, back to electric cookers, food readily available from shops and even my old telly. Living wild and free was not all it was cracked up to be, I had had enough. I was having a good old fashioned wallow in misery when a strange sound began to register on my gloomy mind.

Silĕre was already staring off into the trees when I finally took notice of the strange snuffling grow that approached. Both horses were becoming very restless, ears pricked and eyes wide. I peered in the same direction but as yet I could see nothing to justify Silĕre's attentive pose. I began to get very worried as she slowly drew her sword, her body language portraying apprehension. Naturally, her anxiety immediately transferred to me, even though I didn't know what I feared. But then I saw it, a dark shape amongst the trees heading straight for us. Silĕre glanced over at me then to my staff, I knew she was telling me to be ready so I pressed the little hidden switch on my staff and released the blade held within. Now armed with a spear, I remained silent beside Silĕre as a huge shape hurtled towards us. I had never seen Silĕre so frightened and I was glad I had not dined on a huge breakfast, my own fear squeezing my stomach. With a slight nudge to my arm, Silĕre turned her horse and kicked it into a run, I rode after her, totally mystified at the sight of Silĕre's fear.

Amongst the trees and snow, our horses could not escape the pursuit of the snuffling creature. It was gaining fast. Silĕre led me to a small clearing in the woods, an area about ten yards across, a fallen and rotting tree the obvious cause for the unusual space in an otherwise crowded forest. Coming to a halt in the centre of the clearing, Silĕre sprang down from her horse and allowed it to run off, I did the same with Fred the third, reluctantly but I understood Silĕre's actions. She hoped whatever was stalking us would go after the escaping horses. It didn't. The creature watched the horses run off into the woods with barely a flicker of interest. Then it turned back to us.

Silĕre spun to face the direction of our pursuer, her body poised and her sword ready. Then, from the trees burst the huge bear-like creature but moving much faster than the shambling of a bear. I scarcely had time to note its long brown fur, the thick tail and the short bandy legs. Oh and the teeth, I forgot to mention the teeth. I dived to the right, Silĕre jumping to the left as the beast charged straight at us. Immediately the beast whirled around and shot after me. There was little time, I stabbed my staff at its face but with lightning reflexes, it dodged nimbly away. I blinked and it was charging me again, this damn thing was fast, very fast I thought as I jumped away, no time to use my staff. As soon as my feet touched the ground it was there, growling in a low continuous sound as it teeth flashed towards me. Again I leapt away, again it was almost on me. Despite all my animan speed and reflexes, this huge bear-like beast was faster.

While the beast concentrated on catching me for its dinner, Silĕre had dashed in, trying to stab the thing as it strove to sink its teeth in me. In a blinding demonstration of speed, the beast turned and sprang at Silĕre before her sword even touched its back. I knew this thing was better than us, we couldn't fight it but we also couldn't outrun it without the horses. Oh, how I wished for a gun. I watched Silĕre spring up a tree, the beast inches behind her. Silĕre jumped back to the ground, the beast followed immediately. I simply could not believe its speed and tenacity, it was utterly fearless. What the hell was this thing? Silĕre was trapped, her back against a tree as the beast darted towards her, teeth and claws at the ready. Did I mention the claws? No? Well sorry, but the thing had claws, massive razor sharp claws and they were reaching for Silĕre. I knew I couldn't reach it in time to stop it rendering her into mincemeat so I shouted, I shouted as I ran at it, my staff held in front of me like a lance.

Again with unbelievable speed, the damn thing spun and ran at me. I stopped my forward dash and turned tail, leaping for a tree branch and swinging myself up and out of its way. The beast stopped, momentarily confused as it stared up at me clinging to the branch. Up it leapt, its claws trying to gain purchase on the frozen trunk of the tree. Then it found a grip and started to climb up to render me into little pieces. I stabbed down with my staff, the blow not hurting the creature but was enough to loosen its grip on the icy trunk, breaking its hold and causing it to slide back down to the ground. Its confusion didn't last long, it couldn't reach me so it turned and shot straight at Silĕre again.

'Up!' I shouted, 'Up in a tree. Now!'

Silĕre's lithe form bulleted towards the nearest tree and with agility spurred by fear, she virtually flew up high into its branches. The beast stopped in its tracks, staring up at Silĕre for a moment before looking back at me. I could almost see its mind angrily working as it contemplated the problem. I watched with mounting horror as the beast padded confidently back to the tree in which I perched. With a sniff and a growled, the damn thing again leapt at the trunk and began to climb towards me. Oh crap! What the hell do I do next? One swipe of those huge claw armed feet and my legs would be shredded. I couldn't climb any higher so I prodded with my staff and again dislodged the beast. It slipped back to the ground but leapt up again. This happened several times, proving the determination of the animal.

Suddenly, it secured its grip and began making its way up to me. If it reached me I would be well and truly buggered, I had to do something. I shifted my weight and balance into a more stable position on the tree limb, grasped my staff and pointed it down at the beast. It took no notice of the blade at first, until it climbed within reach. Frantically I began stabbing down at its snapping jaws, my higher position giving me the advantage, but only slight. I stabbed down, aiming for the creature's eyes and nose, matching my animan speed against that of the animal. It put up a ferocious fight, snapping with its jaws or swiping with those clawed feet as it attempted to get past the blade of my staff. The creatures speed and reactions were amazing, each time I stabbed down, it moved, dodged or swiped the blade aside with the ease and accuracy of a highly trained boxer. All the while it moved closer. Then at last I caught it, my blade sliced along its muzzle, leaving a deep red cut that almost punctured through its cheek.

That was too much for the bearlike creature, with a grunt it jumped down from the tree and shuffled off into the forest, occasionally stopping to paw at its injured face and look back at us with a snarl. It disappeared into the trees, the sound of its passage gradually fading. I waited several long moments before carefully climbing down out of the tree, my staff held ready in case the creature returned.

As the fear left me I slumped to the ground in shock, what the hell was that? I asked myself. I had never encountered such a persistent and ferocious animal in my life, neither as a human or animan. Sadly Silĕre could not tell me, I would have to wait till we got back to town. Sometimes having a mute companion was frustrating. Once Silĕre had descended from the safety of her tree, we continued cautiously in the direction of the town on foot, finding the track from which we had strayed and moving as fast as we could to catch up on the time spent avoiding becoming the creatures breakfast. We had been lucky I thought, two escapes in one day.

Chapter 13: United

Our rate of travel increased greatly as we threw caution to the wind and followed in the flatten tracks made by the Ursidae soldiers. Many animan feet had flattened a swath through the snow as efficiently as a plough, cutting the undergrowth as they went. Now we were running, travelling in a ground eating lope as the sounds of aggression reached our ears. The town was close now and we could make out the shouted insults and jeers of the two armies as they came face to face.

At the last moment, Silĕre and I peeled off the track and headed under cover of the trees, it would not have been wise to run straight into the rear ranks of the Ursidae army. From the trees, we could see the battlefield, the Lupus soldiers formed in lines with Indutiae behind them. I noted their numbers had increased. Clearly, some of the reinforcements had arrived in answer to Crudelis's call for help. Matching their number, the Ursidae army lined up facing the Lupus with the trees from where Silĕre and I hid, at their back. Somehow Silĕre and I needed to avoid the attentions of both armies and get back to the town. There was no need to warn Pugnator, he could see for himself. Over the heads of the soldiers, I could make out figures on the palisade, the townsfolk of Indutiae anxiously awaiting the outcome of the forthcoming battle. Their future and possibly their lives depended on the whim of the victor.

The two armies were in the posturing stage, soldiers from both sides busy shouting insults and taunting each other while the senior officers conferred. I realised this was probably similar to the medieval battles humans once fought before the art of killing became a long range affair. I do not doubt that modern human politicians would not be so keen to start a war if they were to be in the front line and armed only with a sword or spear. Guns and missiles can kill from a distance, this battle would be face to face, hand to hand. Leaders were expected to lead from the front, not from some office hundreds of miles away. Would the Iraq war have happened if Tony Blair and George Bush had to personally face the enemy on the battlefield? Something tells me it would not.

Seeing everyone busy with battle preparations, Silĕre and I chose that time to make our move. Keeping just inside the treeline, we circled to the right and slowly neared the town. I hoped no Lupus scouts or guards remained wandering about the place. Surely they would have been recalled as the Ursidae army approached? I hoped so. Safe among the trees I watched as General Crudelis and Commander Aequus rode across the divide between the two armies and met each other. I couldn't make out what they were saying but it was obvious both were very angry. Suddenly General Crudelis drew his sword and made to strike out at Aequus. The Ursidae commander dodged the poorly aimed blow and drew his sword in defence. More angry words followed before Crudelis again attempted to attack Aequus. This time the Ursidae commander was ready and a duel began between the two leaders. The sight of their leaders fighting spurred both armies into action.

With shouts and roars of defiance, both armies surged forward, in moments the two leaders were engulfed in violent and bloody combat with their opponents. The engagement had begun. Now Silĕre and I ran as fast as we could towards the town, no fear of being spotted as both the Lupus and Ursidae soldiers focused on staying alive. The battle raged as we approached the main barricade, shouting as we ran to be let in. I didn't know who issued the order but ropes were flung out, ready for us to climb over the barrier and into the relative safety of the town.

'Where on Terra have you two been?' was Pugnator's greeting as he along with Secuutus met us when we climbed off the barricade.

'Hi, nice to be home,' I replied between gasps for air. 'We had a little trouble with the Ursidae, seems they liked us so much they decided we should stay.'

'What? You mean they imprisoned you? Even after you had rushed to warn them of Crudelis?' asked Pugnator incredulously.

'How did you escape? Did you use magic?' asked Secuutus with anticipation.

'No of course not,' I replied, somewhat irritated. 'Anyway, enough about us. What's the plan?'

'It appears we are impotent at this moment, we can do nothing until a clear outcome of the battle,' Pugnator gestured at the two armies. 'Then we'll know where we stand.'

'Or fall,' added Secuutus.

I climbed up and looked over the palisade at the battle beyond the town. I could see both armies appeared evenly matched and from the screams and cries of despair and pain, it was a fierce contest. The green uniforms of the Lupus and brown of the Ursidae were merging into red as blood spilt from both sides. I could see the Ursidae commander whirling like a Dervish, his blade slashing and cutting, seemingly at several opponents at once. I searched for Crudelis, looking for his bright green uniform amongst the melee, then I saw him, encircled by his officers who fought off any attempt to get at their general. I noted his sword still gleamed clean, no blood yet soiling its blade.

Amid the melee, horns began to blow and Pugnator and the others joined me to see what was to happen. As the horns continued to sound, both armies gradually began to move apart, soldiers on both sides retreating from the fight. I concluded this initial battle was a result of the two leaders clashing in front of their respective armies. Now the period of anger was sated, the time for planning and strategy arrived. None can win if both sides go at each other in pure hate, the result would be the annihilation of all.

Once the armies retreated, teams were sent out from each side to collect the wounded, the dead were left where they had fallen. The town of Indutiae breathed a sigh, for now there would be a period of peace. How long it would last depended on the strategies of Crudelis and Aequus. Pugnator led the way as we filed down off the palisade and returned to the publican for our own planning session. The arrival of the Ursidae meant we would have some respite but the future of the town was still very much in question. As for myself, I could not see any benefit in Crudelis continuing his campaign against Indutiae now the Ursidae were here. If I were in his place, I would choose a different action and I worried that the Lupus general may have reached the same conclusion. I didn't voice my suspicions to the others as it was only a suspicion, one based on human reactions, not those of the animan. But still I worried.

Once seated, fed and plied with battery acid, the talking began in earnest. For the moment I was distracted by the strange drink as I realised I didn't know what it was. Did it have a name? What were the ingredients? Did I even want to know? I decided I did so I left the others to their planning and sought out the publican.

'I've been drinking this stuff since I got here,' I began when I had the publican's attention. 'But may I ask what it is?'

The publican looked at me as if I were an alien or a small child. One of those assumptions was correct at least, but I refrained from commenting.

'It's called Ignis aqua, everyone knows that,' he replied sullenly. 'We make it by distilling fermented grain with piperis for heat. Apart from vinum, it's what most animan drink.'

I was still none the wiser but was slightly relieved to discovery the battery acid was actually made from grain, much like most of our alcoholic beverages at home. I returned to the group of town leaders which included Secuutus and Silĕre. The conversation was directed at Silĕre but she wasn't answering, gestures

317

and mime only go so far. As I sat down, the questions came at me, most asking what the Ursidae base was like and where was it, or who the Ursidae commander was. These questions I answered, each answer confirmed by a nod from Silĕre. I informed those present about the layout of the base. I depicted our capture with some embarrassment, before describing Commander Aequus. I explained that although a strong character, I believed Aequus did not care for Indutiae. His sole reason for being here was to ensure Crudelis remained bound to the treaty between the two Casts and allowed Indutiae to continue as a neutral trading town on the border.

'I don't think Aequus will attack, I think he is only here because of Crudelis. If Aequus is successful, he and his army will return to their base. However, if Crudelis wins, the town is doomed. That's how I see it. I could, of course, be wrong,' I finished.

Pugnator had listened quietly, leaving the others to put forward questions, but now he spoke, asking the only question no one wanted to consider. 'Will we survive a full on military attack by Crudelis? Or Aequus for that matter?'

Silence fell sharply, all talk ended as if a radio had switched off. No one knew the answer but more to the point, no one wanted to contemplate our situation. The town of Indutiae had until now repelled the Lupus military, but could it withstand another full on attack? If Crudelis threw his entire reinforced army at the town and its makeshift defences, we all knew Indutiae would fall. Unless that is, we came up with a line of defence that Crudelis could not cross. Yes, we had a plentiful supply of Molotov cocktails and gunpowder 'bombs' but would that be enough? The simple answer was no. If Crudelis defeated Aequus, the town would fall under his command and we would be helpless to resist.

'We have one choice,' I broke into the conversations that had begun to circle endlessly. 'We can't defeat Crudelis. That we all know. There is only one way of protecting Indutiae. We must use all our resources to ensure Aequus wins the battle. We must side with the Ursidae and together we may beat Crudelis once and for all.'

Everyone turned to stare at me, the truth of my statement hitting home. We must put our faith in the Ursidae army and Commander Aequus, but it could be the tail of the snake, the head may yet turn and bite us.

'I believe Harry is right, we have no choice. We know Crudelis wants control of Indutiae. That's a fact. What we don't know is, can we trust Aequus?' asked Pugnator quietly. 'Who is to say he won't look on us once Crudelis is defeated? None can, but Harry thinks the Ursidae wish to honour the treaty and leave us alone. Therefore we must trust Aequus and in doing so, we must help. We have to join the fight and attack the Lupus army.' There it was, in black and white. To remain a neutral town, Indutiae must choose a side.

What the hell had I gotten myself into this time? Here in this land where humans had not evolved, a land ruled by four main predators, four Casts, the Tigris, Leo, Ursidae and Lupus. In a land where the sword was king and science was called magic. Was the world of Totus-Terra in another dimension to my world? Had I somehow travelled into the future, sent by the green jade box? Perhaps I was in the deep dark past of the universe's history? Scientists now believed there had been more than one Big Bang, some believed the universe grew before collapsing into itself and growing anew. Was I on a world that preceded the human race? Of course I had no idea. Wherever or whenever I was, if I wanted to eventually return home, the one necessity was that I stayed alive. This was no fantasy.

Suddenly I realised Pugnator was talking to me, 'It must be you Harry, you must get into the Ursidae camp and let Commander Aequus know of our plans. You, and Silĕre of course, are the only two who have met the commander.'

'Huh?' I began intelligently. 'What plan? Do we yet have a solid plan? Simply telling Aequus that we will help him is not enough. He will need details, times and strategy. We'll both need to discuss the appropriate intervention from Indutiae. However, no one has taken Crudelis into account, his plans will differ from ours so any scheme must be flexible. When we have a solid plan, then and only then will I risk speaking with Aequus. Hopefully without losing my head in the process.'

'Agreed,' said Pugnator. 'I suggest we each rest, eat and ponder on this matter. We'll meet up again here in two hours. Yes?'

All acknowledged their agreement, especially me. I was knackered and my thoughts were jumping all over the place. I needed sleep, I knew it wouldn't be much but any would help. While the gathering of townsfolk vacated the publican, I made my way to the room I rented. All thought of war and fighting dismissed in favour of a pillow. I realised Silĕre was right behind me and cursed myself for being so self-absorbed, I had forgotten I was not the only one who had lived through being captured, escaping and fighting off a wild animal. Silĕre had been there with me the whole time.

Remembering that strange animal, I turned and called down to Pugnator, catching him just before he left the publican. I described the creature and its actions and asked him what it was.

'Sounds like you met and survived a Gulo gulo,' he replied. 'You are both indeed lucky!'

Huh! I thought. What the hell is a Gulo gulo? Then I remembered, my fellow ex-human turned animan Sage had spoken of the Gulo gulo. If I recalled correctly, it was another creature that evolved to become a top predator, just like the Hyaenidae. The evolution of lions, tigers, bears and wolves had left a huge gap in the ecosystem and other animals had evolved to fill that gap. The Gulo gulo had evolved from the wolverine. A creature that though small, was so ferocious and tenacious, even far larger predators would avoid it. Here in this land, the wolverine had grown to the size of a grizzly bear, but without the pleasant attitude. No wonder it had Silĕre and me defenceless against its speed and viciousness. Thanking Pugnator I continued to my room, hoping fervently I never met another Gulo gulo as long as I lived.

I entered my room, thankful that Secuutus had somewhere else to sleep. Having my friend and fellow ex-rider here would have surely resulted in little rest. It would be a case of horrendous snoring or endless questions, alone I could sleep. I turned to close the door but found to my surprise, Silĕre had entered the room behind me. I paused, not knowing what to do but she took the initiative and folded her arms around my neck and lay her head on my shoulder. Oh crap I thought. It looks like I wouldn't get any sleep after all. However, Silĕre was as tired as me it seemed. She released her grip and moved towards my bed. As I dumbly stared, she undressed and climbed between the covers, laying to one side and leaving room for me. I followed her lead and joined her, together in each other's arms, we slept.

A thudding on the door woke us two hours later. I staggered from the bed while Silĕre snuggled down deeper under the covers. Adserviŏ had been sent to fetch us as a planning session was about to begin. A raised eyebrow was the only reaction from Adserviŏ when he saw my bed companion, and I was grateful for his tact. A few minutes later and still half asleep I joined Pugnator and the town leaders in the bar once again. Pugnator was already speaking but broke off when I arrived.

'Ahh Harry. I'm sorry you could not sleep longer but time is not a choice we have. My colleagues and I have been discussing plans but I admit, we've not come up with anything sound. Get yourself some food and when you're ready, we'll pool our ideas. If we have any that is.'

Silĕre arrived then so I ordered food for both of us and paid the publican, who it appeared, was also feeling the strain. I realised it must be difficult for him, trading as a publican in between guard duties or fighting for his life at the barricade. Perhaps the fact our meetings created more business for his establishment balanced the hardship somewhat? Once we had finished our light 'breakfast', the plotting began. Night was falling fast and we all feared a resumption of the action under the cover of darkness, but luckily, armies tend to stick firmly to a set strategy and would be unlikely to attack until dawn. We had the night to construct a plan, maybe longer if the two armies occupied themselves. Nonetheless, we could not be certain.

Ideas bounced around the table for some time with none producing a firm plan of action. These animan were just traders, shopkeepers and farmers. What did they know of military strategy? I was certainly little help, Silĕre could not speak so that left Pugnator as the only one with any form of experience. Yes, Tigris warriors were fighting for the town, but Tigris are mainly assassins or mercenaries, mostly working alone. So we waited upon Pugnator and adding our own ideas and suggestions when called for.

At that moment a thought struck me, where was Eustace? Being an ex-human soldier, maybe he could add something. I excused myself from the gathering and went off in search of the Leo. It didn't take me long, sure enough, he was in our little shack at the back of the publican. Looking around, it was evident he had made the place his home, unwisely perhaps as he was surrounded by gunpowder. But it was his choice and I didn't object. I asked him to join our planning party, explaining we were seriously short of party games. Back in the bar, everyone there looked on Eustace with suspicion, I remembered only I knew his full story, and that could never be told. So I began to fabricate a background for Eustace that would hopefully be credible and justify my reason for including him.

'Some of you will already know my friend Eustace,' I began.

'Eustace? What kind of name is that?' queried Secuutus.

'My name is Harry,' I reminded him.

'Oh. Right,' he responded, implying both our names were strange and that explained why we were friends. Secuutus knew more than that of course, he knew where we had come from and how. He alone knew the significance in my reply but his acceptance quietened the others.

'Eustace was a soldier in his past, he has knowledge, like Pugnator, of these things. I brought him in to assist in our plans. To be fair, we're not doing too well. Agreed?'

I peered about the room and saw begrudging nods of acceptance, none voiced any objection. Now with the added input from Eustace, the ideas began to flow. The two ex-soldiers bouncing off each other in an exchange of experience and knowledge. Ultimately a suggestion was made that all agreed on. I would sneak into Aequus's lines and inform him, if I survived, that upon his next frontal assault on the Lupus army, we, the fighters of Indutiae, would strike at the general's rearguard. The intention being to split the general's force's to justify the old rule, divide and conquer. I could not help but be slightly amused, it was the same plan as our original idea, but without all the talking. That's committees for you, the simplest idea is always the last to be agreed on. Now all I had to do was get past the Lupus camp, find a way to the Ursidae, avoid being captured; avoid at all costs being killed, find the commander and outline our plan. Simple.

The trouble with plans is that they often have a tendency to go wrong, a plan is like a living thing and can change its mind. Suddenly from outside, shouts and cries of alarm pierced the night. As one, everyone piled out the publican door, some rushing to defend the barricades, others running home to hide under their beds. I followed Pugnator with Silĕre; Secuutus, Eustace and Adserviŏ right behind me as we sought the reason for alarm.

It soon became very clear, General Crudelis was attacking the town! So much for planning I thought as I rushed to the palisades, my adrenaline flowing. It only took a moment to understand the general's plan. Catching everyone by surprise, his whole army had ringed the town un-noticed by the sentries and lookouts. Battles already raged along the perimeter as desperate town fighters fought determined Lupus soldiers. I could make out movement in the Ursidae camp, but it was clear they too had been caught out. No help would be coming from that quarter for some time, an army takes time to assemble and prepare. It was up to us to hold off the Lupus until the Ursidae arrived. But with the whole lupus army attacking the town, it was going to be a hard fight.

Without warning, the head of a Lupus soldier appeared right in front of me, catching me by surprise, a moment that almost cost my life. He scaled the palisade, swinging his sword down at my head. Fear overcame me and my reflexes burst into action. With speed born of desperation, I whipped up my staff and rammed the end into the soldiers face, smashing his nose and causing him to fall backwards. I risked a glance over the palisade and saw the Lupus army had been busy, makeshift ladders sprouted up all around the town. The general had given up on his attempts to gain access via the barricades. He was going to come in over the top. I screamed, 'Repel borders!' before realising the animan wouldn't understand, so changed my cry accordingly. 'Beware the palisade. Beware the walls!'

Indutiae fighters flocked to all points of the town where access over palisades, wall or roofs was at risk. I noted all this in an instant as Lupus soldiers were climbing over in large numbers. Two now faced me and all was forgotten as I fought for my life. I brought my staff up horizontally, jabbing its butt into one soldier before pushing the bladed end into the face of the other. Beside me, the fighting was ferocious, every male, and many female animan fighting, their animal heritage showing a brutality I couldn't believe possible. I admit humans were cruel, but the animan, when stirred, could show the humans a thing or two about cruelty and viciousness. I pummelled another Lupus as a question arose in my mind. Why was Crudelis attacking the town when his main enemy was behind him? It smacked of desperation but for what reason? I didn't have time to give it any more thought as a huge Lupus battered his way through the town fighters and headed in my direction. I had never seen such a large Lupus, how he'd gotten so big was a question for later, for he was charging right at me. Quickly I sidestepped but found my way blocked by other bodies, each fighting for their lives.

On raged the bull Lupus, a hideous snarl distorting his features. I could not retreat or move to the side, so I did the only thing I could do, I charged straight towards him. Up swept his sword in a double-handed grip that would have cleaved me in two. On instinct I dropped to the ground and barrelled into his legs, the forward momentum of his charge aiding my efforts and down he went, face down in a sprawl. Immediately I jumped to my feet and slammed the staff butt down onto the back his neck, halting his attempt to regain his feet. In the blink of an eye, his back resembled a pin cushion as many blades stabbed into him. He had no chance, every fighter within range brought their weapons down on him. He wouldn't get up again but others were ready to replace him.

More and more Lupus soldiers scaled ladders and the fight became ferocious, the town defenders fighting desperately for their town, their homes. I peered around while gasping for breath, feeling the fatigue aching in my muscles. I knew all the fighters would be feeling the same. We fought solidly against an enemy far fresher than ourselves, each soldier to climb over the defences faced an opponent who was already tired. The numbers of town defenders now began to fall, we were losing this battle.

As I stabbed out at yet another Lupus I found Eustace beside me, fighting with all the killer skills taught to the modern human soldier. Blood covered him from head to toe, his sword sporting a coat of flesh from his victims. With a shock, I realised I looked the same, my clothes were stained red and gore hung from my staff. I was no longer a science lecturer, I was a killer.

'Why the hell are they attacking us?' I screamed across at him while withdrawing my blade from the eye of a luckless soldier.

'They want the town!' he shouted back.

'I know that. But why attack now?'

'The general wants to gain control of Indutiae before the Ursidae can stop him. Once his forces are inside, they will stand a better chance of winning this battle.' With that, we both faced new opponents making any further conversation impossible. I slashed and whirled with my staff, occasionally resorting to my knife if pressed too close. Every muscle ached, every stab or slash becoming an effort. I was covered in small wounds as my speed and mobility slowed with exhaustion. I began to wonder if this would be my end, cut to shreds on the palisade of an animan town in this alien world.

A faint sound began to reach my ears over the screams of the wounded and clash of weapons. A horn was sounding somewhere in the distance, a sound I was too busy to locate. Eustace and I were fighting back to back as more soldier's scrambled up the palisade and began to encircle us. My staff darted in and out, held one handed as I slashed and stabbed with my knife. I kicked, elbowed and head butted any soldier close enough, using the whole of my body as a weapon. When a lowly karate student, I never dreamed I would be forced to use those skills on a battlefield. Against a few drunks on a Saturday night in Manchester maybe, but not like this. I wondered if Silĕre was still alive, or Secuutus. I had not heard my friend's roar for some time and feared the worst for him, though at this rate, I would be with him soon, one way or another. My entire body screamed out for rest, my weapons so heavy I could barely lift them, only fear kept me going, desperately clinging to life.

Nearer now, I could hear the sound of a horn but still it failed to register on my tired brain. Eustace and I were virtually leaning on each other as the constant tide of Lupus soldiers surged around us. The end would not be long in coming.

Chapter 14: Three Armies

My knife slid from my hand, my fingers no longer had the strength to hold it. I could barely raise my staff and resigned myself to the agony of a killing strike. The horn kept blowing but I didn't care as I slumped to the floor, beaten and exhausted, defeated. I closed my eyes and quietly said goodbye to all my friends, past and present, the too few loved ones and my life. I knew Eustace lay near me, his chest heaving in an effort to drag in the breath of life. Slowly he looked over at me, his huge Leo frame now frail and worn out, I looked back at him, knowing he was seeing the same in me. We had fought and we had lost. Two ex-humans beaten in a war between animan that neither of us could avoid. I closed my eyes again and awaited the inevitable.

Then it came, I was manhandled upright while voices shouted at me. I didn't care, my eyelids were too heavy to open and I had no wish to look my killer in the eye, as they did in all the cowboy or war films I had watched so long ago. My only wish was they would get on with it instead of dragging me to God knows where. It seemed like eons later I felt myself gently lowered to the ground. Huh? Since when has an enemy gently lowered a defeated opponent to the ground? I forced my eyes open to see blurry faces peering down at me. Voices now began to register on my consciousness, voices I recognised. Slowly my eyes swam back into focus and I saw the faces of Silĕre and Secuutus staring down, concern on their features. I was in a room I didn't recognise and assumed it was someone's home. I was laying on a rug that felt like a feather bed at that moment. Now the adrenaline of battle was fading all I wanted to do was sleep. It had been a long night.

'Wake up Harry! No sleeping on the job, there's still much to do. Come on, wake up,' urged Secuutus with all the sympathy of an ant.

'Huh, yeah, I'm fine thank you Secuutus. Least I think I am, do I still have all my limbs?' I asked as I struggled to sit up.

'Yeah you're fine. I think you just overdid things a little. After a rest, you'll be fine,' replied Secuutus with a grin.

Overdid things a little he said. Overdid things? What the hell else was I supposed to do? It's not like overdoing the daily exercise or too much wine. I didn't intentionally exhaust myself, I was trying to stay alive for Pete's sake! What the hell did he expect? Before I could retort, Silĕre reached down and laid a hand on my shoulder, no words were needed as her actions spoke volumes. She handed me a mug of warmed thin vinum and some form of bread. I accepted both gratefully, surprised at how hungry I was. Just before I took a sip, a thought came to me.

'Eustace?' I asked.

'He's fine,' replied Secuutus. 'He's lying over there sleeping off his exertions. He fought well, even for a Leo, so we've let him sleep for now.'

'Okay. So Eustace gets to sleep while I get awakened by you two. How come I get the special treatment?' I asked grudgingly. Then I suddenly remembered. 'Did we win? How goes the fight?'

'No we didn't win but Aequus finally arrived,' Secuutus explained. 'He attacked the general's forces and Crudelis was forced to draw back his troops to face the new threat. The battle still rages, but for the moment we have some respite. I'm not sure how long it will last and neither is Pugnator. That's why we woke you, Pugnator has called for a council of war, and we, including you, having been ordered to attend.'

'A council of war huh? Seems a little late to be forming such a committee, the war has already arrived.' I muttered in between mouthfuls of bread and sips of vinum.

'Well we did have several meetings before but we all underestimated Crudelis. We thought the armies of Ursidae and Lupus would keep each other busy and not pester us until one side or the other won. By choosing to attack the town first, Crudelis messed up all our plans, thus we need to renew our thinking. So, a war council was formed and you're in it. So how about getting up now?' Secuutus reached out a massive hand to accompany his words.

The council of war, as Secuutus called it, was being held yet again in the publican. I couldn't help but wonder if the town survived, perhaps they should build a town hall. Least then the town leaders would have somewhere 'official' to meet and discuss whatever it is small town politicians discuss. Glancing around the room, I could see faces I recognised as town leaders, I had not bothered to discover their names. There was Adserviŏ and Eustace, his presence surprised me but I was glad to see him. Pugnator was once more doing most of the talking, the others in the room content to listen. That animan was a born military leader and excelled in the situation we found ourselves in. However, how would he cope in peacetime? A soldier is one thing but it takes a different calibre to be a politician. One thing for sure, I didn't have any intention of getting involved past surviving the next few days. I still wanted to find the green jade box and attempt once again to return to my own life as a human. Least that's what I told myself, but as I glanced over at Silĕre, doubt crept in and I suddenly felt unsure. I shrugged it off and began paying attention to what was being said, especially as it appeared to concern me.

'It is clear that we, the animan of Indutiae must play a part in shaping our own future,' Pugnator was saying. 'Outside our gates, the Lupus fight the Ursidae for control of our town when it is we who should be in control. In this land we have members from all Casts and as such, no individual Cast should rule us. Nonetheless, we first have to ensure Crudelis is not victorious before dealing with the problem of Aequus. He has stated to Harry that he has no interest in Indutiae, but once the fighting is over, what then? Will the Ursidae decide they do desire control of our town? Is it a risk we wish to take?'

'No, I don't think so. First, we must protect our town, then we must take control of our country and bring a halt to this battle for power between the Lupus and Ursidae.'

'Fine words,' interrupted one of the town leaders who introduced himself as Carnifex, he owned a butchers shop in town. 'But how are we to achieve this state of independence? Our fighting animan consist of shop keepers, farmers and simple working folk, we don't have an army nor have we the numbers of animan that this plan would require. I ask you Pugnator, how do we claim rule for ourselves?'

Several of the town leaders voiced their agreement with the questions posed by Carnifex, including me. Science I understood, military tactics and local government not so much. My interest was spiked though, how was Pugnator going to achieve this? Once the grunts, nods and muttering had died down, Pugnator cleared his throat and began again.

'My wish to live in a self-governing country with no interference from any one Cast wanting to rule will be a matter for discussion later. But we must deal with the matter in hand, how do we defend Indutiae? To this end, I have sent those riders who could be spared out to all four corners of this country. They ride with a message, a plea for help, and an appeal for unity. It is time the Casts of our land stood up and fought back. I don't know how many will come but the call has gone out for all to come to our aid. It is time for rebellion and it will start here, in Indutiae and spread throughout the land of Silva Homines. We, ourselves in our defence of Indutiae, must show the way.'

Blimey, I thought. It's just like the Roman times back at home. Leaders such as Caractacus and Boudicca gathering all the Briton tribes into one massive army to fight the Romans. It is possible Pugnator's plan could work. It will depend on the spirit and courage of the animan of Silva Homines. I didn't know how populated this land is, but one thing is for sure, if Indutiae survives this battle, it will set an example to all and an uprising will ensue. Cool I thought, it's just like living through a history lesson, a lesson I hope to survive. Around the room, townsfolk from all Casts were applauding Pugnator, his personality and the power of his speech had reached every one of them, but not all.

'How the hell did we get from defending the town, to ruling the country?' whispered Eustace in my ear. 'Seems we've heard this type of speech before.'

'You're right,' I replied in a similar whisper. 'However, no one would listen to us, in truth, they'd probably lynch us right here if we told them what we know and how we know it.'

'Right, but it's still a shame. I've made my home here now and since the arrival of Crudelis's army, the townsfolk have accepted me as one of their own. I like it here,' said Eustace. 'Anyway, we first have to defend this town. Bit like cowboys and Indians ain't it?'

I agreed with a smile, the similarity was there but I was reminded of the old western films with John Wayne. One man trying to save a town, in this case, Pugnator. But how long before he turned from John Wayne to Julius Caesar I wondered.

The adulation over, the talk returned to the matter at hand, how to defend Indutiae. Pugnator was laying out a plan and seeking suggestions. 'I think it's imperative that we first remove the threat from Crudelis. Once he is neutralised, then we will turn our attention to Aequus. I know he has said he will not take control of our town but we can't be sure. But first, Crudelis. Ideas anyone?'

I had risked a quick peek over the palisades on my way here and saw the battle outside flowed to and fro in much the same way as they do whenever two equal armies meet. As yet the victor remained uncertain but from the reports from lookouts and scouts, it appeared the battle was swinging in favour of Crudelis. We needed to do something other than talk, and fast. I stood to interject with my own suggestions but Eustace beat me to it. The ex-American soldier had already proved his worth in military strategies and as he stood, the room fell quiet.

'Our original plan was to attack Crudelis from behind. This plan was ditched when he attacked first, nonetheless it was a good plan. I suggest we gather the largest force of militias we can, and using a wedge shaped formation, attack the rear lines of Crudelis's ranks. This will cause a split in his forces and, hopefully, allow Aequus to gain an advantage at the front before we are annihilated. By this time, both armies would have incurred large numbers of casualties so even a force of fifty to a hundred militias will make a difference.'

'It won't work,' growled Carnifex, 'our militias could never face trained soldiers. We would be outclassed and out fought immediately. It would be a slaughter!'

'Yes there will be loss of life, however, if after the initial arrowhead, our defenders will withdraw and begin using guerrilla tactics, then we may have an advantage,' answered Eustace.

Immediately cries of, 'What in Terra is guerrilla? We don't have any gorillas here!'

Pugnator stood and held up his hands for quiet. 'I understand,' he began. 'These tactics Eustace speaks of could be our best method of undermining Crudelis's forces. Guerrilla tactics involve rapid hit and run attacks, darting in and striking at the enemy before running away. We also have two particular weapons ideal for this form of combat. We will use Harry's ignis aqua jugs and some of his incendium pulvis. We can strike at the Lupus soldiers from a distance, dodging and avoiding close contact with the enemy.'

Incendium pulvis? What the hell is that? Then I had it, it was the new animan word for gunpowder. The animan didn't have any understanding of a gun so the word *gunpowder* meant little to them, they came up with their own description.

'Do we have enough gunpowder left?' I turned to Eustace and asked.

'Yeah, I think so. I mixed quite a large amount while you and Silĕre were off on your jollies with Aequus. We'll need to make sure we only use the more sensible town militias though, we don't want them blowing themselves, or worse, us up instead of the enemy.' Eustace replied with a grin. I swear he was enjoying all this. As if to prove my point, Eustace stood once again and made a statement that somehow didn't surprise me.

'I will lead the guerrilla force,' he said to all in the room, 'I have some knowledge of these tactics and I know how to use the gun . . incendium pulvis. I would suggest we get a move on before it's too late. From the reports coming in, Aequus is not fairing too well and could use our help.'

'The matter is set then,' announced Pugnator. 'Eustace and Harry will lead our attack. I want everyone here to help gather a hundred of our militias and be ready to distribute the ignis aqua jugs, Molotov cocktails as Harry calls them, and the incendium pulvis. We will choose who gets what when we see who will accompany the attack, all others will defend with whatever they can. So, it's time to begin our fight back. Now, everyone move, we have a battle to win!'

A brief pause as all those gathered in the room contemplated what was to come before slowly making for the door, each one of them fearful for their future. Morning had arrived and we all needed sleep, the whole town had fought in one form or another all night and I for one desperately wanted my bed. Just before the gathering left the publican, Eustace answered my prayer and called out, 'Get some rest but don't sleep all day. We have much to do before this evening.'

I wondered how many would follow his advice, once in bed, these exhausted animan would be reluctant to rise for a battle many would not survive. But off we all went, the Tigris, Leo, Ursidae and Lupus, inhabitants and now militias of Indutiae. Silĕre and I had the shortest of journeys as we still had rooms in the publican. Secuutus glanced over at me and gave a small nod before leaving with the others. At least he had a home to go to now, his relationship with Socium firmly established. Once again Silĕre shared my bed and again we slept wrapped in each other's arms.

Four hours later we were woken by a banging on the door, it was the publican informing us our presence was required. Back in the bar, we found a hot plate of food awaiting us, Pugnator and Eustace already tucking into theirs. I wasn't really hungry but knew I would need nourishment to face the coming challenge. I also had no idea when I would eat again, so I forced down the meaty stew accompanied by numerous mugs of cool water. I had just finished the last bite when Secuutus and the war council entered the bar. Secuutus patted his stomach, I guessed he had been well fed by Socium. The meal over, Pugnator called for progress reports. Eustace began by stating the hundred militias were ready, and some had been allocated the weapons we had made. Others reported that the defences were well manned, many of the town femina's are now standing at the barricades in place of husbands, fathers and sons who were assigned to the strike force or already lost. Water barrels were full, almost every town resident was armed and faculties for treating the wounded were being prepared. The 'hospital' was to be set up in one of the larger townhouses with others available if the numbers of fallen grew too high. Pugnator reported that the two armies had attacked each other again and it was time we put our plan into action.

I wondered why the Ursidae and Lupus forces had decided to go to war after lunch but of course, I had no way of knowing. Rules of engagement and battlefield strategies would differ from what I had gleaned from television, so in truth, I had no idea. The main fact was that they were at it again, both armies trying their best to defeat the other, one for control of Indutiae, the other to honour a treaty. Our cause was much simpler, survival. Finally, with our attack force ready, a space was cleared so we could sneak out via a small alleyway, an exit through one of the main barricades would have been spotted immediately, and we needed stealth. In a single file, our force made its way around the town perimeter, each fighter hugging the walls closely in an attempt to remain undiscovered. Slowly we crept nearer the rear lines of Crudelis's army. Eustace and I led the way but I conceded leadership to Eustace, he knew what he was doing. He was a trained soldier, I was a college lecturer and my only experience of battle came from my time with Janiz and his riders.

As we drew closer, we had not been spotted amid the chaos of the melee, the Lupus soldiers focus fixed firmly on the enemy in front. No thought was given to the townsfolk, dismissed as victims rather than a threat. Un-noticed amidst the melee the militias were assembled, I held my breath as Eustace roared out the command, 'Charge!' sending the militias leaping into the fray. I had a brief moment to wonder why everyone insisted on using the word, *charge*. Why not, go or forward? But thoughts were immediately replaced with action as the rearmost Lupus soldiers turned to face this new danger. Seeing a bunch of ragtag town animan, some of the Lupus soldiers even laughed, but not for long.

'Light and release!' came the order from Eustace.

The Lupus soldiers stared in bewilderment as a rain of strange objects flew through the air and landed in their midst. Instantly many surprised Lupus found themselves engulfed in flames, flames that burned wherever the Ignis aqua cocktails landed, flames that couldn't be simply brushed away. Screams soon filled the air, only to be abruptly curtailed as explosion after explosion ripped through the ranks, sending bodies and body parts high into the air. Huge gaps opened up in the Lupus ranks as the homemade grenades exploded, flint shrapnel killing or ripping off limbs and wounding dozens. The rear lines began to retreat in fear, only to find their way blocked by the forward lines still battling the Ursidae. Chaos erupted with soldiers running in all directions, screaming in fear as another wave of missiles dropped from the sky. The loss of life was horrific, Lupus soldiers burnt alive or blown to pieces under the attack.

Now the town militias fell upon the survivors, weapons slashing, stabbing and slicing through the terrified ranks. The Lupus army was trapped between two enemies and was being slaughtered. Before the Lupus could gather their wits, Eustace shouted, his command echoing through the militias. 'Fall back!'

This was the devious part of the plan, even by human standards. The militias retreated and seeing this, the soldiers rallied. They turned from their flight and began to chase the retreating militias. Cries of triumph replaced those of fear as the Lupus soldiers charged towards the fighters, narrowing the gap between them. The charge soon faltered as the town fighters stopped running and turned back to face the soldiers. Still buoyed with the belief they had the upper hand, the Lupus troops continued to close the gap.

A few more yards and then cries of shock and fear ripped through the soldiers as they realised their mistake. A new rain of missiles was dropping into their ranks. Immediately some soldiers tried to flee but their way was blocked by those behind who had not yet witnessed the clouds of death about to rain down on them. Other soldiers stood rooted to the ground in shock, one moment rejoicing in victory, the next in fear of death. Again flames burst amongst the soldiers as the cocktail jugs shattered, showering victims with burning liquid. Clothes, hair and flesh burned, adding a sickly stench to the air. Soldiers beat at their flaming garments in panic, others rolled on the ground in an attempt to smother the flames. Many unwittingly rolled into pools of burning liquid that had not yet found a target, until now.

Next came hell itself as the bombs began to explode, depending on the fuse, some exploded at head level, others fell to the ground, bringing death and removing limbs in a plume of smoke and shrapnel. Explosions ripped into the Lupus ranks, tearing into the soldiers. As the sound of the last bomb echoed away, the militias charged again, mopping up those not burned black or blown apart. My staff whirled and stabbed, sliced and slashed at all about me, the fight had died in the eyes of the soldiers, now they were simply victims.

This combined form of attack was too much for the soldiers. As one, those still capable turned and ran in every direction away from the militias and their strange new weapons. Suddenly the front ranks found themselves standing alone against the Ursidae. Seeing the Lupus rear guard fleeing the battlefield, the Ursidae attacked with increased fervour, killing and maiming the overwhelmed Lupus soldiers. Within moments horns were being sounded and the entire Lupus army scattered. The general was attempting to rally his troops away from the joint assault from his foes. In front stood the Ursidae troops, behind was the town militias. General Crudelis had no choice, his army was defeated and forced to retreat. But I knew he would not give up on Indutiae easily. The remains of the Lupus army retreated to their camp to regroup and recover.

As I stood gasping with the other militias, I wondered why the Ursidae commander didn't carry the attack to the

Lupus camp. It appeared that sort of thing was not done for the Ursidae remained in their battle ranks, all eyes on the small Indutiae force. I watched as Aequus strode to the front of his forces and stopped. His eyes wary, his body poised as he waited to see what we would do next. Long moments passed as both sides stared across the blood-stained and burnt snow. The atmosphere was tense, not a bird sang or insect buzzed. Both participants ready to kill and maim in an instant if the other attacked. I wondered if I should make the first move, I certainly did not want to go to war with the Ursidae but nor would I allow Aequus to invade Indutiae. It was becoming an extremely taut situation, the slightest wrong move would result in an eruption of blood spilling and death.

'Commander Aequus?' came a shout that cut through the hostile silence. Quickly I glanced around to identify the owner of that voice. It was Eustace. Now he took a few steps forward and placed himself in front of the militias.

'I am Commander Aequus,' came a reply. 'Who are you?'

'I am called Eustace and I stand for the town of Indutiae. I wish to know your intentions.'

Aequus's eyes roamed over the figure of Eustace, a Leo standing for Indutiae. This fact did not escape the commander, a member of the Leo Cast should never be dismissed lightly.

'I have no intentions regarding you or your town. I am here because a treaty was broken, that is all. Unless you have intentions of your own, I will now order my animan to collect our dead and wounded and return to our camp. There we will remain until the matter of Crudelis and his treachery is settled. We have no issue with the town of Indutiae,' answered Aequus.

'Then the animan of Indutiae thank you,' Eustace replied. 'You may not have come to our aid but your arrival was fortuitous to our victory. We bear no intentions towards the Ursidae, we only wish to return to our homes in peace.'

'Go then. Leave for we will not hinder you.' Aequus raised an open hand in a final gesture of peace before turning to his army and giving the order to return to camp. With the sound of many feet moving, the Ursidae army turned about face and began to march back to their camp.

Soon it was just the town militias standing defiantly outside the walls and defences of Indutiae. Most appeared to be shocked at our victory, many could not believe they were still alive. Very few of our numbers had fallen, mainly due to the tactics and the use of human weapons that depleted the enemy from a safe distance. I knew this plan would not work again, both armies would be aware of our weapons now and when the next attack came, their strategies would change. New plans to be considered. However, the fact remained that in weapons, the animan of Indutiae held the upper hand. Unfortunately, when considering numbers, both the Ursidae and the Lupus could overwhelm the town like a swarm of ants over spilt sugar.

Eustace gave the order to return to town and as one, the militias turned to head back to their loved ones and home. The snow had begun to fall again and the temperature had dropped noticeably. I wondered at everyone's acceptance of Eustace's command but I was grateful. At least the militias were being led by a soldier, not a university lecturer. Another thought occurred to me as I tramped through the fresh snow. In medieval times of the human race, wars were fought during the warmer months, following the planting of crops, coming to a mutually agreed truce when harvest time approached. Of course, a vast number of medieval armies consisted of farmers and labourers, each fighting to support their lord and master. This practice benefitted both lord and serf, the lord would receive no tithe if he didn't allow his farmers to tend their crops. Even the mighty Roman armies stopped the fighting and returned to their barracks when winter fell. Of course, it depended on the intentions of their enemy, but most Roman campaigns came to a halt in winter. Here in this land, they didn't care what time of year they fought, burning hot summer or freezing cold winter, it made no difference. With frozen feet and cold hands, I would happily wait till summer before going to war. Sadly it was not my choice.

My thoughts were halted when Silĕre joined me, momentarily grasping my arm as we made our way back into the warmth of the publican. I was horrified. I had given not a single thought to the welfare of my companions. Silĕre and Secuutus had stood with the militias but not once had I searched to check if they were hurt or dead. I felt ashamed and vowed to pay more attention to my only true friends in this land. I scanned the bar for signs of Secuutus but found none. Immediately my thoughts pictured the worst scenario so I called out to all the others in the bar, 'Secuutus? Anyone seen Secuutus?'

'Yeah, I saw him earlier, heading towards Socium's house. Don't think we'll see him for a while,' the speaker sniggered.

I heaved a sigh of relief and wrapped my arms around Silĕre in a hug. She naturally didn't appreciate my public display of affection and I was roughly pushed away. Ah well, I thought, better luck next time. Looking around, I ascertained Pugnator and Adserviŏ had also survived our skirmish, though I did note a couple of the town leaders were absent. Pugnator was holding court, debriefing all the defenders, trying to gain information about the two armies outside the town, searching for that elusive nugget of intelligence that may give Indutiae the advantage. I wondered how he would react to Eustace, it was the ex-American soldier who had led the battle. Pugnator, as the unofficial town war leader had elected to remain in charge of defences while we faced Crudelis's army. How would the townsfolk and its militias view that?

I was glad to have the leadership of Eustace, however, I may have been biased as Eustace was a fellow ex-human. Pugnator held sway, all the townsfolk still deferring to him as their leader and from what I could see, Eustace was happy with that arrangement. He could lead an assault and fight as well as any of us, but being in overall command is different, the responsibility is enormous. Eustace was accustomed to following orders and the fact that Pugnator remained within the relative safety of the town didn't appear to bother him. Besides, if we had not been successful, it would have fallen on Pugnator to defend the town, a task that may have been insurmountable. No, I understood Eustace's acceptance of Pugnator and I agreed with him. Pugnator was a natural born leader with experience of how the animan go to war. We only had the violent history of the human race to fall back on, but here there were no guns or bombs.

Chapter 15: Desperate Situation

The snow fell heavily that night, making any thoughts of further conflict unfeasible. Not even animan could fight in blizzard conditions. I didn't mind for it meant a full belly and a good night's sleep, eventually. It appeared Silĕre's method of relaxing included some bedroom acrobatics. Again I didn't complain, until the next morning when every muscle in my body ached, and not just from the fighting. However, it was a pleasant change to feel at peace, even though we all knew it wouldn't last. Our lookouts reported no movement in either camp, it was difficult with the snow swirling, whipping icy grit into their faces but I had to give them kudos, they remained at their post throughout winter's blast.

Taking advantage of the lull in violence, Eustace and I rushed to produce more gunpowder and make grenades out of any container we could find. The town potter supplied baskets of misshapen pots he would normally discard, but we needed even more. Lastly, we began wrapping gunpowder in parchment envelopes. I knew these would work as I had used them against the sorcerer. Pugnator set up a rudimentary production line for the ignis aqua cocktails. I suspect it was one of the publican's most profitable periods. The production was generously boosted by the town's folk, who gave up their private supplies of the alcohol for the cause. Pugnator and the other leaders promised to reimburse the publican for his stocks, it was, after all, the most flammable liquid in town. Activity in those conditions was difficult but still animan scurried about, reinforcing barricades, ensuring water barrels were full and not frozen, and fresh bread and meat prepared.

Thus far, the town's supplies were lasting well. Being a commercial town, goods were bought in not just for personal use but also for trade. Many of the bakeries, butchers and grocery stores were donating supplies on an understanding they would be reimbursed from the town's common purse. I did wonder what would happen to any trader who refused in these desperate times. I deduced they would not remain in business, or alive. The town prepared itself and I marvelled at the resolve and bravery. All the animan in town and surrounding purlieu prepared to give his or her life in defending the right of Indutiae to remain neutral.

Eventually but with growing fear, the blizzard eased. The sky brightened and the temperature warmed a little. The sun shone for the first time in days and bird song again filled the air. Preparations done, the town stood in readiness for whatever the enemy threw at them. What fate did decide to lob at the town was feared but unexpected. As the day moved on, reports from lookouts spoke of interaction between the two military camps. None could fathom the reason as apprehension grew. Pugnator sent out scouts to gain information. They never returned.

Pugnator, Eustace and I stood on the palisade, looking out over the two military encampments. In the clear light we could see activity, but far more worrying was the action appeared to involve both forces. Perhaps Aequus is allowing Crudelis time to vacate the area? Maybe Crudelis has surrendered? In truth, none of us knew the answer but I was absolutely positive we would find out soon.

'I think we're going to need help in this one,' I said to Pugnator.

'Yes, sadly I agree,' he replied. 'By now those riders I sent out to get help should have reached many of the other towns; small hamlets, homesteads and farms that cover this land of Silva Homines. I am relying on nationalism and loyalty to spread our plea further. The war between the Lupus and Ursidae has gone on long enough. If the animan of this land join us, we will put an end to this war here and now. I await despondently as in my heart I expect no answer. It's a difficult decision for working animan to leave their homes and go to war. Without aid we are doomed, Indutiae will be lost.'

I have never been an optimist. If you don't expect good things to happen, you're not disappointed when proved correct. However, if you build yourself up with hope, dejection and despair are never far away. Glass half full or half empty? In my case the whole damn thing has probably been nicked, so no damn glass at all! I wasn't expecting any reinforcements or even a response to

Pugnator's plea from his country animan. But I still hoped. Nevertheless, watching soldiers moving freely between the two army camps could only mean someone was going to steal my damn glass again.

'Surely if anyone was going to come to our aid, they would have done so by now?' I finally asked.

'I concur,' replied Pugnator. 'This land is huge and its population spread far and wide. It is likely that no one outside this immediate area is even aware of our fight. This town is one small spot on the landscape, famous I agree but still just one town. Silva Homines is a land mainly occupied by Ursidae and Lupus but the other Casts of Leo and Tigris also live here. Until now, the war has not affected anyone other than those involved. By attacking the neutral town of Indutiae, Crudelis has put all Casts under threat. This could be the breaking point for our country, a time to smash the shackles of a divided country.'

'I'm hoping your fellow Tigris, and your fellow Leo's Eustace, will stand by our cause. Sadly I cannot say if any Lupus or Ursidae will bother, for them the war has gone on too long. They have both accepted the other Cast as their enemy and have grown accustomed to the situation. Admittedly there are some isolated locations where Lupus and Ursidae live together in peace, but this war has smouldered for too long and few will agree to aid us. Regrettably, we can do nothing about it, I fear we are on our own and I'm suspicious of what I see in the camps. In truth I fear the worst.'

'Perhaps we could vacate the town and move to the disused fort?' suggested Eustace. 'At least there we would have stronger defences. This town is too difficult to defend, therefore why not make use of a structure that lies not half-mile away?'

'That suggestion has been raised before I believe,' replied Pugnator with a glance at me. 'But getting all the town inhabitant's moved with all their belongings, animals and supplies would be a major undertaking. I agree the fort would be easier to defend but how would we get there without being slaughtered in the meantime?'

I agreed. 'The idea is certainly feasible but not at this moment. If the town survives then perhaps the notion of moving lock, stock and barrel over to the fort would be advantageous against possible future attacks. But Pugnator is right, there is no way we could move the whole population of the town while still under the scrutiny of Crudelis and Aequus.'

'We stay and fight, perhaps a hopeless cause but it's our cause. We'll defend Indutiae as long as we can but,' Pugnator paused to ensure he had our complete attention. 'I will not sacrifice the lives of animan just to retain this town. If the odds become insurmountable, I will surrender the town.'

'That's understandable,' I replied. 'A town is not a town if none are alive to live in it. So far we have been lucky, with the use of our new weapons, we have held off Crudelis's assaults. Sadly I fear the next attacks may be overwhelming, the enemy has witnessed the destruction our weapons can bring and will plan accordingly. I too have suspicions about Aequus and Crudelis, I worry things are moving against us too quickly. This could be the final battle.'

'Do you believe Crudelis will treat the town fairly or will he pillage and kill as a punishment?' asked Eustace.

'I'm sure no more lives will be lost, only our freedom, although any Ursidae will be in great danger. If Aequus remains, then I don't see how there can ever be true peace, the hate between the Lupus and the Ursidae leaders has laid down deep roots. I believe your Casts will remain safe, no animan in their right mind would start a war against either the Leo or Tigris. It would be more a slaughter than war.'

'Never say that Pugnator, I have seen wars that make any fought here look like a school playground scuffle.' I replied quietly while Eustace nodded in agreement. The human race has excelled in the art of destruction, no swords or spears but guns; bombs, biological, chemical and nuclear weapons. Power of the like the animan could never imagine in the hands of a dominant few, and those few could decide the fate of the whole planet, not just another Cast.

'We will defend one more time,' declared Pugnator. 'Then, if we are not victorious, we will have to allow the Lupus army into our town and accept whatever fate decrees.'

On that statement, the three of us parted to assist or plan the final defence of Indutiae. Pugnator went off to gather the town leaders and inform them of his decision. Eustace returned to his shack and the gun powder while I went off in search of Silĕre. It was unusual not to have her by my side, and I realised I didn't like the experience. I wondered what would happen if I managed to acquire another green jade box. Would I risk opening it now that I had strong feelings for Silĕre? Or would my homesickness overcome my desires? At that moment, in the cold snow covered land of Silva Homines, I honestly didn't know.

I had not given much thought to finding the jade box, I didn't even know if one existed here. For reasons I cannot fathom, ever since finding one on the pavement in Manchester, the jade box controlled my destiny. Of course, there was the chance I will never see one again, and remain in this land for the rest of my days, but somehow I didn't believe that. I felt its presence, I knew it would find me again. The feeling was similar to losing one's key, although it couldn't be found at that moment, one knew it would turn up eventually. The last time I opened the box, Secuutus had been drawn in, did that mean he too was now linked to the box? Again, I had no answers. I could do nothing but wait until it reappeared and then decide if I wished to open it again. In truth, I knew what I would do, deep down in my soul. I would open that damn box in the desperate hope that it would finally send me home.

Having seen no sign of Silĕre, I returned to the publican with hunger leading the way. Once inside, I found Silĕre sat at a table, an empty plate in front of her. I ordered a hot meal and a mug of warm vinum before joining her at the table. She appeared pleased to see me, I had too much experience of women who couldn't stand the sight of me the next day. My mute companion had found some writing materials, not your real paper and pen, but the most basic small square of slate and a soft stone. With these, Silĕre managed to convey all her questions without any ludicrous miming or gesturing. I wondered if the animan had developed any form of sign language but quickly dismissed the thought. Even if she knew sign language, I didn't so it would be no use anyway. I brought Silĕre up to date with Pugnator's plans, and after a few moments contemplation, she nodded. Then she explained further using her slate, she had long considered the attempt to save the town was doomed and agreed we could not fight forever.

My meal arrived and the two of us remained silent while I munched. I felt comfortable in the silence, a fact that worried me somewhat. Was I now so accustomed to the company of Silĕre that I was at peace? It's often said if one can share a silence with another, then that person is either a true friend or a lover. A thought occurred to me and I broached the question to Silĕre. What did she intend doing when this war was decided, one way or another? Almost instantly she began writing on the slate.

It simply said: "Stay with you."

Hah! Now what the hell was I supposed to do? If the jade box turned up, would I leave Silĕre behind? Did I love her? Should I take her with me? After all, Secuutus had arrived here with me, the box had transported him along for just standing too close to me when I opened it. Could I take Silĕre to wherever the box decided to send me? Would it be fair on Silĕre? What if the box returned me to Manchester? How would I stop Silĕre beating the crap out of anyone who she considered to have offended her? The local 'hoodies' wouldn't know what hit them.

Why am I asking so many damn questions which I have no answers for? I thought angrily as I finished the last bite of my meal. I looked over at the beautiful Tigris femina sat opposite and slowly reached out my hand across the table. Without hesitation, Silĕre placed her hand in mine and gave a gentle squeeze before withdrawing it again. That simple gesture spoke volumes. We both knew our lives were a risk, we may not survive the coming battle and even if we did, what then? But for now we were together, the future would take care of itself and there was nothing we could do about it.

Peace lingered for another night, mainly achieved by the snow being too deep for fighting, soldiers and townsfolk alike remained close to their fires to keep warm. The only movement was the occasional journeys of a soldier crossing the short distance between the two army camps. Pugnator grew increasingly worried at this sight, and I understood his concerns. In a three way fight, if two of the combatants began negotiating, it usually had dire consequences for the third party. In this case, the town of Indutiae and all who lived within its walls and fought at the barricades. There was a chance Aequus might be discussing peace terms with Crudelis, but one needs to consider the worst case scenario and prepare. Pugnator was prepared, the whole town was prepared, I was prepared, but for what? We could only wait and see. We received our answer in the morning as the sun rose on an otherwise beautiful day.

I had risen early and breakfasted with Silĕre before Adserviŏ came rushing into the publican. 'Come on you two, things are happening and Pugnator wants you to join him. Have you seen Eustace? I've already woken Secuutus but can't find Eustace.'

'I expect he's in the shack behind this publican,' I answered after finishing my last mouthful of food. 'What's happening?'

'All I know is there is activity in the army camps, I didn't get a chance to look for myself before Pugnator ordered me to round you all up. I haven't even had anything to eat yet,' bemoaned the young Leo.

'Okay so you've found us and you know where Eustace will most likely be,' I replied, 'why not grab some food here before you go charging off again. If the events turn serious, you'll need a full belly. We'll wake Eustace on our way.'

'Thank you,' sighed Adserviŏ, his energetic eagerness overcome by his youthful appetite. In one long stride, he was at the bar and placing an order for hot food with the publican.

As Silĕre and I rose from the table, I wondered how the publican managed to run the bar, which appeared to never close, man the defences and prepare food. But as that thought entered my mind, so a small voice called out from a room that I took to be the kitchen. It was evident the publican had help, useful as his trade had soared recently with paying guests and constant town meetings in his establishment. I realised then that I didn't even know his name. Was he married? Did he have a family? Who was he? I felt ashamed I couldn't answer any of these questions. I resolved to ask him later. I paid him for our breakfast then Silĕre and I went in search of Eustace. The door of his shack, or rather the shack he squatted in while mixing gunpowder was empty, and more to the point, there were no signs of anyone having been there overnight. Where the hell was Eustace I thought with some suspicion?

It was no use hanging around and trying to second guess my fellow ex-human so we continued to join Pugnator. On the palisade, we joined Secuutus and Pugnator as a satisfied Adserviŏ ran up behind us. Moments later Eustace arrived and quickly made his way to my side. In a whisper, he told me he needed to speak with me, but not now, later in private. I acknowledged as we both turned to peer over the palisade. Now I understood the reason for Pugnator gathering us all together. It was a sight I had wished not to see.

Out on the snow covered ground, two lines of soldiers were leaving their respective camps and marching towards us. Lupus side by side with Ursidae and led by Aequus and Crudelis. I realised my qualms were confirmed, the two armies had joined forces. As yet none of us watching from the town could not know the reason, was it to be a truce or war? We were about to find out as the military leaders approached the town.

'Greetings to you Pugnator and the animan of Indutiae,' called Aequus as he and Crudelis halted a short distance from the palisade on which we all stood and stared in bewilderment.

'Greetings to you also,' replied Pugnator. 'I see you have reached some form of agreement. May I ask what that might be?'

'You are correct Pugnator, we have reached an agreement as you wisely deduced,' came the response from the commander of the Ursidae army. 'General Crudelis and I have agreed to a temporary truce between our two Casts. Our truce is a direct result of your actions and those of Indutiae. This is a situation that cannot be allowed to continue, we cannot have a neutral town within the border of our two territories. Therefore a decision has been made by General Crudelis and myself on behalf of the Ursidae Cast.'

Aequus paused to draw in a deep breath then, 'We hereby order you and all the inhabitants of Indutiae to leave. The town of Indutiae will be razed to the ground and no longer stand in the way of either the Lupus or Ursidae in the contest for dominance.'

A shocked silence fell over the town. Initially, Crudelis had only wished to control the town, to be used as a Lupus border post. Crudelis had even offered to allow all Ursidae to leave in safety within a given period of time, and other Casts could remain as long as they recognised his authority. We had sought out Commander Aequus and his Ursidae army for help against Crudelis. We could not have known the two forces would join against the town. Now it appeared all we had fought for, the homes and livelihoods of hundreds of animan, were to be burnt to the ground. To be removed entirely from the landscape. The neutral town of Indutiae was to be destroyed.

'This is an outrage! You cannot destroy a whole town just because it will not choose an aggressor,' shouted Pugnator in horror. 'There are hundreds of animan here, from all four Casts. You cannot simply eject them from their homes and their lives on a whim between two arrogant soldiers! Are you both mad?'

Pugnator's words triggered cries of disbelief and shock throughout the town, cries of anguish that slowly turned into shouts of anger. A low growl emanated from every street and every house, from the palisades and the barricades, a growl of anger and defiance rose from the town. As the sound of hundreds of angry voices reached the two army leaders, looks of uncertainty flickered across their faces. They now realised what they had done, they had awoken a beast that they may not be able to control. Soon shouts of abuse and hate poured from the town, flowing over barricades, walls and palisades and down upon the heads of the military leaders standing alone outside the town.

Suddenly Pugnator roared, his tone smothering the voices like a blanket. He turned his back on the two military animan and faced the crowds that spewed onto the streets of Indutiae. I noticed that almost all were armed, all had expressions of fury, hate and fear. This was a mob, and someone would be lynched, figuratively of course. The threat to burn down their homes and destroy Indutiae had sparked a full-on rebellion, I knew by the faces of those about me that there would be no agreement to Aequus demands, not without a war!

Once a muted silence had fallen, Pugnator called to the residents gathered below and on the defences. 'What is your wish? He cried. 'Do we leave our homes, our businesses, our lives? Or do we fight? Do we fight the evils that wait outside our walls or do we leave? Will we fight? Will we die for our town?' Pugnator's voice had risen with each question, his voice reaching a crescendo with his last words.

'Kill! Kill the soldiers! Kill them all!' came the shouts of the very angry crowd. The ferocity of the cries rained down on Aequus and Crudelis, the fury behind the replies staggering them in shock. Immediately they both ran back to the safety of their armies. The choice had been made. Indutiae would fight, but now they would fight in hate and anger. No quarter, no lives spared. The beast that was Indutiae poised to leap to battle.

Outside the two the armies prepared, forming into lines of attack, officers screaming at their troops in an attempt to bolster courage in those who had heard Indutiae growl. Inside the town the growl was quiet, everyone was busy. All that could fight were armed, older children and the old stood shoulder to shoulder with the militias. Weapons ranged from swords and spears to pitchforks and skillets. Anger remained in power over fear as every inhabitant of

Indutiae made ready to defend not only their town but their very livelihoods. Eustace and I dashed off to gather as many of the homemade grenades as we could carry, Adserviŏ and Silĕre rushed to the publican to collect all the jugs and pots of Ignis aqua. Rocks were gathered by children and placed in piles around the palisades, caltrops were thrown out onto the ground surrounding the town to penetrate feet and cripple any unfortunate soldier who stood on one. Water barrels were filled, buckets of water placed about the town and animals corralled against any panicked escape.

Once back at the palisade, Eustace and I distributed the grenades to those who had wielded them in the previous fight against Crudelis. Others were given the alcohol filled vessels, the cocktails already fitted with strips of cloth for ignition. I noticed the contents of a few cocktails being consumed by scared townsfolk to steady their nerves, no one complained. Braziers were lit in readiness to light the weapons and to provide illumination if the battle raged into the hours of darkness. During all this hustle and bustle I noted not one animan had elected to leave the town, no one ran for safety. Every single animan of Indutiae remained to fight. Tigris stood with Lupus, Ursidae beside Leo. The four Casts of this land were come together as one to face the enemy.

Chapter 16: Surrender?

The attack came within the hour, a combined force of Lupus and Ursidae troops marched towards the town, Crudelis and Aequus leading the way. The soldiers were well-armed, well trained and in a life they had chosen. They all knew they would be killing members of their own Cast but orders were orders and they had to obey. Feet trampled the snow, creating a furrow that gradually deepened as it drove straight for the main barricade of the town. Crudelis called a halt and stood staring at the town, his features full of arrogance. His whole posture indicated his belief that Indutiae would fall quickly.

'I speak to all the animan of Indutiae,' he shouted. 'We will give you one more opportunity to leave this town and go on your way unharmed. Evacuate now and keep your lives.'

Pugnator stared down at the general for a heartbeat before turning to the animan of Indutiae. In a loud firm voice, Pugnator echoed the general's words.

'If any of you wish to leave, you may do so without blame or ridicule. I will not force anyone to fight. Come forward those to leave in peace and a way out of the town will be made for you. Who amongst you chooses this path?'

I held my breath, visions of animan running to escape the town filled my mind. But no one moved. No femina, no child nor elderly came forward, not one soul moved. I looked on with a mixture of astonishment and pride, astonished that none chose to save themselves and pride in the animan's bravery and determination to stand for their town. I am sure if this situation were to occur back in my human world, women, children and those sick, injured or old would be escorted out of the town. But I could see fault in that gallant approach. Those who left would face an uncertain future, no food or water other than what they carried. No home or shelter to hide from the cold, no defence against wild animals or bandits that inevitably roamed the land. At least by remaining, they were with their loved ones, they were helping to protect their homes and they stood where they wanted to be. No, leaving was not the safest action they could take, and none did.

'I will take your silence as my answer,' shouted Crudelis. 'I am sorry but it is your choice. Now you have chosen death and destruction and I pity you.'

'Prepare to defend yourselves.'

With those his last words, Crudelis walked calmly back to his ranks of soldiers, squared his shoulders, raised his sword and ordered, 'Charge!'

That single word created a chain reaction in both the military and the town as both forces went to war. A rain of caltrops fell onto the ground in front of the first rank of soldiers with an immediate effect. Suddenly dozens of both Ursidae and Lupus soldiers dropped to the ground in agony. Officers screamed at them to get back on their feet, they were well within reach of spears and other missiles. The next rank of soldiers rushed forward, trampling on any comrade who didn't or couldn't move away fast enough. This rank carried ladders and, under a rain of stones and more caltrops, the ladders were pushed against barricades and palisade. I stood awaiting my first opponent when I realised the army was splitting into three, the first group attacked the main barricade. The other two deployed in opposite directions and moved rapidly to the sides. I recognised the manoeuvre and shouted a warning to Pugnator. The combined military was initiating a pincer movement.

Pugnator rushed off to warn the other defences, leaving myself, Silĕre, Secuutus and Eustace to lead the fight at the front. The first head appeared over the palisade right in front of me. I didn't stop to think as I stabbed my bladed staff in his eye and pushed him backwards and off the ladder. Within moments another had reached the top and before I could react, he jumped over and landed so close his nose almost touched mine. My staff was useless at such close range but my evil knife was not. Up it swept as it sliced deeply into the soldiers gut, ripping upwards and carving him open, venting his steaming innards. Withdrawing the knife I pushed the dead soldier away just in time to defect a blow rushing down at my head. A sword flashed into my vision as Silĕre stabbed her blade into the face of my attacker. I didn't have time to thank her as I was instantly confronted by two more soldiers, each attempting to remove my body parts. I whirled and danced whilst my staff slammed and stabbed.

Suddenly a blow knocked me to the ground, robbing the ability to move from my limbs. My vision blurred and raising a hand to my head I discovered an egg shaped bulge rising nicely. Strong hands grabbed me and I lashed out, fearing an enemy. My feeble attempts were brushed aside and Eustace swam into sight as my vision cleared, my would be slayer prone at his feet.

'Get up Harry! Move!' he shouted while helping me up. 'I've found the jade box,' he screamed over the sounds of fighting and dying.

'What?' My brain couldn't comprehend what he was talking about, my thoughts were still engaged in the small matter of staying alive. The green jade box was the last thing on my mind as blades flashed around me.

'I said, I've found the jade box,' repeated Eustace as he held me steady until my equilibrium returned. 'I was rooting around the shack for more pots when I remembered an old sack which I knew contained bric-a-brac. I emptied out the sack and there it was. I swear it wasn't there the last time I checked because I filled the sack in the first place! I recognised the box immediately and I have it safe if you wish to get out of here?'

'What?' I replied, still in shock. 'Why would I leave? I'm needed here, we're both needed here. We can't leave now.'

'Oh I'm not going anywhere,' grinned Eustace as he helped me back to the palisade and pushed my staff into my hands. 'I am staying here forever, live or die today I will stay.'

Then he was off, charging at a group of soldiers that had Adserviŏ pinned in a corner. I followed and between the three of us, the soldiers were soon dispatched. But now the battle raged fiercely throughout the town. Buildings burned and animan died, the sword not distinguishing between soldier or shopkeeper, all died the same. I looked for and found Silĕre and rushed to her side, finding Secuutus close by. I knew I would have to inform Secuutus that the jade box had been found, but now was certainly not the time. Soldiers spilled over our defences and I saw the main barricade being torn apart.

The soldiers had a clear run into the town and hundreds flooded in, to be met by a wall of steel held in the hands of simple townsfolk. Indutiae residents who fought for a cause and the cause was theirs, a cause that leant strength to their arms and fire to their gut. They fought with a ferocity that the soldiers, though greater in number, could not match, they were simply following orders. A vast difference in motivation.

My brief contemplation was ripped apart as an Ursidae soldier lunged at me, his sword ready to skewer my middle. I leapt to one side, smashing my staff down at his head in one fluid movement, but it was not enough. The soldier dodged away and my staff flashed through empty air. Immediately he attacked again, swinging his sword at my head while I was unbalanced. I had no choice, I dropped down and barrelled into his legs, both of us ending in a tangle on the ground. His sword remained firmly in his grasp and now he began trying to stab me.

We were scrambling about on the ground too close for either sword or staff. Neither of us was gaining any advantage over the other as weapons were discarded in favour of fists. I was tall and strong, but he was stocky and stronger. His blows felt like a hammer while mine appeared to have little effect on his solid head. Time to fight like a human I decided as I brought my knee up sharply between his legs. That certainly had the desired effect, immediately his hands dropped from battering my face to grasp at his painful pride and joy. I shot to my feet, grasped my staff and stabbed down into the soldier's neck, twisting and sawing the blade in ensure his demise. I felt a brief twinge of guilt at having killed the soldier in such a way, his final position in death saw him curled on the floor with both hands protectively grasped about his genitalia.

My guilt, or amusement lasted but a second as more soldiers streamed into the town and several headed in my direction. The town was being torn asunder as skirmishes and individual fights spilled out from the main battle. Everywhere I looked there were soldiers killing townsfolk and town fighters slaughtering soldiers. I saw Pugnator remove the head of one soldier while continuing to scream orders and encouragement to the animan of Indutiae. I saw Secuutus roaring like the bear he evolved from as he slashed and tore about him, a sword now in each huge hand. Eustace and Adserviŏ were standing back to back fighting a small group of Lupus soldiers. But then I saw Silĕre fall. Moving with every ounce of speed left in me I rushed to the spot where she went down, arriving just in time to ram my blade through the exposed back of her assailant, and immediately halting his intent. In fear, I looked down at the Tigris femina who lay dazed upon the ground. Reaching out I grasped her hand and dragged her upright, checking her over for serious wounds. Relieved I saw that apart from cuts, gashes and bruises, she was in no worse state than myself.

Another Lupus soldier bore down on us. I wrapped one arm around Silĕre's waist, holding her up while stabbing out at this new opponent. I saw him grin, he knew he had the advantage and I would either be forced to release Silĕre to her fate or die protecting her. I made my choice and retained my hold on my unsteady companion. The soldier gave a short laugh as he advanced slowly on me, his sword ready, easily deflecting my staff swings. Without warning, a huge shadow fell upon the soldiers back and a shape rose up behind him. A flash of steel and the soldier's still grinning head flopped wetly to the ground.

'Having fun?' grinned Secuutus before he turned and dived back into the thickest of the fighting. I shouted a thanks to my huge Ursidae friend, wondering again if I really wanted to return to my former life. But this was no time for pondering, the fight was not over. Silĕre shook her head and released herself from my support, a smile indicating her gratitude. Another Lupus soldier foolishly rushed at us but against two Tigris, he stood no chance. In a moment Silĕre and I were plunging deep into the battle again, the foolish soldier lying lifeless behind us. Now it was almost two against one as the greater number of soldiers began to sway the battle from the town and into the grip of the coalition. During a brief respite from killing, I looked around and from what I saw, I knew we would not, could not win.

Indutiae would fall.

'It's no use Harry, we are defeated,' came Pugnator's voice from behind me. I turned to face the town leader and found a bloody and bruised figure looking back at me in anguish.

While the battle raged around us, Pugnator's shoulders dropped and he stared at me, exhaustion and sorrow lining his face. For a moment the world and the killing faded as I looked upon a brave animan who knew he was beaten, his town was finished. I stepped towards him and laid a hand on his shoulder.

'We must surrender,' he whispered before continuing louder. 'We must surrender Indutiae and save as many lives as we can. There's no point in this slaughter. We must stop it now!'

I didn't know what to say, this courageous animan had given his all. We both knew that he would die if we surrendered. As the leader of Indutiae, he would shoulder the entire blame for these events. The Lupus and Ursidae armies would execute him and all his officers. A sudden realisation, Shit! That includes me. I would certainly be put to death alongside Pugnator and the others. But what could I do? In order to stop the killing and save the lives of those townsfolk still standing, I too must die.

'I understand Pugnator,' I said. 'The animan of Indutiae have fought bravely but the war is lost. We put up a good fight but this must end before every single one of us is slaughtered.'

Although the town resisted bravely, against the combined forces of the Lupus and Ursidae, we stood no chance. Pugnator lowered his sword and climbed to the top of the palisade wall. I saw him fill his lungs ready to shout for surrender when a hush began to fall. It began outside with the soldiers and rapidly spread into the town. Pugnator stopped, his eyes turning to the forest that surrounded the Indutiae. Some still fought on unawares but most were halted by a perception that something else was happening. I leapt up to stand beside Pugnator and saw what caused his voice to falter.

From the tree line that surrounded the small clearing and the town of Indutiae, animan were emerging from the forest. First just a trickle but then a flow that became a flood as hundreds began to appear. In complete silence they walked towards the town, a few soldiers attempted to stop them but to no avail, the tide of animan kept coming. Animan armed with swords, spears, farming tools and even wooden clubs. The numbers kept coming, a mass of animan emerging from the darkness of the forest all around Indutiae and marching silently towards the town. All fighting ceased as both soldiers and townsfolk stared at the horde approaching from the trees, hundreds grew into thousands and hundreds of thousands, and still they came. Ordinary animan from all points of the compass, a tide of bodies moving in silence towards the town. I could see this approaching mass consisted of all the four Casts of animan, Leo, Ursidae, Tigris and Lupus. Male and female, old and young walked in silence as in and around the town, attackers stood side by side with defenders as they watched in surprise and shock at the multitude approaching the town. The horde did not attempt to avoid trampling the tents and paraphernalia of both army camps as they continued their advance.

Shattering the unnatural silence a cry was heard. Crudelis was ordering his soldiers to the fore to face this unexpected surge of animan. Some of the Lupus soldiers near me looked at each other but did not move. The vast number of animan emerging from the trees swamped the numbers of the Ursidae and Lupus coalition. They were powerless and Crudelis impotent.

To be honest, I was beginning to feel somewhat uneasy as I watched the sea of animan silently flowing towards us. The scene reminded me of those zombie films so much in favour back home before I opened the jade box. A silent horde marching together towards Indutiae. I grasped my staff tighter as apprehension brought sweat to my brow, the sheer number of the horde would tear us to shreds in seconds, overwhelmed under a sea of bodies. Silĕre and Secuutus moved quietly to my side, fear and bewilderment on their faces, a mirror of my own trepidation. Under the winter sun, the tide of animan surged and flowed closer like an incoming tide. I heard the sound of sobbing behind me, whispered words of comfort or sorrow, emotions rising in all who watched the spectacle grow around the town and the would be conquerors.

Then from the silence came a shout, 'There's my mum!'

Then another, 'And mine!'

'That's my dad!

'My sister!'

'My son!'

Voices began to fill the air as Lupus and Ursidae soldiers recognised family and friends amongst the horde. Unexpectedly a single stout female Lupus emerged from the mass. Her arms outstretched and tears in her eyes as she walked slowly towards the dumbstruck armies. No one made to stop her as she approached. Then suddenly a heartfelt cry came from the lines of Lupus troops. A young soldier broke from the ranks, threw down his sword and ran into the outstretched arms of the Lupus femina, crying over and over again, 'Mum, mum, I'm here mum.'

The horde stopped just yards from the town perimeter, every animan halting and standing, still without a word spoken. I could feel thousands of eyes upon us as we waited to see what was to occur. Even Crudelis and Aequus were silent in their shock and fear. A heartbeat later, the clatter of weapons being dropped rippled through both armies as soldiers left their ranks and ran into the horde, there to be met by fathers; mothers, lovers, sisters, brothers, sons and daughters. Amidst the sobs of happiness and tears, I heard an Ursidae soldier near me throw down his sword with a sigh. 'That's it!' he said to all who could hear, 'I'm not fighting my own family, my loved ones. Not for anyone!' That said, the soldier walked off towards the crowd, quickly followed by other soldiers from both sides. As I watched soldiers from both sides discarded their weapons and fled to the horde, searching for their loved ones.

Then from the depths of the rapidly growing horde, four animan emerged like wraths from the grave and moved forward alone. This small quartet made their way through the leading edge of the horde and came to stand directly in front of the main entrance to the town, where once a mighty barricade had defended Indutiae. The four animan held my gaze for a moment before I turned again to stare at the host of animan surrounding Indutiae. I noticed brown and green military uniforms scattered throughout the horde, soldiers from Lupus and Ursidae stood shoulder to shoulder with farmers and shopkeepers. Now I was totally confused, what the hell was happening here?

The four animan, one from each Cast, stood and stared at the town and the armies in silence, none approached them, and none tried to stop them. The Leo of the group took a step forward. Seeing the strength and posture of the Leo, I was immediately reminded of Janiz, a prince of his realm with whom Secuutus and I fought a sorcerer, so long ago it seemed. An imposing figure, radiating the majesty of his Cast. Wide shoulders and flowing fair hair gave stance to features that demanded respect. A short pause before he spoke, in the unnatural and foreboding silence his voice boomed out for all to hear.

'Those in change, step forward. Now!' the Leo roared.

Aequus and Pugnator made their way to the threshold of the town before stopping and looking back in search of Crudelis. From amongst the shocked soldiers, an indignant voice shouted in protest, 'I will not be ordered about like some common animan, I will hear what he has to say from here. I will remain where I stand!'

It was Crudelis, the Lupus general's arrogance still very much in evidence, but now, no one was taking notice. In response, several hands reached out and grabbed the general, hands that belonged to Lupus soldiers I noted. Despite his angry shouts and threats of court martial and death, the soldiers dragged General Crudelis forward and deposited him beside Pugnator and Aequus, facing the four animan and the horde behind them. The numbers were so great that the horde entirely encircled the town hundreds deep, a ring of flesh with one single mind.

'I demand to know the reason for this disrespectful behaviour,' shouted Crudelis. 'The Lupus army shall hear of this and bring wrath upon your heads!'

'I don't think so,' replied the Leo calmly. 'I am Mortes. My friends are Pestilentia, Bellum and Fames. We four represent the animan of Silva Homines, all four Casts of this land. Who is Pugnator? Who are your leaders?'

Pugnator followed by Aequus introduced themselves before explaining who Crudelis was because he stoutly refused to answer. The four animan stared at the three leading opponents in the war of Indutiae for a long moment before the Tigris member stepped forward.

'We heard your call for help Pugnator and we came, all of us. For we have long travelled this land attempting an end to this conflict between the Lupus and the Ursidae. This land has suffered and the animan now say no more war. None wished to be ruled by either Lupus or Ursidae and we have made our wishes known, sometimes with force, mostly with peace. We were already heading this way and our supporters have grown with each town we've freed. Now we are many and no army can stand against us. We,' the Tigris gestured to the horde surrounding us, 'are the animan of Silva Homines!'

'I am Bellum of the Tigris Cast. On behalf of all the animan of Silva Homines, we demand you lay down your weapons and cease. The animan of this land have grown tired of this petty war and all order it stopped.'

This statement shocked both soldiers and townsfolk in its implication. Gasps were heard as I watched the surreal scene from the palisade. The Tigris who now stood before the trio of Pugnator, Aequus and Crudelis was one of my own cast but would tower over me in both height and physical presence. His hair tied back from a wide and somewhat cruel face topping a muscular body, a huge sword hung from his belt and a round iron shield was strapped to his back. A true and mighty Tigris warrior. I hoped I never had to face him in combat, the outcome would certainly not be in my favour.

The roar of his words brought an instant reaction from Crudelis, with bluster and puff, he drew himself up ramrod straight, stared Bellum in the eye and responded with all the gusto we had come to expect from the general. He ranted and raved, threatened dire consequences and a lifetime of war if this charade continued. The Tigris did not answer, he took a step back and allowed another of the four to come forward, and it was the Lupus member of the four.

'I am Pestilentia of the Lupus Cast and you will heed what we say. You are nothing to the animan of Silva Homines, a cancer that must be cut out before the body dies.'

The thin but still imposing figure of the Lupus peered at Crudelis, a wicked or perhaps evil glint in his eye. Again, this member of the four stood tall, taller than many of his Cast. His grey features set stern under short cropped grey hair. He too possessed a huge sword, smaller than that of the Leo and Tigris but that was understandable. Amongst the animan, those two towered over all. Again the bluster came from Crudelis as he screamed for his soldiers to kill these arrogant animan. Not one Lupus soldier moved, none dared for they all recognised a true Alpha when they saw it, and Pestilentia radiated danger.

The final member of the four, the Ursidae, stepped forward, taking Pestilentia's place. His brown eyes settled on Aequus for a moment, causing the other to lower his gaze in submission. The Ursidae was built like a tank, his large extended belly framed by a rippling body of muscle. I thought there and then that this Ursidae could wrestle an elephant, and win. He too sported a shield strapped to his back while a broad sword hung from each side of his belt. A small cap made of some form of metal perched on his huge head, his hair as black as coal.

'I am Fames,' he called out in a deep rich tone. 'I demand all Ursidae to relinquish their weapons, now! This war is finished, the Casts of Silva Homines will no longer stand for such slaughter in this power seeking struggle. Both Ursidae and Lupus will halt their squabbles for power, no one Cast shall have rule over this land.' The huge Ursidae paused and glowered at all before him, others of his Cast avoided his menacing gaze.

'On the command of the animan of Silva Homines, a government will be formed with repraesentativa from all Casts. You and your petty war are void.'

As soon as he finished speaking, every soldier and every one of the townsfolk dropped or sheathed their weapons. The presence of the four animan stood at the entrance to Indutiae with the horde behind them left no animan in any doubt of the consequences of refusal, all bar one of course. General Crudelis roared out his defiance and swept his ornate sword from its scabbard before lunging at Fames. The huge Ursidae appeared to barely move, but in an instant, the generals head fell to the ground, followed a second later by his dead body. It had all happened so fast, even my feline eyes had difficulty in following the movements of Fames. Fames bent and wiped his sword on the Crudelis's blood covered tunic before carefully sheathing the weapon.

Another one I'll avoid in future I decided.

Silence rested on the town and its attacks, all stared at the four leaders of the horde. The world fell hushed, the quiet spiritual in its completeness, even the birds in the sky omitted not one song. I felt the hairs on the back of my neck stand on end in this overpowering stillness. It lasted several heartbeats before the silence was broken by a huge resounding sigh, a sigh that emanated from every animan present. A shuffling of feet followed as all awaited further instructions. Everyone, including me, suddenly found themselves at a loss at what to do next. The four impressive animan stood shoulder to shoulder and glared at all who caught their eye. After what seemed an age, the huge Leo called Mortes demanded an answer.

'Will there be peace? Or will you die?' he roared so all could hear.

'Peace! Peace! Peace!' the cry resounded throughout Indutiae and the surrounding area, the animan responding in one voice. Townsfolk, militia and soldiers, all gave vent to that single word, echoed by the massive horde.

Pugnator stepped forward and approached the repraesentativa of the four Casts. Stopping in front of them, he turned to the town and held up his arms, signalling for quiet. A hush settled and Pugnator turned back to the repraesentativa.

'It is on behalf of the animan of Indutiae that I speak, I cannot speak for the two armies but Indutiae calls for peace. Long have we lived in peace despite our warring neighbours, we wish to live in peace once more. The Indutiae animan will lay down their weapons and consider this 'government' you speak of.'

Having said his piece, Pugnator turned to look at Aequus who acknowledged with a slight nod. He moved forward, dropping his sword and ripping off his military tunic. Standing in front of the repraesentativa and side by side with Pugnator, Aequus surrendered his animan of Ursidae and though he could not speak for the entire Ursidae army, Aequus promised to abide by the will of the animan of Silva Homines.

'Who will speak for the Lupus army? Demanded Mortes, his eyes flickering to the headless body of Crudelis before him.

One animan emerged from the ranks of Lupus soldiers and walked towards the gathering outside the main entrance to Indutiae. 'I am, was second in command so now have the responsibility for this Lupus army. I am called Fiduciary and it is I who will speak for them. The Lupus army surrender to the animan of Silva Homines and we place ourselves at your mercy.'

I stood quietly watching as the scene unfolded, wondering at the power of these four repraesentativa, four powerful warriors were bringing peace to this land. I wish the same could happen back in my world but unfortunately, there are too many politicians involved. When all had agreed the war was over, Mortes turned back to the horde and raised both arms high in victory. Immediately a cheer rose from the horde, growing increasingly louder as the news was passed throughout the massive crowd of animan. A cheer that resounded through the air, a cheer that came from the heart of all.

Pugnator then took over the preceding and invited the repraesentativa into Indutiae as guests of the town. Both Lupus and Ursidae armies dissolved as I watched, a few bewildered soldiers scattered, some joined the horde where perhaps families or friends could be found. Others simply headed off in their own direction, possibly towards their homes. Those left remained together, still in ranks as their training demanded, but now uncertain and afraid. The arrival of the horde and the four repraesentativa had brought peace so quickly, no one knew what to do. Now as peace descended, fires could be seen flaring up amongst the horde, tents were raised and the masses of animan settled, making ready for the night, preparing meals and trying to keep warm in the snow covered land. Mortes informed us that the horde would be on the move again after a day's rest. Indutiae was not the sole location of aggression between Lupus and Ursidae.

Aequus and the new Lupus commander, Fiduciary rounded up all those bewildered soldiers with nowhere and no one to go to and therefore wishing to remain in the respective armies, and organised the rebuilding of their camps. Pugnator led the repraesentativa into the town amidst much cheering and celebration. Families hugged in relief, some sobbed at the loss of family or friends. Traders opened for business and rushed out to sell their wares to any willing customers within the horde. It was a business opportunity not to be missed. Along with the celebrations, the remains of the barricades and hastily constructed wall were dismantled. Animan extinguished fires, rounded up frightened stock and began the repair of homes and property. Others sought refuge where they could as they had no home to go to, destroyed in the battle for Indutiae. Life was returning to the town.

Pugnator ushered the four into the publican. Where else? I followed along behind with Silĕre and Eustace. All of us sore and carrying wounds that required attention. Moans and screams of the wounded and dying still pierced the cold air around the town while carers from both town and horde moved amongst them, saving those they could, giving succour to those facing the ultimate end. Though it seemed surreal now, there had been a major battle with animan killing and animan dying. Peace may have arrived in a short time but some wounds would not heal quickly.

Weapons lay discarded on the ground, no one wishing to remove them. Some animan simply sat where they had fought, too exhausted or traumatised to move. Others knelt beside prone and lifeless bodies of loved ones, friends and family, despair crumpling their features. The shock and fear of the war remained, peace had arrived so quickly many could not apprehend what had happened, many sat and cried. I felt a dampness run down my cheeks as I witnessed the aftermath of such horror that can only come from war. My heart was torn from my chest at the sight of a little girl, no more than three or four, desperately seeking a response from her dead mother. I could stand no more and turned away, guilt and hopelessness washed over me and the dampness became a flood.

A flood of tears.

Finally, my soul spent, I looked for my fellow ex-rider but saw no sign, Secuutus had already disappeared back to Socium, obviously eager to celebrate in his own way. An idea I would entertain, as soon as I could drag Silĕre away from the meeting now underway between the repraesentativa, Pugnator and those surviving town leaders. Aequus and Fiduciary had promised to join them later, once they had reorganised their troops. A war had been ended by the will of the animan, and no doubt, by the persuasive manner of the four mighty animan collectively now known as the repraesentativa, Mortes, Pestilentia, Fames and Bellum.

It was the next day before I remembered Eustace's news about the jade box and following a hot breakfast, I went in search of the American. The horde was relaxing, welcoming lost family back into the fold. Even the repraesentativa merged back into the thousands of animan who traversed the land, putting an end to the struggle for power between the Casts of Lupus and Ursidae. During the meeting the night before, Pugnator had been nominated to represent Indutiae when a government was formed after all hostilities had either ceased or been squashed by the horde. Pugnator had agreed with the town's blessing. I was pleased for him and proud of all the animan who had stood up for their land, their country and their freedom. I was also rather pleased with myself, I had fought in a war, fighting for a cause even though it had little bearing on my life. I smiled and wondered what my students would think of me know, a humble university lecturer turned veteran warrior. I was also very pleased following a night of more action, this time with Silĕre.

Chapter Seventeen: A Question

Despite the vast number of animan camping all around the town of Indutiae, calm had settled over the land. Fiduciary and Aequus were deep in talks with the repraesentativa, along with Pugnator and other prominent members of the town. I asked Eustace why he was not attending the peace discussion but he replied, in his own words, 'Not interested in all that hot air!'

He then reminded me again about the jade box, he knew where it was and there would not be a better time to get it. I was about to agree when Secuutus appeared. I hadn't seen him since the end of hostilities but wasn't surprised, the big Ursidae had found love. My old friend and ex-rider had been by my side through many adventures, guiding and protecting me as I built a new life amongst the animan. Something was different this time, Secuutus didn't charge up with his normal confidence, instead his approach appeared subdued. I knew something was wrong and I suspected I knew the reason. I was right.

'Hi Harry, can I have a word, alone please?' he asked quietly with a glance at Eustace.

I knew what was coming so assured Secuutus that Eustace would understand what he was going to tell me. At first, my friend seemed reluctant, still not sure of the ex-American. I smiled and nodded and with a slump of his huge shoulders, Secuutus explained.

'When you leave, as I know you will, I cannot come with you this time. Your 'magic box' brought me here and although I miss my home and Janiz, I have made a new home here with Soci. I want to stay here with her. I'm sorry.'

'I understand,' I replied. 'I knew this was coming and I'm happy for you. To be honest I've not yet decided what to do next. I too have found someone. I don't know if she will want to leave with me or stay here where she is accepted with no more shame. Eustace also knows of the 'magic' that brought us here, and he and I are just about to er . . . go and find the magical box. Then I will speak to Silĕre, further than that I can't say.'

I watched my friend Secuutus, his big brown eyes glistening and his lower jaw trembled slightly. He had been ripped from his home and life with Janiz and the riders and dumped straight into a war zone. I hope Soci would bring him the peace and stability he so desperately needed. I was happy for him, he had found his home.

'Please don't be sad, you have a new life here and someone to share it with. I'm happy and I will never forget you. Who knows? I may even stay myself. Go now my friend, go with all my thanks, my friendship and my thoughts. Go and be happy.'

I should have expected it but I didn't. Without a word, Secuutus grabbed me in his arms and gave me what could really be called a bear hug. His strong arms embraced me, his power reaching deep into my soul. Then just as quickly, the truest friend I had ever had gently let me go, turned and walked away, away from me but now walking into his new life with Soci in Indutiae. I choked up and had to turn and hide the tears that threatened to well up inside me. My friend would never know how much I would miss him. Eustace laid his hand on my shoulder, understanding on his face. He too knew the pain of being ripped from one's home and he knew the value of a true friend. However, it was my turn to decide my future so with a deep breath, Eustace and I went off to find that damn green jade box.

A short time later I had the key to my future, good or bad. The green jade box was in my possession. Eustace had already declared his decision to remain in Indutiae and had willing given the box to me. I dared not open it yet, a conflict raging in my soul. I needed to talk to Silĕre and knew her decision would govern my own. The box lay heavy on my person, my fingers frequently caressing its surface, my mind now throwing up more doubts. What if it didn't work? Was it the 'real' jade box that had changed my life so much? I knew I would have to wait, I couldn't even contemplate opening it at this time, but the urge, the desire was strong. I had to find Silĕre before temptation overcame me.

As I walked I remembered, I remembered my previous life in Manchester, that sprawling city in England where I had grown into a man. I recalled the time spent trying to pound knowledge into reluctant students and wondering if I had been of the same ilk during my own academic studies. But now none of that mattered, I had a decision to make. Given the chance, would I return home and continue my life as a nondescript human being in an overpopulation world? Or would I stay as an animan, a biped tiger in a world of evolved animals? Here I had found true friends for the first time in my life, friends that would lay down their lives to save me, friends I trusted. Here I had also found love, a love that bypassed all the mushy stuff of wine and roses. There had been girls in my past obviously, some I remembered fondly, others I would rather forget. But now, here on this strange world I had met a true soul mate, a person that mirrored my own being in so many ways. Which future did I want?

'Hello Harry, you appear preoccupied.'

It was Pugnator, I had been deeply engrossed in reflection as I trudged through the town that I had failed notice him approaching. Looking at him now, he appeared younger than I remember, a grin on his face I had not seen before. In my infinite wisdom, I concluded Pugnator was – happy!

'Hi Pugnator, yeah sorry. My mind was elsewhere. Any news? What's happening with this self-rule thing you and the four horde leaders?'

'Oh, it'll take some time before anything is set in stone. For now we are just talking, nothing to report so far. You know how much leaders like to examine every single aspect of every single decision on every single item. This period of building a government for Silva Homines and Indutiae will take time. This is a big land and there are many other animan who must be consulted. At least the burden of civil war between the Lupus and Ursidae will soon be a thing of the past. The animan have shown their unity and the military of all Casts must now bow to an elected committee or government of the animan, by the animan, for the animan.'

Pugnator turned and gestured at the surrounding horde that ringed the town of Indutiae, dwarfing it into almost insignificance. 'There is the army of Silva Homines now. Casts shoulder to shoulder with other Casts, brother alongside brother, friends beside friends. Now we truly stand united.'

I nodded politely as Pugnator spoke, his faith and vision obvious to see. As for myself, I knew I'd heard this rhetoric before somewhere in my past as a human. That simple statement helped build America, for better or for worse? Your decision. I was happy for him and admired his vision, but I had troubles of my own, troubles he could never understand. I made some polite comments and then bide him farewell, not know if it was a *farewell* for now or forever.

Moving on I finally spied Silĕre coming out of the blacksmiths and rubbing down her sword with a rag. I assumed she had attended to her weapon, getting the dents knocked out and the blade sharpened after the recent fighting. A wise move I thought, perhaps I should have my weapons attended to, but they would have to wait. Greeting each other with no physical contact of course, Silĕre was certainly not the hugging type. We made our way back to the publican. Once seated in a secluded corner, Silĕre gave a slight smile, no doubt assuming I wished to be romantic. I didn't of course, well not at that particular moment I didn't.

'Maybe you should get out your writing stuff,' I began. 'I have something to say and I need you to listen closely, it may shock you.'

Silĕre stared at me in puzzlement for a long moment before getting out her slate. I began, I told her about my other life as a human, though I avoided mentioning humans evolved from apes. I remembered the hilarity and derision I had faced from Harron and his family after my arrival in this world. I told her some aspects of my previous life, how I was a man of learning, an academic in a city far bigger than she could ever imagine. I told her of Sophos and Janiz, how I'd met Secuutus and how we had travelled here. I told her about the green jade box.

Throughout my confession, Silĕre remained still, her eyes watching me intently for any signs of mirth or lies. She had heard snippets of my story but never the whole story. Her slate remained untouched even though questions must be flooding into her mind. I was thankful she hadn't run from the room in fright, away from the delusive madman who told her such tales. Finally, my account came up to date and it was time for *that* question. I laid the jade box on the table and looked at her, the beautiful Tigris femina who had been by my side through most of my journey in this land. A female I had shared my bed with, a warrior who had saved my life, a woman I loved.

'It is time for me to make a choice,' I began. 'Do I remain here, in this town, in this land with you or do I open this box? You must know I would want you beside me. Unfortunately, if I open this box, I can't say where it will send me. It may be back to the world of humans or somewhere else in this world. I don't know, it may even send me to some foreign world where neither humans nor animan exists. I have no way of knowing but I am sure wherever I go, I want you beside me.'

I waited for a response, or a knife in the ribs. One could never be sure with Silĕre, she was a free being, independent and very capable. Conclusively, I asked the question.

'Should I open the box?'

I sat in the weak winter sun outside the publican and watched as the town of Indutiae rebuilt its life. Outside the town, the animan horde was readying themselves to move on, on to another town or village where the war between the

420

Ursidae and Lupus still blighted the lives of animan in Silva Homines. I had not yet received a reply from Silĕre but in truth, I had no timetable to keep. Things would happen at their own pace. Pugnator had offered me work at his side, part adviser, part armed guard but I could not reply until I received my answer. Secuutus and Soci had performed the animan ritual of marriage and were now officially a couple. They both seemed happy and I truly wished them well. Eustace had become quite popular following his bravery during the battle, and I notice he was attracting lots of femina interest. I wished him well too. As for me, I just sat and watched the animan world go by until the slim athletic figure of Silĕre approached. She said nothing because she couldn't, instead she just handed me her slate and on it was the word.

Open.

I asked if she was sure and upon receiving a nod of confirmation, we walked off to gather our meagre belongings. A short time later and both with a small bag of extra clothing and of course, all our weapons, we emerged from the new home of Secuutus. I could not leave without saying goodbye and wishing them both a happy future. Now Silĕre and I stood in a cold but bright street and watched as the horde slowly moved off. My last sight of them was the four figures of Mortes, Pestilentia, Bellum and Fames mount huge horses and ride off into the distance. Somehow this revelation disturbed me. However a nudge in my ribs brought me back from my reverie and hand in hand with Silĕre, I opened the small green jade box.

Blackness.

Finis